Blackfeet Eyes

Blackfeet Eyes

Leonard Schonberg

SUNSTONE
PRESS

SANTA FE

Sunstone books may be purchased for educational, business, or sales promotional use. For information please write: Special Markets Department, Sunstone Press, P.O. Box 2321, Santa Fe, New Mexico 87504-2321.

Book design — Vicki Ahl
Body typeface—Adobe Garamond Pro
Printed on acid free paper

Library of Congress Cataloging-in-Publication Data

Schonberg, Leonard, 1935-
Blackfeet eyes / by Leonard Schonberg.
   p. cm. -- (Blackfeet mystery series ; 1)
   ISBN 978-0-86534-703-8 (softcover : alk. paper)
 1. Siksika Indians--Fiction. 2. Blackfeet Indian Reservation (Mont.)--Fiction.
3. Indian reservations--Montana--Fiction. 4. Montana--Fiction. I. Title.
   PS3569.C5258B63 2009
   813'.54--dc22

                              2008051644

WWW.SUNSTONEPRESS.COM
SUNSTONE PRESS / POST OFFICE BOX 2321 / SANTA FE, NM 87504-2321 /USA
(505) 988-4418 / ORDERS ONLY (800) 243-5644 / FAX (505) 988-1025

Prologue

According to Blackfeet Indian legend, Napi came upon a flock of birds gathered around the base of a tree in the forest. The birds had exhausted themselves flying to the top of the tree to watch for approaching danger. Napi watched as one of them sent his eyes up at intervals to scan their surroundings. Amazed by this feat, Napi asked the bird to teach him the chants and rituals that would allow him to accomplish this. The bird refused, telling Napi he would abuse the gift if he gave it to him. Napi swore he would not and the bird relented. He taught Napi the chants, but told him he could send his eyes up to the top of the tree no more than four times in a day. The birds then flew away.

Napi was eager to use his new gift. He performed the chants the bird had taught him. Deer, badgers, and skunks gathered round to watch as Napi sent his eyes to the top of the tree, then called them back. More forest dwellers came to watch as Napi again performed his magic. Unable to restrain himself from showing off, he sent his eyes up two more times, then realized he had used up his four chances for the day.

Napi hesitated. Then he convinced himself that he was stronger than any bird and could certainly send his eyes up to the top of the tree as often as he wanted. He did it again, then called them back. But his eyes did not return. No matter how often Napi called, his eyes would not come back.

A coyote watched as the drama unfolded. Napi had often teased this coyote and subjected him to practical jokes. The coyote walked up to Napi and waved his paw in front of Napi's face to be sure that his tormentor was blind. As Napi tried to feel his way through the forest, the coyote, seeking his revenge, lay down in his path and tripped him. Again and again the coyote tripped him, leaving Napi sprawled on the ground each time. Napi realized what was happening. He moved his feet gingerly. When his toes touched the coyote, he reached down and grabbed the coyote by the scruff of the neck. He covered the coyote's face with his hand and gouged out one of the coyote's eyes. Napi breathed on it before placing it in one of his empty sockets. Napi could see again from that eye. The coyote begged him not to take his other eye, but Napi ignored him. He gouged out the other eye and placed it in his remaining empty socket. Napi could see again. The coyote whined and begged for help. Napi picked some gooseberries and pressed them into the coyote's empty sockets. The coyote, too, had his sight restored. Because the gooseberries glowed green and bright, his eyes always shone in the darkness of the night.

*R*aymond Two Teeth drove the Tribal Police *Ford Explorer* as if he didn't have a care in the world, which, at the moment, was true. He'd spent the night with Mary Anderson, whom he'd known since high school and had a crush on ever since. In spite of how long they'd known one another, their present relationship was new. Mary's husband, Double Runner, had wiped himself out on Heart Butte road four months ago during an unexpected June snowstorm. Raymond was on duty when the call came in and he was the one who identified Double Runner. The body was sprawled in the road, the snow settling softly on him like a downy white blanket. Raymond knew by the awkward angle of Double Runner's neck that he must have broken it when he was ejected from his car. Except for that, there wasn't a mark on him. One other thing caught Raymond's attention. Double Runner's fly was open, his sex hanging out enveloped in a shroud of snow.

The tree Double Runner hit had cleaved the front of his old Chevy, leaving the twisted remnants of the hood wrapped in a metallic embrace around the pine's trunk. Pieces of glass from the windshield and headlights crunched beneath Raymond's boots as he plodded through the snow around the wreck. His flashlight beam danced ahead of him and settled on a second victim. Raymond recognized the woman hanging out of the partially open passenger door, her long black hair draped on the snow. Hell, every man in Browning knew LuAnn Starshine. Most of them had slept with her. Her pretty face wasn't so pretty anymore. Shards of windshield glass were embedded in the skin and there was a dark blue depression on one side of her forehead. Her eyes were open and staring, but they weren't seeing anything. She must have been giving Double Runner head when they hit the tree, Raymond thought. That was one hell of a climax.

The car stank of whiskey. Raymond spotted the bottle on the floor in front of LuAnn's feet. Seagram's, and there was enough left for a decent swallow. Raymond, tempted, sniffed at it before tossing the bottle back on the floor. He'd been dry for almost a year. No sense spoiling things now.

"Ambulance ought to be here any minute," said a voice behind him.

Dewey Wilson's tow truck sat idling on the other side of the road. Raymond figured it was Dewey who had called in the accident to the Tribal Police dispatcher. He'd been so intent on studying the wreck he hadn't heard Dewey come up behind him.

"Ambulance won't do them much good. Did you see it happen?"

"No, but I heard it. I got here less than a minute later. They were both dead."

"Shitty night to be out on these roads."

"Tell me about it. Well, at least Double Runner died happy."

"How do you—oh, yeah," Raymond said, realizing Dewey had seen the unzipped fly.

"You gonna tell his wife?"

"I'll have to. It's the part of the job I hate."

Raymond helped load the bodies onto the ambulance. It drove away without its flashing light or siren. Speed wasn't going to help Double Runner and LuAnn. The falling snow obscured the ambulance's tail lights in a matter of seconds. Raymond climbed into his cruiser. It was time to head to the Anderson place to break the news to Mary.

"Drive carefully," Dewey Wilson called to him. "I don't want to have to come out again tonight."

The house Mary lived in had belonged to her parents when they were still alive. Mary's old man had built the place with his own hands. Its handsome wood construction set it apart from the neighboring houses, the prefabs and double-wides that dominated reservation architecture. The dull glow of a lamp was visible through the curtained living room windows. It was past two in the morning. Mary, fully dressed, opened the door moments after he knocked. She blinked in confusion.

"Oh, hi, Raymond. What time is it? I was waiting for my husband to get home and must have fallen asleep on the sofa."

"It's late. Can I come in, Mary."

She was wide awake now. "He's dead, isn't he?"

Raymond nodded. "He hit a tree on Heart Butte Road. The roads are bad. Four inches of snow down already."

"Was he drunk?"

Raymond shrugged. "There was a bottle in the car. Almost empty."

She studied Raymond. "What else?"

Raymond's tongue flicked across his fleshy lips. "He must have been killed instantly. His neck was broken."

"That's not what I meant."

"What do you mean?"

"Was anyone with him?"

Raymond hesitated.

"Let me guess, that whore, LuAnn."

"How did you know?"

"I'm not stupid. Is she dead, too?"

"Yeah."

"I wish I could say I'm sorry, but I can't."

"Do you want me to break the news to your daughter?"

"Delia's spending the night at her girlfriend's house. She doesn't have to know until tomorrow. Besides, she gave up on her father a long time ago."

Raymond figured Mary had given up on Double Runner a long time ago, too. What puzzled him was why she had married him in the first place. Like everyone else in town, Mary knew he was always sniffing after every female and couldn't keep a job because of his drinking. If she had given Raymond the time of day back then, he probably would have married her. Instead he ended up with Erica, and that had been a disaster. Well, that was all in the past.

Raymond was glad Mary wasn't one for pretence. She must have figured three months was more than enough to give the semblance of mourning. She was the one who called him for their first date, dinner at her house. They'd been seeing one another once or twice a week since. Raymond had been divorced for three years. He missed having regular sex and a woman to cook for him, but he was in no hurry to tie himself down again. The arrangement with Mary suited him just fine, and now that he was off night shift for all of October, it worked out even better.

Working days was a hell of a lot easier, Raymond thought as he drove past Blackfeet Tribal Headquarters. Less chance of bloody car wrecks involving drunken kids, alcohol-fueled bar fights, and domestic violence. Well, that last wasn't strictly true. With eighty percent unemployment on the reservation, some guys seemed to think beating up on the old lady was the only way to pass the day. Raymond's lips twisted into a smile. Yeah, for the most part the demons came out at night. At some point, his turn for nights would come up again in the work rotation schedule. But no sense worrying about that now.

It had been a fairly quiet day and in another hour his work day and work week would end. Mary had called and asked him to come by for dinner and spend the night again since Delia was sleeping over at her friend's house.

"That's the best invitation I've had since last night," he'd told her. "But I promised Standing Bear and Leonard Nye I'd go hunting with them tomorrow."

"So you'll get up early and meet them."

"You know how hard it is for me to get out of bed when I have you next to me."

"Don't worry, I'll kick you out."

She didn't have to ask a second time.

"I'll stop at home to pick up my bow on the way here," he told her.

The dusting of snow that covered the fields around Browning earlier that day had pretty much disappeared, blown away by afternoon winds sweeping off the front range of the Rockies. North-slope patches that weren't blown away were quickly melted by the sun, which broke through the clouds in mid-afternoon. Black clouds had hugged the mountain ridges the entire morning, but now the peaks were framed against a turquoise sky. As he drove past the Blackfeet Stampede Park, Browning's new rodeo ground, the Sweetgrass Hills, the same hills where he'd be hunting the next morning, glistened in the distance.

It hadn't been much of a day and that was fine with him. Two kids shoplifting at the *Ben Franklin* in Tepee Village. He'd apprehended them both. They were no more than ten or eleven years old and Raymond knew their families. Knowing what they'd face at home if Raymond told their fathers, they swore up and down they'd never do it again. Raymond acted as if he couldn't hear a word they were saying, but he never had any intention of making things tough for them. He let them sweat for a while, then told them that against his better judgment he'd let them go this time. He'd no sooner sorted out the kids than he got a call from the commodities building. The store had run out of bulk cooking oil, which made some of the women unhappy enough to take it out on the clerk, Sammy Redtail. Poor Sammy. It was all Raymond could do not to laugh when he let Sammy out of the storeroom where'd he'd barricaded himself. His last call had been a woman having a seizure outside the Senior Citizen Center, where the old folks went for their free meal in the afternoon. He had dropped her off at the hospital. Since then it had been quiet.

He made a final swing past the deserted pencil factory. When he was a kid that factory had three shifts going. The tribe shipped pencils all over the country. Well, that was then and this was now. Most businesses had pulled out of Browning in the sixties and seventies. Now there wasn't much work for anyone, especially in the winter. Things got a little better in the summer thanks to Montana's fire season. There was always a place for Blackfeet on the fire lines.

A flock of squabbling magpies caught his eye. They clustered on the ground along one of the metal sheds on the pencil factory's grounds. More birds screamed at them from the roof. Must be a dead animal, Raymond thought. He drove through the wide-open entrance gate toward the shed. The birds lifted off the ground as the car approached.

Raymond eased his big frame out of the driver's seat. He was two inches over six feet. Up until a year ago he'd worked out with weights fairly regularly and bulked up. It was strange, but when he stopped drinking he didn't feel like pumping iron anymore. During the past year he'd gotten himself a paunch that was starting to show. He wasn't happy about it. Both of his parents had been obese and diabetic. He'd seen his father lose his toes, then his legs, before he died. And his mother had died of a stroke brought on by her diabetes. What the hell are you thinking about that now for? he fumed. Reaching back into the car he slammed the plastic lid down on the open can of cashews he'd been nibbling from.

The birds pecked at a pile of rags strewn against the wall of the shed. Why the hell would the birds be interested in that? he wondered. He walked closer. "Jesus!" he said softly. The rags were clothes—a sweater, a blouse and a long skirt—and they were on the body of a young woman. She was barefoot, lying face down. Raymond didn't know if he was imagining it but he thought he heard her moan softly as he approached. He knelt down next to her and placed his hand on her shoulder. He heard the sound again, like the soft mewing of a cat. Gently, Raymond rolled her onto her back. He recoiled immediately and crossed himself. He hadn't been to church in years but making the sign of the cross was instinctive. "What the fuck," he whispered to himself. She was young and blond, no more than a child, fourteen at most. Her face was bruised and swollen, as if someone had beaten her with his fists. Her lips were caked with blood and tracks of crusted blood ran down her cheeks. She didn't look at him. She couldn't. She had no eyes. Someone had gouged out her eyes. Clotted blood and torn eye muscles clung to the inside of each socket.

"Can you hear me?" Raymond asked, his fingers touching her face. Her skin was cold, its color as gray as death in the shadows of the shed.

Her head moved slightly. He wasn't sure if she was trying to nod. With her empty sockets, she reminded him more of a skeleton than a living being. As her lips parted, Raymond again heard the plaintive mewing sound. He stared in horror at the girl's gaping mouth. Her tongue was gone, sliced off near the base.

Raymond staggered to his feet and yanked the rear door of his car open. He grabbed the two army surplus blankets he kept folded on the back seat and spread them out to cover her, then got on his radio and called for an ambulance. While he waited, listening for the wail of the siren, he squatted next to the girl. "Who did this to you?" he asked, taking her hand in his. "Can you print the letters of his name on my palm with your finger?" She made no sign of having heard him. He rested his fingers on her neck. She still had a pulse. He wanted to comfort her but didn't know how. What words could he say to a child like this?

2

awn's first light crept over the rolling hills to the east as the late model GMC diesel four-by crested a rise and rolled down a rough dirt track. It came to a stop in front of a dilapidated cabin of hand-hewn logs with a rusting metal roof. Smoke curled from the chimney. White Calf stepped out of the cab and stretched his arms. His gaze darted from the cabin to a smaller weathered wood-frame house a hundred feet to the southeast. Lazy bitch hasn't started a fire yet, he thought.

White Calf peered into the bed of his pickup. It contained only a rolled-up blue tarp held down by a few flat rounds of firewood. He looked at the tarp impassively, then walked toward the cabin and pushed the door open. His large frame filled the entrance. Two Bear Woman, his wife, stood at a wood-fired stove toasting slabs of bread. Turning her head, she gave him a cursory look. White Calf's two sons, seven and ten, sat at the kitchen table. Both boys were barely awake. The younger one rubbed sleep from his eyes with his fists while the older rested his head on his arms.

"*Oh kee*," said White Calf, sitting down at the table. A place had already been set for him. He reached for the kerosene lamp and turned up the flame. It was still too early for light to enter the cabin from outside. The older boy sat up straight when he heard his father's voice and mumbled a reply to his greeting. Two Bear Woman set a cup of watery coffee in front of each of them, then carried the toast and a stick of margarine to the table. She sat down opposite White Calf and ate in silence.

Let her be pissed off, White Calf thought, spooning sugar into his coffee. He knew she was wondering where he had gone in the middle of the night. It was four in the morning when he'd rolled out of bed to take care of the business he'd left unfinished earlier in the evening. She must have heard him drive out in the truck. Let her wonder. He knew she'd never ask him anything.

The coffee had done nothing for his sugar craving. He took two cans of *Mountain Dew* from a box near the front door and drained them in quick succession. His two boys watched wide-eyed.

"Can we have some, Mama?" the older boy said in a voice barely above a whisper.

"No, drink your coffee."

Two Bear Woman averted her eyes from her husband. White Calf ignored her and his sons as he stood up and headed out again.

He walked up a fifty-foot slope to an outhouse set on level ground. When he emerged, he passed the rear of the cabin and stopped behind a flatbed parked adjacent to the building. Aalford, his boss, would be wondering why he hadn't brought the flatbed back the day before. White Calf would have to drive to Valier to call him, but first he had to talk to Sharon.

Three sheds separated the cabin from the wood-frame building to the east. The largest, White Calf's toolshed, was sided in corrugated metal. The other two had been carelessly thrown together with rough pine and plywood. White Calf paused momentarily in front of the one nearest Sharon's house. His eyes narrowed as he remembered what had taken place there hours earlier.

Sharon Aalford looked up as he entered. He could barely see her in the darkness. She sat at the table, a baby at her breast. White Calf lit the kerosene lamp on the table, illuminating the woman's pale face and haggard features. Her blond hair hung limply to her shoulders and dark shadows encircled her eyes. She was seventeen but looked ten years older. White Calf ignored her and started a fire in the woodstove. Turning, he saw his two-year-old son curled up asleep on the sofa, his thumb in his mouth. From the adjoining bedroom came the sound of coughing and a child's faint cry. White Calf, irritated, turned to the woman.

"What the hell are you sitting in the dark for? It's freezing in here."

"Rebecca didn't come home last night," Sharon said, her weary voice a dull monotone.

"That's because she sneaked out of the house while you were asleep. I found her in the shed when I went out there before going to bed. I yelled at her and she ran out. I saw her heading down the road. She wouldn't come back when I called."

"She found a kitten yesterday. I told her you don't like animals and she should get rid of it. Maybe she hid it in the shed."

"I've told you and your sister that no one is to go into the sheds. Anyway, I don't know where she went. I couldn't find her in the dark, so I got up early to look for her."

"I heard you drive out about four."

"You were awake?"

Sharon lowered her eyes. "Something must have happened to her."

"What could happen? She's thirteen, old enough to take care of herself. When she gets hungry enough she'll come back."

They sat in silence broken only by the coughing from the bedroom and the harsh breathing of the boy on the sofa.

"The kids are sick," Sharon said. "I'm afraid the baby will get it."

"If you didn't keep the place so fucking cold they wouldn't be sick. I'm going out again. It's light now. Maybe I'll find your sister." He avoided looking at her as he walked to the door. He hesitated for a moment before stepping outside, expecting her to say something. Had she seen him coming out of the shed during the night? he wondered. He felt her eyes on his back, but the only sound as he closed the door behind him was the coughing from the bedroom.

White Calf climbed into his truck. His hooded sweatshirt wasn't warm enough for the morning's chill and he shivered as he backed away from the cabin. He caught a glimpse of a face at the cabin window and knew Two Bear Woman was watching him. The bitch was always watching him. Ever since he installed the white woman and her younger sister in the small house four years ago, his wife made a habit of watching him. In the beginning, he had tried to explain to her that he was following his religion, the religion the prophet had converted him to. She had laughed scornfully at him and spat on the ground. He slapped her across the face, drawing blood. Since then she knew better than to provoke him. Now he no longer cared what she thought. What mattered was whether either of the women had seen anything during the night. They couldn't have, he reassured himself. Two Bear Woman had been asleep when he crawled out of bed and it was too dark for Sharon to have seen him prowling around and depositing his bundle in the truck.

The sun hadn't risen yet as White Calf left the reservation but a pink glow lit up the sky above the eastern horizon. It took him almost a half-hour to reach the first gas station outside of Valier. The station was closed but the payphone was outside. He dialed Aalford's number.

"Aalford Farm," said a female voice.

"Is the prophet there? This is White Calf."

"Where are you?" said Aalford, coming on the phone before the woman could reply.

"Valier."

"I thought you were coming back yesterday."

"I was busy. And I had to straighten out some problems here."

"What kind of problems?"

"Personal problems. It's all taken care of."

"And my merchandise?"

"You don't have to worry. It's safe. When do I have to deliver it?"

"Check with me again on Tuesday. I should know by then."

"What about the flatbed?"

"Keep it at your place for now. If I need it before you make your delivery, I'll let you know Tuesday."

White Calf was about to hang up when Aalford spoke again. "You're sure nothing is wrong?"

"I told you, it's all taken care of."

"I know my stepdaughters can be difficult. Don't let them forget that only total obedience will get them to heaven."

"They won't forget."

*I*n his rear-view mirror Raymond Two Teeth saw the shadowy figures of his fellow officers watching him as he drove away from the lot. Leonard Nye and Ira Sands had arrived while Raymond was helping to load the girl into the ambulance. They'd all done what Raymond considered a half-assed search of the crime scene, but with the gathering darkness it was difficult to see anything.

Gashes of pink and purple slashed the western sky above the mountains as Raymond headed back into town. What light remained would soon be gone. Arriving back at Tribal Police Headquarters to write up his report, Raymond struggled to find the right words to describe what he had seen. He glanced at the wall clock. Almost seven. Mary would be waiting for him. Leaning back in his chair, he dialed her number. As he listened to the ringing of the phone, he shook his head, trying to dispel the image of the girl's mutilated face. He wondered if that face would haunt him for the rest of his life.

"I'll be a little late," he said when Mary answered.

"How late?"

"I don't know." His words were more curt than he'd intended.

She hung up and he knew she was pissed off. But dinner was the furthest thing from his mind right now. After what he'd seen at the pencil factory his stomach churned at the thought of food.

Before going back to his trailer to change clothes, Raymond stopped at the hospital. He had to find out how the girl was doing. At the same time he really didn't want to know.

"Hi, Raymond," said the round-faced woman at the Emergency Room desk. "I haven't seen you in a while." She smiled flirtatiously. Raymond frowned. He was in no mood to play games.

"The girl who was brought in earlier. Which doctor saw her?"

"What girl?"

Annoyed, Raymond pointed at his eyes. The woman's smile disappeared.

"Were you the one who found her?"

He nodded.

"Poor thing."

Raymond didn't know if she was referring to the girl or to him.

"Doctor Hartman and Doctor Rule saw her. Doctor Rule is busy in back with a drug overdose, but Doctor Hartman and his wife are having dinner in the caf."

Raymond spotted them as soon as he entered the cafeteria. The doctor's wife was hard to miss. She was a knockout. Hartman, wearing green scrubs and a white jacket, was pushing his stew around the plate with his fork when Raymond came up to them. I guess he doesn't have much appetite either, Raymond thought.

"Mind if I join you?" Raymond said.

John Hartman made an open-handed gesture toward the chair next to his wife.

Raymond didn't know Hartman or his wife all that well. They'd begun working at the Blackfeet Community Hospital four months earlier. He knew they'd come up from the Navajo rez in New Mexico, where they'd put in a lot of years. It was unusual for an Indian Health Service physician to spend more than two years with the agency. Hartman had to be dedicated, nuts, or a misfit. Judging by what he'd heard from his friends at the hospital he figured it was the former. The hospital had gotten lucky. Not only had they landed a good pediatrician, but they'd gotten Hartman's wife, a nurse practitioner, in the bargain.

"How are you, Officer Two Teeth?" Beth Hartman asked.

"Please call me Raymond. And to answer your question, not too well at the moment."

"You're here about the girl?" John asked.

"Yeah."

"Your chief came by right after she was brought in."

"Homer? I thought he'd already left the office."

"He arrived minutes after the ambulance." John placed his fork on the table and sighed.

"I'm sorry. I don't want to interrupt your dinner."

"It's okay. I wasn't very hungry anyway."

"I know what you mean. I've been with the Tribal Police for almost twenty years and I've seen a lot of stuff, but nothing like this. How is she?"

John gave him a puzzled look. "Nobody told you?"

"Told me what?"

"She died minutes after Chief Whitecloud left."

"She's better off," Raymond said, unconsciously picking up a spoon from Beth Hartman's tray and bending it in half.

"She was pretty far gone when the ambulance brought her in. We did what we could." Hartman closed his eyes for a second before he resumed speaking. "Her hands, feet, and ears were frostbitten. She must have been out there on the ground for at least twelve hours, maybe more. Besides the obvious things—the missing eyes and tongue—she'd also been beaten badly. We took postmortem X-Rays of her face and skull and they showed fractures of her orbit and facial bones. I took some photos postmortem, too. We don't have a digital camera but I should have the pictures for you by Monday. You have no idea who she is?"

"I know all the white kids in town. She's not from here. How old do you think she was?"

"About thirteen."

"The chief probably asked you all these questions, but since I was the one who found her, I thought—"

"It's okay. I understand."

"Was she raped?"

"There were no signs of trauma to her genitals, but she wasn't a virgin."

Raymond had arrested a number of teenage prostitutes on the reservation, but never one as young as this girl. "So some fucking sadist took it into his head to do this to her for no reason at all?" he said, thinking out loud. He turned to Beth. "I'm sorry. This business has me—"

"John and I feel the same way," Beth said, resting her hand on Raymond's arm. "No need to apologize."

"I can't speak for the reason," Hartman said softly. "I don't know how much it will help you, but whoever did it might have cuts on his hand from her teeth. The front incisors and bicuspids were loose from the beating she took."

"Jesus," Raymond said softly, his eyes narrowing. "How could someone do this?"

"I wish I could help you more," John said. "Maybe the medical examiner will come up with something. I'll have those pictures for you by Monday."

"Yeah. Well, thanks, Doc. I'll let you folks get back to your dinner."

Beth gazed thoughtfully at the cafeteria exit through which Raymond had disappeared.

"What are you thinking?" John asked.

"I was just remembering a patient you took care of in the hospital in Gallup, a young girl who'd been raped."

"The one whose vulva was so badly torn up she had to be put back together in the operating room?"

"Yes."

"What made you think of her?"

"Don't you remember how they caught the man who did it? It was dark and the girl never saw his face."

"The buckskin tassel at the rape scene?"

Beth nodded. "Who says objects can't talk?"

"Raymond and the chief didn't say anything about finding an object."

Beth shrugged. "Maybe they just have to look harder."

John pushed his plate away. "I'd better go back upstairs and check on the baby I admitted this afternoon."

"Which one?"

"The one with a high fever and seizures."

"You didn't tell me about that."

"I got sidetracked by—" He made a vague gesture with his hand. Beth knew he was referring to the mutilated girl.

"What do you think is wrong with the baby?" she persisted, trying to distract him from thinking about the dead girl.

"You're going to love this. The mother's a chronic meth user. There were crystals on the baby's pacifier."

"Oh, John, that's horrible. You think—"

He nodded. "I thought nothing could be worse than that. Until they brought that girl into the ER."

4

*H*omer Whitecloud, the Blackfeet Tribal Police chief, sat at his desk with the door to his office open. He looked up in surprise when Raymond ended.

"What the hell are you doing in uniform? Your shift ended a few hours ago."

"And I thought you'd gone home earlier.'

"Well, I haven't," Homer said testily.

Raymond nodded in understanding. "I'm supposed to be somewhere for dinner, but I don't have much appetite."

"Yeah, I can believe that." The chief leaned back in his chair. He suddenly looked older than Raymond had ever seen him. He opened his mouth to say something but it took a few moments for the words to come. "I couldn't face going home after what I saw tonight."

"Yeah, I know," Raymond said in commiseration. "I stopped by the hospital a little while ago and talked to the pediatrics doc, Hartman. He told me you'd been there earlier. The girl died right after you left."

The chief said nothing for a moment, then blew out a long exhalation. "I hate to say it, but it's better that way."

Raymond nodded.

"Well, you're the one who found her. Any ideas?"

"I don't know what kind of sick pervert could do this. We looked around the lot, but it was getting too dark to really see anything. Leonard and Ira were still there when I left, but . . ." He raised his hands in a gesture of helplessness.

"The doctor told me the girl had been out in the cold at least twelve hours," Homer said.

"He told me the same thing. Hardly anybody goes near that factory anymore. If I hadn't seen those birds near the shed I would have driven right past."

"I'll be bringing the feds in on this in the morning. They'll want to go over the crime scene. Maybe they can come up with something."

"I'd like to go with them."

"I thought you were going hunting with Leonard this weekend."

"Yeah, but that was before this happened."

The chief pushed himself to his feet and peered out the window into the darkness. "I think you should go."

"How can I think about hunting when I can't get that girl's face out of my mind?"

"That's exactly why you should go."

"I'm okay. It was just the shock."

The chief stepped away from the window and approached Raymond. Homer Whitecloud was not yet fifty, only six years older than Raymond, but his thinning hair, worn in a pony tail, had turned gray during the past few years. His days as an all-state defensive tackle for Browning High School were in the distant past. He had retained his bulk but the muscle had turned to fat. His abdomen sagged over his belt as he stood in front of Raymond, breathing heavily.

"That's an order, Raymond."

"What is?"

"You're taking the weekend off."

Raymond started to protest, but Homer cut him off. "Go on, get out of here."

Raymond glared at him, but said nothing. They'd been friends for years, but Raymond knew there were times when it was best not to argue with the chief.

5

*I*t was almost nine when Raymond arrived at Mary's. The television droned through the door. Raymond knocked but got no reply. Annoyed, he pushed the door and it opened.

"Mary?"

She sat on the sofa in the living room, her legs curled beneath her. She ignored him, staring at the TV screen.

"Sorry I'm late."

"Your dinner is on the table. It's cold," she said, not looking at him.

Moments like this made Raymond know why he was in no hurry to get married again.

He slumped into a kitchen chair and leaned his head against its back. He was dying for a drink but pushed the thought from his mind. The second thing he was dying for was the oblivion of sleep, anything to push the image of the girl's face out of his mind.

"So that's it? No excuses? You're just sorry?"

"Something happened at work."

"Something that made you two hours late for dinner? What was her name?"

"You've got me mixed up with someone else. I'm too tired to argue."

"So what happened?"

"I found a body out at the old pencil factory. It was just before the end of my shift."

"Who was it?"

"A girl. A white girl."

Attentive now, Mary swung her legs out from under her and leaned forward. "What happened to her?"

"You don't want to know. She was still alive when I found her, but she died right after she got to the hospital."

"Come sit by me, Raymond. I'm sorry I got bitchy."

He pushed himself to his feet and sat down heavily next to her. Mary rested her head against his shoulder and took his hand in hers.

"How old was she?"

"A kid. About thirteen."

"Who'd want to hurt a girl so young?"

Raymond didn't answer.

"Let me heat up your dinner and make some fresh coffee. You'll feel better."

He shook his head. "I can't eat, Mary."

She took his face between her hands and looked at him sympathetically. In spite of her apparent concern, Raymond felt annoyed. Minutes earlier she had been ready to bite his head off.

"Tell me, Raymond. What happened to her?"

Raymond hesitated. He liked leaving his cases down at headquarters where they belonged. But this one was different. He had to talk about it. He barely recognized his own voice as he described the girl's injuries in a dull monotone. Seeing the horror in Mary's eyes, he thought she was on the verge of fleeing from the room.

Instead, she covered her eyes with her hands. "My God," she said softly. "What kind of monster could do this?"

"I don't know. I keep asking myself the same question. I've come across some real bad-asses and psychos, but I don't think I've ever met anyone capable of doing this."

"Raymond, I'm so, so sorry for how I behaved. You're right. I had you mixed up with someone else."

Raymond made a dismissive gesture with his hand.

"I've never gone out with a cop before. I guess I'm going to have to get used to things like this.

"Are you still going hunting tomorrow?"

"I'd rather stay here and work the case, but the chief thinks I need to get my head together."

"Did he say that?"

"He didn't have to. I saw the way he looked at me. He ordered me to take the weekend off."

"Maybe it is better."

"Maybe. But hunting deer is the furthest thing from my mind after what I saw today. What I want to hunt is the—" He bit off his words abruptly.

Mary stroked his neck and kissed his cheek. "Being out in the woods and away from here for a couple of days might be a good idea. You're sure you can't eat anything. It'll only take a minute."

"I really can't. I've got a knot in my stomach."

"I know it's early, but let's curl up in bed and I'll hold you. You'll feel better after a good night's sleep." She stood up and took both of Raymond's hands in her own.

Raymond followed her to the bedroom like an obedient child.

6

Mary was right. Raymond did feel better the next morning. She had snuggled up against him when they crawled into bed. Feeling the warmth of her body and the soft pillow under his head, Raymond was asleep in a matter of seconds. He awoke at four-thirty, Mary's arm draped across his chest. Raymond never had to depend on a clock. His internal alarm never failed him. Sliding out of bed carefully so as not to wake Mary, he dressed silently and left the house, pulling the door shut gently until he heard the click of the lock.

He felt rested and took a deep breath of frigid morning air. It cut into his chest like a cold knife. Raymond jumped into his pickup. As soon as he started the engine, he set the heater on high. He knew it wouldn't kick in until he was almost at his destination, but knowing it was on made him feel a little warmer. He was glad he'd thought to bring along his thermal underwear. If they decided to camp out, he'd need them.

Leonard and Standing Bear were already in the *Red Crow* cafe when Raymond pulled into the Tepee Village lot. Judging by the cars parked outside the café they wouldn't be the only ones hunting this morning.

"How you doing?" Standing Bear asked, his deep voice almost a growl.

Standing Bear was a cousin to Raymond on his mother's side. The two men were the same age, forty-three. They'd practically grown up together. Like Raymond, he was a big man, and wore his hair plaited into two long braids. Unlike Raymond, whose skin was smooth and hair still black, Standing Bear's skin was creased and his hair graying. Raymond attributed his cousin's more noticeable aging to the *Marlboros* he chain-smoked.

Standing Bear had a reputation as the best mechanic in Browning. Two weeks earlier he'd replaced a water pump and brake linings in Raymond's old Chevy pickup.

"How's the rig doing?" he asked Raymond.

"Just like new."

"You must have had a good mechanic."

"I must have. You guys already had breakfast?"

"Just coffee. We were waiting for you."

"I passed your place this morning," Leonard said, "but I didn't see your truck. I thought you'd already be here."

"I spent the night at a friend's."

"How is Mary?" Standing Bear asked.

Raymond looked at him in surprise.

"I keep telling him he'd make a good detective," Leonard said.

"This town is too fucking small," Raymond grumbled.

Standing Bear chuckled, more of a rumble than a laugh.

Raymond's appetite had improved. Each of them packed in a breakfast of toast, eggs, bacon, and home fries. Standing Bear was the first one to push himself back from the table. He tossed a ten dollar bill next to his plate.

"That should cover my share," he said. "We can go in my truck. I'll wait for you outside."

"I'll bring your change," Leonard said, looking at the check the waitress had left on the table.

"You and Ira find anything in the lot after I left?" Raymond asked.

"Uh-uh," Leonard said, extracting some bills from his wallet. "Too dark to really see anything."

"Homer's calling the feds in on it today. I told him I wanted to be there but he jumped all over me."

"If there's anything in that lot, the feds'll find it."

"Maybe."

"Let it go, Raymond. Come on, Standing Bear is probably waiting for us in the truck."

Each man removed his hunting gear from his own vehicle and placed it in the bed of Standing Bear's pickup.

"Feels like a sauna in here," Raymond said as they climbed into the cab.

"When did you ever go to a sauna?" Standing Bear asked.

"My ex-wife's brother had one outside his house in St. Cloud."

"Weren't those Swedes afraid the red color would wash out of your skin?"

"Very funny. Anyway, Erica was only half-Swedish. Her mother was Flathead."

"It's a miracle you two didn't kill one another."

"We came close a few times."

Standing Bear drove northeast out of town, the first streaks of dawn coloring the sky in front of them. The three big men jammed into the cab lapsed into silence as their full bellies and the early morning hour caught up with them. Raymond thought of Mary, her warm body stretched out next to him when he awoke. He wished he was back in her bed.

"You fuckers better talk to me before I fall asleep," Standing Bear complained. He turned off the heat in the cab and rolled down the window a crack.

"I have a question for you," Raymond said.

"Good. Anything to keep my eyes open."

"You've been around the block a few times, cousin. Did you ever meet anyone who was a sadist?"

Standing Bear gazed directly ahead, averting his eyes from the road only when oncoming headlights approached.

"You still awake?" Raymond asked.

"Yeah, I'm thinking."

"No wonder there's a burning smell," said Leonard.

"That's a funny question. Why are you asking?"

"No particular reason."

"Don't bullshit me, Raymond. You never say anything without a reason. You mean someone who just likes to hurt people?"

"Yeah," Raymond said. "Someone who likes to do things to people you and I couldn't even imagine."

Standing Bear glanced at him. "What the hell's got into you? It's a nice morning, we're going hunting, and you're talking about torturing people?"

"Jesus, Raymond," Leonard said, seconding Standing Bear.

"Raymond, you need a long vacation," Standing Bear said, fishing a *Marlboro* out of his pack with his lips.

"We'll suffocate in here if you smoke that," said Raymond.

"If you're that big a pussy, I'll just pretend."

A spikehorn whitetail leaped out of the darkness on the opposite side of the road. Standing Bear swerved, his right front tire catching the edge of a shallow ditch. He fought to gain control as the truck crossed the center line into the opposing lane. Raymond and Leonard clutched the dashboard until they were back in their lane, moving smoothly along.

"Good thing no one was coming toward us," Leonard said.

"I got only one thing to say," Standing Bear said. "I'm lighting this fucking cigarette and anyone who doesn't like it can get out and walk."

arrell Walks Alone looked up from his desk as Beth Hartman entered his office. In spite of his Indian name, Darrell's appearance reminded Beth of the BIA bureaucrats she had dealt with during her years working at the hospital in Gallup. Whatever physical traits Darrell had inherited from his Blackfeet father had been submerged in the genetic pool he'd received from his white mother. He was not yet forty, slight in stature, and his hair, one step above a crewcut, was flecked with gray. He peered at Beth through wire-rimmed glasses and smiled.

"This is a nice surprise on a Saturday morning."

"I need a favor, Darrell."

"Have a seat."

"It concerns a patient I saw in the clinic yesterday."

He nodded. "Let me guess. A meth addict."

"Yeah, a really pathetic one."

"Aren't they all?"

"This one is pregnant."

"And?"

"She's been using crystal meth for months. She looks like hell—missing teeth, skin's a mess, malnourished. And signs of abuse—lots of bruising. I'm really concerned for the baby."

"How far along is she?"

"About four months."

Darrell shook his head. "Not good."

"No, it isn't. That's why I'm here."

"We're filled up, Beth. The Chemical Dependency Center only has eighteen beds."

"But you keep two extra beds for emergencies, don't you?"

"Is she suicidal? Showing signs of psychosis?"

"I'm not a shrink, Darrell. All I know is that she has to get out of her present situation if this baby is to have a chance."

Darrell picked up a pencil and twirled it between his fingers. "How old is she?"

Beth hesitated. "Sixteen."

Darrell placed the pencil back on his desk. "Beth, you know there's nothing I can do. We can't house adolescents."

"Can't you make an exception this once?"

"I wish I could make exceptions all the time. I get the same request from other docs at least three or four times a week. I've been a counselor here for eight years, Beth. I used to think it was all alcohol abuse, but now I know better. It's only after we talk to our patients that we learn they're also addicted to meth. It's become an epidemic on the reservation. More and more kids are getting hooked. I'm sure you hear the same thing from John."

"Yeah, he sees enough of it in the Peds Clinic."

"Does John know about this patient?"

"He was the one who suggested I see you. I know what you're up against, Darrell, but what am I going to do with this girl?"

"Where is she now?"

"John admitted her, but she's not happy about being in the hospital."

"If you can hold her until Monday, I'll try to make arrangements to get her to Spokane. Do you think she'd be willing to go there?"

"I'll have to talk to her. How long will it be for?"

"Could be a few weeks or it could be for three months. That's up to them. Afterward, when she comes back to Browning, we can see her for her aftercare."

"That's the best we can do then," Beth said, standing up. "I'll talk to her this morning and see how persuasive I can be."

"I'm sorry I can't be of more help. Did you and John see a lot of meth use among the Navajos?"

"During our last couple of years in Gallup, it was becoming pervasive on the rez. Whenever we got domestic abuse cases or victims of violent crime, meth was involved more often than not."

"Speaking of which, I heard about that girl who was brought into the ER yesterday. The one who was mutilated. That's one of the worst things I've ever heard. Do you think meth was involved?"

Beth grew thoughtful. "I don't know."

"But it's crossed your mind?"

"All I know from what John told me is that this went beyond abuse. It was too sadistic." Beth headed for the door and paused, turning to Darrell. "She was white, you know."

"So I heard. And no one knows who she is?"

"Not that I've heard."

"Strange that she was found in Browning yet nobody knows who she is. Anyway, call me Monday and I'll let you know if I was able to get your patient into the center in Spokane."

Beth stepped outside into the gloomy light of an overcast morning. She shivered in her light jacket as she walked to her car. Two young boys huddled together on the grassy strip running along the parking lot. They looked no more than ten or eleven. One wore only a tee shirt. They passed a cigarette back and forth and Beth caught a whiff of marijuana as she opened her car door.

f Homer Whitecloud thought a hunting trip would take Raymond's mind off the murdered girl, he was mistaken. For the two days Raymond trudged through the Sweetgrass Hills, he could think of nothing else.

On Saturday night they camped out in a dilapidated cabin belonging to one of Leonard's relatives. Even without the scurrying of mice all night, Raymond wouldn't have been able to sleep. The girl's mutilated face haunted him. He was so distracted he missed his one clear shot at a six-point buck on Sunday morning, the arrow embedding itself in a tree immediately in front of the whitetail.

The buck was off the ground in his first leap to escape when Standing Bear's arrow caught him in the neck. The animal fell onto his side, twitched for several seconds, then grew still, its eyes glazed over by the time the men approached it.

"I never saw you miss an easy shot like that," Standing Bear said. "You must be getting cock-eyed from all that nooky you're getting."

Raymond let his cousin's taunt go and walked away while Standing Bear gutted the deer.

"What's eating him?" Standing Bear asked Leonard.

"It's a case we're working on."

"That why he was asking those weird questions in the truck?"

"I guess so."

"And you don't want to talk about it either, right?"

"Right." He walked away to join Raymond when Standing Bear began sawing through the breast bone.

Raymond had leaned his bow against a rocky outcropping. Absorbed in his thoughts, he stood with his hands thrust into his *Carhart* jacket pockets.

"Can't get it out of your mind, huh?" Leonard said.

Raymond shook his head.

Leonard clapped him on the shoulder and walked away.

Raymond and Leonard remained subdued on the drive back to Browning. Standing Bear made a few attempts to engage them in conversation before finally giving up. "I haven't had this much fun since I was at the deaf-mute picnic," he grumbled.

When they drove into Browning's Tepee Village parking lot on Sunday evening, Raymond was relieved to be back in town. Standing Bear dropped them both off by their vehicles. "I'll bring you some steaks as soon as I can," he called as he drove away.

"See you in the morning," Leonard said to Raymond. "I hope I can drag myself out of bed."

Morning couldn't come soon enough for Raymond. His sleep was troubled, marred by a grotesque dream in which Standing Bear was gutting the murdered girl, who then metamorphosed into a deer with no eyes. In the dream, Standing Bear stood up from his butchering and turned toward Raymond. He was barechested and his face was devoid of features. Raymond was no longer certain it was his cousin. Another figure, a woman wearing a blue flowered dress, ran up to the faceless man. She had her back to Raymond and he was unable to see her face, but he knew who it was. "Don't!" Raymond cried, as she embraced the man.

He awoke with a start, his heart pounding. Winds sweeping off the Rocky Mountain Front rattled the windows of the trailer. The sky was pale blue in the dawn light. Raymond threw off his blanket and sat heavily on the edge of his bed. He rubbed his eyes with his knuckles, then pushed himself to his feet and padded toward the bathroom. His bloodshot eyes stared back at him in the mirror. He grimaced and stepped into the shower, wishing he could wash away the images from his mind as easily as the dust from his body.

*I*ra Sands was the first person Raymond met when he walked into Tribal Police Headquarters. Ira looked up from the front desk as Raymond came through the door. "How'd it go?" he asked.

"Standing Bear got a six-pointer. Anything new here?"

"The chief'll fill you in. He's got someone in there but he said I should send you in as soon as you got here."

Homer Whitecloud's visitor sat with his back to the door when Raymond entered the room.

"Raymond, this is agent Perkins," the chief said from behind his desk. "He's the FBI's new man in Browning."

"Raymond Two Teeth's the officer who found the girl," Homer said to the agent.

Perkins, who had turned in his chair when the door opened, stood up and shook hands with Raymond.

Oh shit, it's him, Raymond thought. Three weeks earlier Raymond had stopped at the *Red Crow* café for a sandwich and coffee and found the *Great Falls Tribune* on his table. He'd been amused by a feature article on a Native American FBI man who'd been assigned to the Blackfeet reservation. The token red man for the lily-white feds, he'd thought. And now the same face he'd seen in the newspaper was right in front of him.

"You feel any better?" Homer asked Raymond.

Raymond ignored the question.

"Chief Whitecloud gave me the details of the girl's mutilation," Perkins said. "I can understand what you must have felt."

Raymond, glancing at Perkins, did a quick study. During his years with the Tribal Police, he'd seen his share of federal agents when felonies were investigated on the rez. But this was the first time he'd seen one with high cheekbones and copper-colored skin. No suit and tie could disguise the fact that he was an Indian. He was slender, mid-thirties at most, and at least four inches shorter than

Raymond. He's not Blackfeet, Raymond thought, trying to recall whether the newspaper article had mentioned Perkins' tribe. Raymond knew that Perkins was studying him just as intently and turned away from the man's appraising look.

"The FBI's Evidence Task Force combed the parking lot over the weekend," the chief said. "They didn't find much."

"There was a boot print that looked recent," said Perkins. "We made a cast of it."

"It could have been mine. There are probably lots of footprints in that lot," Raymond said. "Kids sometimes go there to party."

"This print was near where you found the body. And there was a trail of old blood on the ground. We figured he carried her from his vehicle. We tried to follow the blood to tire tracks, but like you say, it's a party place. There were tire tracks everywhere."

"The blood could have dripped when we loaded her into the ambulance. There was enough of it."

Is this the best the FBI can come up with? Raymond wondered. This guy hasn't told me anything that might be useful.

As if reading the cop's mind, Perkins nodded at Homer, who held up a frayed length of rawhide. "We found this on the ground not far from where the body was," Perkins said.

"Maybe he had the girl tied up before he dumped her," Raymond said.

"There was no mention of ligature marks in your report."

Raymond's irritation mounted. "Maybe it has nothing to do with our case."

"There are two things I'd like to do this morning," Perkins said to Homer. "I'd like to go back to the parking lot with Officer Two Teeth. Sometimes it helps to be there with the person who found the body. And I haven't been out to the hospital yet. I'd like to talk to the doctor who saw the girl in the emergency room."

"Raymond will drive you to the lot," the chief said. "Then he'll take you to the hospital."

The early morning promise of a nice day disappeared as they drove away from Tribal Police Headquarters. The sun was obscured by a threatening low pressure system that rolled in from the mountains. By the time they reached the road leading to the factory the sky was leaden, appropriate for Raymond's bad mood.

Raymond couldn't argue with Perkins' remark about revisiting the crime scene with the officer who found the body. He himself had done the same in other cases. The chief's telling him to drive Perkins to the hospital afterward was what irked Raymond. Raymond had already talked to the doctor and it annoyed him to be chauffeuring the agent around. Besides, he had planned to visit Dr. Hartman by himself later that day to see if the promised photos were ready. Those were pictures Raymond had no desire to look at. He was having enough problems with the images in his dreams. He didn't need Perkins along for company while he went through the ordeal.

To a man, the Tribal Police looked upon the feds as a necessary evil. They appreciated the expertise they brought with them, but their presence on the rez was an intrusion on Tribal Police turf. For some reason, this particular agent had rubbed Raymond the wrong way from the get-go. Working with white men was one thing, Raymond thought, but a red fed in a fancy white man's suit was something else.

"Looks like a snow sky," Perkins said, the first words either of them had spoken since getting in the car.

Raymond grunted.

"How long have you been a cop?" Perkins asked.

"Twenty years next spring."

"Long time."

"How long you been with the feds?" Raymond asked, keeping his eyes on the road.

"Since I got out of law school. Nine years."

"Where'd you go to school?"

"Nebraska."

"That where you're from?"

"No, South Dakota, just the other side of the line. Pine Ridge."

Raymond glanced at him for the first time. "You're Lakota," he said, remembering now that the article in the paper had mentioned it.

"That's right."

"Full blood?"

"Three-quarters."

Raymond lapsed into silence for a full minute.

"Why so quiet?"

"That's the factory," Raymond said, "up ahead on the right." He nosed the Ford up to the gate, now closed with a padlock on it.

"The chief told me this was once a pencil factory," Perkins said.

"Yeah. Once."

"What happened?"

"You came off a rez, you ought to know what happened. Everything went to hell in a handbasket in the sixties. We weren't part of the Great Society."

Raymond opened the lock with the key given to him by Homer. "Right there," Raymond said, pointing to the shed. "I found her at the side of that shed. The magpies were all over the place."

"I know," Perkins said sympathetically.

"Well, if you've seen everything you want to see, let's get to the hospital. The doctor who saw her in the emergency room said he'd have some photos for us today. We can get them circulated all over the state. Maybe someone will recognize her."

"I know the Evidence Task Force searched the lot," Perkins said, "but I'd appreciate it if you'd take a few minutes to look around with me."

"What are we looking for?"

"Let's start with the spot where you found the body."

Raymond walked to the side of the shed and pointed. "Right there. I thought it was a pile of old rags at first."

Perkins squatted and brushed at the ground with his fingers. Raymond stood watching, his arms folded across his chest. Bored by the agent's meticulous search of every inch of ground near the shed, Raymond walked away, his eyes scanning the lot. A small white rock about twenty feet away caught his attention. What made the rock unusual was the hole in it. Raymond knelt down and studied the tire track that passed directly over the rock. He pushed away the earth around the rock with his fingers. This ain't no rock, Raymond told himself. A minute later he had the object completely uncovered.

Raymond carefully lifted the five-inch long animal claw from the ground with his handkerchief. Its pointed tip was broken off. The 'hole in the rock' was a hole that had been drilled in the claw's base.

"Find something?" Perkins asked, coming up to him.

Raymond held up the claw.

"What is it?"

"*Oh muk ky yo.* Grizzly," Raymond said.

"How the hell did that get in here?"

"Looks like someone was wearing it. It's got a hole drilled through it."

"Hey," Perkins said, "that piece of rawhide the agents found. Maybe that—"
Something in Raymond's face stopped him in mid-sentence. "What's the matter?

You look like you've seen a ghost. You know who that claw belongs to?"

"I don't know. I may have seen it before."

"There can't be too many people who walk around wearing a bear claw."

"Black bear maybe, but not grizzly."

"If the girl's killer was wearing this, it's the first real thing we have to go on."

"If," Raymond murmured. "I just wish to hell I could remember where I've seen it."

"So this doctor took photos of the girl before she died?" Perkins asked as Raymond drove to the hospital.

"The pictures were taken after she died. She only lived for a couple of minutes after reaching the hospital."

"Oh? Sometimes postmortem photos help, sometimes they don't."

"Well," Raymond said irritably, "unless you're planning on resurrecting her that's what we're going to get."

"The chief told me there are no reports of a missing kid in Montana fitting the girl's description."

"Maybe she's a runaway from someplace else. It'll make our job even tougher. Which means we may never know who she is."

"You're an optimist, I see," Perkins said, suppressing a smile as Raymond glared at him.

"The chief said you went bowhunting this weekend," Perkins said after a few minutes of silence. "Get anything?"

Remembering his missed shot, Raymond frowned and shook his head.

"Do you mind if I call you Raymond since we're going to be working on this case together? My friends call me Will."

"What did your mother call you?"

"Son."

"Very funny."

"Okay, I'll tell you. *Ta-oya-te-duta*, Little Crow. I was named after my great-great-grandfather, a Santee Sioux."

"I guess Will goes better with the suit, huh?" Raymond said, not looking at him.

"You have a problem with that?"

"With what?"

"The suit."

"Hey, you're a fed, right? So you have to wear what every respectable white man wears."

"That's a big chip you carry on your shoulder."

"I just call it the way I see it."

"Someday when you feel like hearing it I'll tell you what it took to get where I am."

"That's the hospital just ahead of us."

Raymond turned into the parking lot and the two men got out of the car in front of a sprawling one-storey building. A large metal sculpture was displayed prominently in the lot on a rectangular brick plinth. Perkins stared admiringly at the easily recognizable figures—a buffalo, an elk, a bear, and a brave holding a rattle. "Nice work," he said, expecting to find Raymond beside him. "Where the hell did he go?" Perkins said aloud, puzzled by his companion's disappearance.

He found Raymond standing in front of the Emergency Room reception desk, waiting while the clerk paged Doctor Hartman.

"You trying to shake me?" Perkins said.

Raymond feigned being engrossed in a "patient's rights" form he had picked up from the desk.

John Hartman, walking briskly through the waiting room, smiled in recognition when he saw Raymond. Perkins and the doctor shook hands after an introduction by Raymond. The two men followed Hartman to a cubicle that served as John's office in the pediatric wing.

"Please," John said, indicating two chairs. When the men were seated, he opened a desk drawer and removed two manila envelopes. He handed one of them to Raymond.

Raymond hesitated momentarily, then opened it and withdrew three eight by ten color photos. He glanced at them quickly before passing them to Perkins.

"Jesus!" the agent said softly, staring at the empty eye sockets in one photo, then at the bloody root of a tongue as the girl's mouth was held open by rubber-gloved fingers.

"Maybe we can get someone to identify her from this one," Perkins said, handing the photo to Raymond. The girl's eyelids and mouth were closed. She might have been asleep or unconscious, but her gray pallor indicated otherwise.

"She'd been dead for fifteen minutes at most when I took those," Hartman said.

"There's a lot of bruising," Perkins said, the tip of his finger touching the left side of the girl's face.

"She was beaten very badly." Hartman stood up and carried the second manila envelope to a viewbox on the wall behind his desk. He hung two X-rays on the viewer and waited for Raymond and Perkins to approach. "Her left orbit was fractured," he said, pointing to shadowy lines marring the depression's smooth surface. "And there are multiple fractures of the facial bones on that side. That's what all these lines are. Whoever hit her was probably right-handed."

Raymond and Perkins stared at the films in silence.

"You have any thoughts on this, Doc?" Perkins asked.

"With all the alcoholism in families on the reservation, and now the spread of meth, my wife and I see a lot of cases of abuse. She's a nurse practitioner in the Medical Clinic and sees the wives and girlfriends who've been pounded on. I see the kids who've been abused or neglected by their parents, but I've never seen anything like this.

"The trauma, the beating she took, must have occurred before she was mutilated. She was probably unconscious when that was done to her. The reason for it? That's something I can't fathom. Whoever did it must have been deranged."

"Or angry," Perkins said softly.

"Well, we should be going," said Raymond. "Thanks, Doc, for the information and the photos."

"You know what came to mind when I looked at these pictures?" Perkins said when they were back in the car. "The statue of the three monkeys. You know the one I mean?"

"No," said Raymond.

"One monkey is covering his eyes, another his ears, and the third one his mouth. It means see no evil, hear no evil, speak no evil. It made me wonder if the girl saw some evil and that's why her eyes were cut out."

"And her tongue so she couldn't tell what she'd seen?" said Raymond.

"Yeah."

"I heard you say someone who was angry might have done this. I've seen a lot of angry guys, especially drunks, guys who wouldn't hesitate to shove a broken bottle in your face or break a chair over your head. But this was too—too methodical. To gouge out a kid's eyes and cut our her tongue, that has to be more than anger."

"Maybe anger's not the right word. I meant a homicidal rage, a rage that was meant to send a message."

"A message? To who?"

"I don't know. Maybe in the warped mind of the guy who did it, the message was meant for the girl herself. Shit, Raymond, all I know is that I want to nail this creep."

"Me, too. And I hope he resists arrest."

11

*A*alford Farm was large enough so that the small white church set back behind the house and barn did not seem out of place. From a distance, the hay pastures surrounding the steepled structure might have been construed as a vast village green, but it would have been a village with only one residence.

The dozen children filing out of the church headed toward the Aalford ranch house. They ranged in age from four to twelve. The two oldest girls held the hands of the two youngest. The children conversed softly with one another, showing none of the exuberance to be expected after being confined for three hours. Dirk Aalford, a slender man of about forty, followed them down the path. Like most farmers, Aalford's face was tanned. He had squint wrinkles at the corners of his eyes and his blond hair was thinning. Unlike the average hay farmer, Aalford was dressed in a white shirt and tie, beige slacks, and a coffee-colored sports jacket. The late autumn sun, at its zenith, glinted off the high polish of his shoes.

The path to the house skirted a stubbled hayfield on the eastern part of the property. Large rolls of cattle hay weathered on the far side of the field. The procession passed a barn constructed of weather-stained raw pine boards, the entire structure tilted slightly toward an overhang built off one side. Beneath the overhang, a tractor and baler were parked.

South of the barn, they arrived at a sprawling white ranch house with a detached garage. Both buildings had dark green metal roofs. A Ford F-150 truck with a crushed right front fender sat outside, while within the garage, a five-year-old Honda *Accord* was parked.

"Go inside and get ready for lunch," Aalford said. "Tell your mothers I'll be along shortly."

Aalford walked to the edge of a large hayfield on the western side of the house and peered out at a rectangular stack of bales covered by tarps. Early that morning he had received a call for ten tons, a large order for so late in the year. He had more than enough hay remaining from the summer's crop, but he had no way to deliver it until he made contact with White Calf. That wouldn't be until Tuesday. The Indian had always been reliable during the years he'd worked for Aalford, but his not having a phone was a nuisance. Aalford had had to stall the delivery until the coming week.

The children were seated at two long tables lined up end to end in the dining room. A dinner plate and glass of water was set at each place. Standing next to the stove were three women, the youngest an adolescent and the oldest not yet thirty. Each might have been considered as pretty in her own way if not for the pallor and drab clothing they shared. A cotton print dress, faded from frequent washings, hung loosely on each woman's thin frame. They watched Aalford intently as he entered the room, waiting for him to sit down at the head of the table.

As soon as he had taken his place, each woman sat down. Constance, the oldest of the three, sat opposite Aalford at the end of the table, while the other two took a seat on either side of her.

"Let us thank the Lord," Aalford said, lowering his head. He recited the same blessing the women had listened to before every meal in their years under this roof with their husband.

The moment Aalford raised his eyes, the women stood up. The youngest, Ellen, moved a wheeled table holding two loaves of bread and a large cutting board, to Aalford's place at the table. Aalford methodically sliced each loaf of bread until sixteen slices rested on the board. As Ellen circulated with the bread, Constance filled bowls with soup from a tureen. Jessica, a few years older than Ellen, set a bowl at each place. The soup was a thin chicken broth with small strands of meat floating in it. Not until everyone had been served did the women take their places at the table. Soon the only sound in the room was that of spoons making contact with the bowls. One of the younger children slurped his soup and received an admonishing glare from Aalford. The boy's cheeks flushed and he carefully sipped the remainder of his soup. As soon as every spoon had been set down, the two younger women cleared the bowls and served mashed potatoes, carrots, and small portions of boiled chicken. Salt and pepper were conspicuously absent from the table.

The ringing of a telephone in an adjoining room broke the silence. Ellen looked at Aalford, who nodded. She jumped up from the table and left the room, returning moments later.

"A man wants to speak with you," she said. "He wouldn't give his name."

Aalford stood up and left the room. It was as if an oppressive weight left with him. For a few minutes at least, the women were able to smile at each other and at the children.

"Eat your vegetables," Jessica whispered to the youngest child. "Constance baked a pie for dessert."

The smiles disappeared as they heard Aalford's footsteps approaching. He sat down and resumed eating, paying no attention to the women and children. His thoughts were on the call he'd just taken, one he'd been waiting for since the past week. He now had a date and time to give White Calf, for a delivery far more important than ten tons of hay.

12

B y the end of the week every newspaper in Montana had run the story of the mutilated girl found on the Blackfeet reservation. Her photo, copied from the print John Hartman had given Raymond, appeared on local TV stations and in store windows. For anyone living as far south as Great Falls, or in any town between Kalispell and Havre, it would have been virtually impossible not to have seen the girl's face in newspapers or on bulletin boards in supermarkets. The Canadians cooperated by running the story in Cranbrook and Medicine Hat in southern Alberta province.

The FBI and Blackfeet Tribal Police chased down numerous anonymous tips, but by the time Friday rolled around they were no closer to identifying the girl. They were frustrated, too, by the silence emanating from Missoula's State Crime Lab. It wasn't unusual, Homer and Perkins knew, for weeks and even months to go by before the Lab released postmortem findings. As bad as the delays in Missoula were, they were even worse when dealing with the FBI's lab in Quantico. Homer had seen six months elapse before receiving lab results in rape cases.

Perkins had made a point of speaking personally with the director of Missoula's lab, impressing upon him the importance of any information he could provide to help them. "When you see this girl," he'd said, "you'll know what kind of person we're looking for. The longer we wait, the better the chances he'll get away. We can't let that happen." The director was sympathetic but made no promises.

Raymond, too, had been in a funk the entire week, irritated by lack of progress on the case and annoyed by having agent Perkins always at his side like a shadow he couldn't shake. Making routine passes through the town or driving the rez's primitive roads to outlying areas, he had Perkins in the passenger seat.

"Chief, how much longer am I going to have that *ee mah tusk kee* with me?" Raymond complained to Homer Whitecloud.

"Hell, Raymond, no need to call the man a dogface. He's working the case with you."

"What's there to work?" Raymond grumbled to himself, not pleased by Homer's reply. "We don't have a goddamn thing." The bear claw he had found in the factory lot had been sent down to Missoula, but he did not expect anything to come of it. Whatever prints had been on the claw must have been erased when it was ground into the dirt by a car's tire.

With less than an hour to go on his Friday shift, Raymond drove back to Tribal Police Headquarters, Perkins sitting beside him. Raymond tried to cheer himself up by remembering Mary had called him at home the previous night and invited him for Friday dinner, the first good thing that had happened to him all week.

"Chief wants to see you in his office," the officer at the desk told them.

Homer, his face pensive, looked up when they knocked and opened his door. "Looks like your phone call did the trick," he said to Perkins. "The Crime Lab just called."

Raymond and Perkins sat down and waited expectantly.

"They put the girl's age at thirteen and figure she was dumped in the lot a week ago Thursday evening."

We already knew that, Raymond thought, wondering what Homer was holding back.

"The Lab came up with a few more things. Hay on the girl's clothes and a few hairs that weren't hers on her sweater. It'll give us a DNA sample to compare with when you find the guy."

Raymond appreciated the chief's use of the word *when* rather than *if*, but at the moment he didn't feel all that confident.

"Except for the fact that there were no prints, they had no comment on the claw or the piece of rawhide."

"Not much to go on," said Perkins. "What about her teeth? Any dental work?"

"I asked them that. She had a couple of cavities but no dental work in the past. Any other suggestions?"

"It's hard to believe this girl hasn't turned up on any missing persons list."

"It happens, especially with runaways. With the homes some of those kids come out of, their parents are sometimes happy to get rid of them."

"We can send her photo out to every school in the state."

"We can, but we don't even know if she was going to school. Or if she's from Montana." The chief turned to Raymond. "You're awfully quiet. Any ideas?"

Raymond shook his head. "None."

That wasn't entirely true but for the present Raymond wanted to keep his own counsel. The moment he arrived home he rooted in a kitchen drawer for the telephone directory. Sitting at his kitchen table, he compiled a list of ten names, people he'd been friendly with in elementary and high school and who might still be on the rez or in Toole or Pondera Counties. He glanced at his watch. He had an hour to himself before heading over to Mary's. That would give him time to track down his cousin, Standing Bear.

13

S tanding Bear had his head buried beneath the hood of a Toyota pickup when Raymond found him in his garage.

"Hey."

"Hey. Let me just get this hose on and I'm through for the day. There's coffee on the counter.

Raymond poured himself a cup and grimaced at his first taste. He raised the cup to Standing Bear as his cousin approached, wiping his hands on a rag. "When did you make this, last week?"

Standing Bear shook his head. "Last month."

"I believe it."

"Your truck giving you problems again?"

Raymond shook his head. "You're supposed to be your own boss. What are doing here after six on a Friday night?"

"Being my own boss means I got responsibilities, right?"

"Doesn't Jessie get pissed off with you?"

"She's happy I like my work."

"How is she doing?"

"Starting to feel a little better. It's about time, huh? It's eight months since she had her surgery."

It always made Raymond uncomfortable when Standing Bear talked about his wife's illness. Out of politeness, though, he had to ask. He remembered being at Standing Bear's house when Jessie complained that her skirts were getting tight. He and Standing Bear had teased her about eating too much. Now her skirts hung on her. The surgeons had removed a big cyst from her ovary and fluid from her abdomen. She had almost died from the chemotherapy they put her on in Great Falls. For months she'd been so sick it was difficult for her to hold anything down.

"I'm glad she's feeling better," Raymond said. "You tell her hello for me."

"So what are you doing here on a Friday night, cousin? No date with Mary?"

"As a matter of fact, I'm having dinner there at seven. But I wanted to talk to you about something."

"I'm listening."

"Do you know anyone who ever killed a grizzly?"

"It's illegal."

"No kidding. But do you know anyone who did?"

"I've heard tell of people who claimed they did it in self-defense."

"But no one you ever knew?"

"Why are you asking me that?"

"Did you ever know anyone who wore a grizzly claw as a piece of jewelry, you know, like an ornament?"

"One griz claw?"

"Yeah."

"I've seen my share of claws, teeth, and feathers, but one claw . . . He fell silent for a moment. "It's strange. When you asked me that, something flashed through my mind."

"What?" Raymond asked.

"I know I once saw a man wearing a claw like that, but I'll be damned if I can remember who he was or where I saw him. Maybe it was when I was a kid. What's this all about?"

"I've been having this dream all week. You were butchering a deer, or I thought it was you. But then your face disappears when you stand up. This person has no shirt on, just a grizzly claw hanging from a leather strip around his neck. Then a woman shows up, a woman in a blue dress. I only see her from the back as she goes to hug this guy."

"You sure you're okay, cousin? It's just a dream."

"So you don't remember anything like that happening in real life?"

Standing Bear shook his head. "Maybe you should take some time off, Raymond. I worry about you, man."

"I'm okay. Listen, if you remember where you saw that claw or who was wearing it, you'll call me?"

Standing Bear shrugged. "Sure. Want some more coffee before you go?"

"I'd need a stomach transplant if I did that."

Standing Bear's laugh followed Raymond out the door.

14

"Was Darrell able to get that girl placed?" John Hartman asked his wife at dinner.

"Spokane was full but he found an opening at the center in Oregon."

"She was willing to go?"

"It took some persuasion, but she'll do it. She realizes she can't go on the way she is."

"How long will Oregon keep her?"

"Darrell didn't say. I hope they'll let her stay as long as possible. She needs to be away from here. Her mother's an alcoholic and uses meth, too. There's no father in the picture, but the mother has a live-in boyfriend. The girl refused to talk about him."

"The girl is pregnant. Do you think the mother's boyfriend . . . ?"

"I didn't go there, John. The girl clammed up whenever I steered the conversation toward the situation in the house."

"So what happens when the girl comes back from Oregon?"

"Darrell talked about doing aftercare at the Browning center if the girl was willing, but if she goes back to her mother's house, what chance does she have to stay away from meth? She'll be back in the same boat."

"Does she talk about the baby?"

"When I mention the pregnancy, it seems to take her by surprise. I think she's in denial. God knows what's going to happen to that baby."

"Sometimes I think life was simpler in Dinetah," John said. Displeased with himself for bringing up the subject of the young meth addict at dinner, he pointed his fork at his plate. "The chicken *mole* is delicious."

"I don't get much chance to cook anymore."

"But when you do, it's great."

"Do you really think life was simpler in Navajoland, John?"

He shrugged. "Maybe after all the years there I'd just gotten used to it, warts and all."

"But the problems you faced there weren't all that different from what we see in Browning."

"That's true. Maybe I'm just a little homesick. I know it sounds funny, but Dinetah was really home to me. Still is."

"I understand. I really do. Dinetah is so much a part of me also, and not just because I'm half Navajo. It's where we met and where we married. It spurred me to go to nursing school, which makes it possible for us to work together. And we'd probably still be there if the hospital had found a position for me."

"I'm still upset about that, even after all these months here. It's not like there wasn't a need. Remember how long patients had to wait to be seen in the Medical Clinic?"

"Well, at least in Browning we can work in the same hospital. And don't forget, John, things were changing in other ways at the hospital in Gallup. Except for Tom Whitman, all our old friends in Gallup had left. Maybe it was just time for us, too."

He smiled. "Maybe so. Tom promised to visit next summer, but I'll have to see it to believe it. Take him out of Navajoland and he'll be like a fish out of water."

"And we've heard nothing from Bill Moore since he left. That surprises me. I've always counted Bill one of our closest friends."

"He said he wasn't sure if he'd stay with the Indian Health Service. He was really pissed off about a lot of things going on at the hospital. When they refused to hire you as a nurse practitioner, it was the last straw. Maybe he's still at loose ends, trying to figure out what to do."

"I always thought that Bill was like you, one of those dedicated people who'd work with Indian Health Service as long as he was in medicine. Wouldn't it be great if you could persuade him and Ellen to come to Browning? I'd bet the hospital here would be delighted to have him."

John chuckled. "First I'd have to find out where he is. And you forget one thing. Ellen wasn't as adaptable as you. Remember how much she hated cold weather and snow? We haven't gone through our first Montana winter yet, but it's pretty damn cold at night already. No, if Bill stays with the Health Service he'll try to land a spot in warmer climes. That's my guess anyway."

"Now tell me the truth. Why did you say life was simpler when we were in Gallup? You forget, you almost died there from pneumonic plague. That kind of simplicity I can do without."

"I'm not unhappy in Browning, Beth. Maybe it's just that I keep thinking about that girl they brought in the other day. I can't get her out of my mind."

"Darrel mentioned her when I went to see him Saturday. We got on the subject of domestic abuse and he asked me if I thought meth was involved."

"Who knows? I'm beginning to think it's the cause of every violent crime on the rez. That's another thing bothering me, Beth. God knows the problems in Navajoland were bad enough, but here there seems to be more hopelessness. Sure, unemployment and alcohol abuse was just as bad in Gallup, but the drug scene and the violence in Browning seem to be worse. I'm seeing fourteen-year-old kids who are snorting meth or overdosing on *Oxycontin*. And last week a twelve-year-old was picked up in the schoolyard trying to sell her mother's *Oxycontin*. I ask myself who the hell is prescribing this shit to their parents?"

"Not every doctor has your ethics."

"I tell you, Beth, the despair in this place gets to me. And that poor girl in the ER pushed me over the edge."

"I'm not used to seeing you like this. We've always known how bad the problems are on the reservations. Montana, New Mexico, it's all the same. Gallup was no picnic for you, and I don't mean only because of the plague outbreak. Remember the young kids you admitted with cirrhosis? Tuberculosis? Malnutrition? But you never let it get you down. You just did what you could to make things better. We've met some nice people in Browning, people who really care about the community and are doing their best to make things better."

"Here we are having a nice dinner and I'm ruining it by crying in my beer." He lifted his coffee cup. "Well, in my coffee anyway. I'm sorry, Beth. It's been a tough week."

Beth regarded him in silence.

"What?" John asked. "Suddenly you look so pensive."

"I have something to tell you, but I'm not sure if this is the right time."

"Something good or bad?"

"Well, I think it's good." A faint smile crossed her face.

He looked at her questioningly.

"I think we better ask the lab to run a pregnancy test. I've missed two periods."

John's mouth fell open. "But how?"

Beth laughed. "Oh, the usual way, Doctor."

"No, I mean how, when? We were always careful."

"I figure it was that day in September when we went camping and decided to throw caution to the winds. Are you upset?"

John stood up and held his hands out to her. "Upset? I'm ecstatic." He drew Beth to him and took her in his arms. Even while holding her, John had to make a conscious effort to push the painful memories of his past from his mind. The deaths of Gabriella and Valentina. Gabriella, the beautiful little girl he had fathered with Valentina, a married woman, the little girl he had last seen in her blood-soaked yellow dress, her murdered mother in the room with her. Gabriella, innocent victim of a deceived husband's rage. Tears welled in his eyes and he bit his lip. Eight years had passed since that terrible day in San Diego. The memory of the gruesome scene in Valentina's bedroom did not afflict him as often as it used to, but when it did, the old pain came back. It was something he had had to live with by himself, something he had never revealed even to Beth. And now he was going to be a father again. He had failed Valentina and Gabriella. What guarantee did he have that he wouldn't fail Beth and this new baby?

He was suddenly angry with himself. Don't be a fool, he thought. It's time to stop dredging up the past. He held Beth closer, inhaling the delicious fragrance of her hair. No, he was no stranger to tragedy, but perhaps that was a good thing. It might help him to be more watchful, more protective of the happiness he had found with Beth at a time in his life when he thought he could never love again.

15

*B*obby Dubois had his head under the hood of an '89 Chevy pickup when Raymond Two Teeth drove his own Chevy pickup into the station. Thinking it was a customer wanting gas, Bobby wiped his grease-covered hands on a rag and headed outside. He looked first at the overcast sky, then at Raymond.

"Damn, I would have known you anywhere," Bobby said, extending his hand, then pulling it back. "Grease," he said apologetically.

"What's a little grease," said Raymond, seizing Bobby's hand in a firm grip. "It's good to see you."

"I couldn't believe it when you called yesterday. Twenty years since we last saw one another."

Raymond laughed. "You haven't changed much either. How the hell do you stay so skinny?"

"Yeah, I don't seem to remember this when we were in school," said Bobby, patting Raymond's belly. "So tell me. After all this time how'd I pop up on your radar?"

"I had no idea you were still in the area. I took a chance and found you listed in the phone book. How long have you been in Valier?"

"I bought the station three years ago, after moving here from Great Falls."

"See, that's the problem with being your own boss. You have to work on Sundays."

"Hey, don't tell me you never pull Sundays as a tribal cop."

"Did I say that?"

"We really have some catching up to do. I'll be closing up in an hour. Can you come home with me for dinner, meet my wife?"

"I wish I could, but I'll have to make it some other time."

"It's chilly out here. Let's go in the office where we can talk." Raymond followed him into the small cluttered office, where a desk overflowed with bills, receipts, and papers. Bobby dragged out two chairs, scooping newspapers and magazines off them and adding them to the pile on the desk. "So how long have you been a cop, Raymond?"

"Almost twenty years now."

"Well, fill me in. Married? Kids?"

Raymond shook his head. "Divorced. No kids. You've had better luck, I take it."

"Yeah, one wife and two kids. We just had our eighteenth anniversary."

"That's great." Raymond made an encompassing gesture with his arm. "So you own this place. Funny thing is I pass it a couple of times a year but never knew you were here. I remember in high school how car crazy you were."

Bobby's narrow bronze face broke into a grin. "Yeah, but now I'm fixing them instead of stealing them. Having a wife and kids took the wildness out of me. Anyway, I know you didn't drive to Valier just to socialize. When you called you asked me about a griz claw."

Raymond nodded. He was about to say more when a car pulled up to the pumps.

"Sorry, be right back," Bobby said.

"I'm working on a case," Raymond said when his friend returned. "We think the person we're looking for may have worn a grizzly claw. Not a necklace, just one claw. You said you know someone who wears a bear claw like that."

"I still don't get it, Raymond. How'd you know to call me about it?"

"I didn't. I know that I've seen someone wearing a claw, but I don't remember where or when. You remember my cousin, Standing Bear? When I mentioned it to him, he said he remembered it, too, and he wondered if it was someone we saw when we were kids. That got me thinking, so I made some phone calls to see if someone who went to school with us remembered. You were about the eighth person I called."

"But if it's someone you remember from when you were a kid, it can't be this guy. He must have been a kid himself back then. I don't even think he's from Browning."

"Hey, at this point any lead might help. Who is this guy?"

"His name's White Calf. He delivers hay to people all over this part of the state—Teton County, Pondera, Toole, Chouteau."

"You know him well?"

"Not really. Every now and then he stops in to gas up his truck."

"And he wears a claw."

"Yeah, for as long as I've known him. Hell, you don't see many five-inch griz claws."

"When was he last in?"

Bobby shrugged. "A month ago, maybe."

"You know where he lives?"

"Sort of. His place is south of the Two Medicine River, about fifteen miles northwest of here. At least that's what I've heard. He's not the kind of guy who likes to socialize."

"What do you mean?"

"Like I said, I don't really know him very well, but I do know he ain't the friendliest guy. Big son of a bitch, too. I wouldn't want to tangle with him."

"Does he have another name besides White Calf?"

"I never asked him. He always pays in cash. Never writes a check or uses a credit card."

"Funny, in all my years traveling around the rez I've never bumped into him."

"I'm not surprised. He's not the kind who looks for company. What do you think he did?"

"I just want to ask him a few questions. Maybe he can help us, that's all."

Bobby shook his head. "You always were close-mouthed, Raymond."

"Well, when you don't say much, people can't find out how much you don't know."

Bobby laughed and clapped him on the shoulder. "I really wish you'd come home with me. We can talk about old times and you can meet Cheryl and the kids."

"I'd really like that, Bobby, when I have more time. But I better head back to Browning. This case is keeping me busy."

"Well, I hope you didn't come out here for nothing."

"No, you've been a great help. I really appreciate it."

As they left the office, Raymond pointed to the pickup Bobby had been working on. "What year is that?"

"'89. Looks good, huh?"

"My Chevy isn't that old and it doesn't look half as good," Raymond said, pointing to his truck. "If I didn't have Standing Bear patching it back together it would have fallen apart a long time ago."

"You mean those roads on the rez are as bad as they used to be?" Bobby said in mock surprise.

"Nah. They're all like paved now."

"In your dreams.

"Come back to see us," he called as Raymond climbed into his truck.

16

W hite Calf waited until late morning Tuesday to call Aalford. "Any news about the delivery?" he asked.

"Yeah, Friday night. I'll give you the details when you bring back the flatbed."

"How soon you need it?"

"We got an order for ten tons over in Hingham. You can drop the hay off Friday. It'll be on your way."

"Hingham? That's near Havre, isn't it?"

"Yes. It's a new customer."

"Where's the meeting spot Friday night?"

"Near Fort Belknap. I'll tell you when I see you. Listen, you're going to have to get a phone. Not being able to reach you is getting to be a nuisance."

"I'll bring the flatbed up," White Calf said, ignoring him.

"That's fine. You can get it loaded and stay here till Friday if you want. Everything all right at home? Are the girls behaving themselves?"

"I told you last time. Everything's fine."

Yeah, real fine, White Calf said to himself as he climbed back into his truck. He wondered what Aalford would say if he learned Rebecca, the younger girl, was missing. Her sister, Sharon, was becoming a problem, too. Always a long face now, accusing him with her eyes, as if she knew what had happened.

Sometimes he thought he was better off when Two Bear Woman was his only wife. But over the years while working for Aalford, he'd begun to listen to the man's religious spouting. To White Calf, the white man's religion, whether Catholic or Protestant, had always been just another way to enslave the red man. But what Aalford preached made sense. Whenever White Calf was working at the farm, Aalford encouraged him to attend the religious classes he gave his children five days a week. At first, White Calf had looked at it as a chance to escape from his chores, the bucking of bales and the never-ending fence repairs required on the property. White Calf's thoughts were often far away as Aalford preached, but gradually the words penetrated his consciousness. "Making money is good," Aalford said. "The Lord admires a rich man. And if we have to do things that those who don't follow our religion think are evil, it doesn't matter. We can steal from those people, we can swindle them, we can lie to them, and it's all good. And why is it good? Because we are lying for the Lord."

Aalford's beliefs made sense to White Calf. Getting rich had always been his dream, too, and taking advantage of white men never caused him to lose sleep.

"You see this man who has joined us," Aalford said to his children, looking directly at White Calf who sat on one of the rear benches. "He is not yet a believer but it will come to pass. His ancestors are descended from the lost tribes of Israel, and during the last days before Christ returns to us, this man and his people will again become white. They will join us in our struggle against those who do not believe in the way of the Lord. They will help us to destroy them and pave the way for the coming of the Lord. And they will join our people in heaven, where the pleasures we enjoy in this life will be multiplied a thousand-fold.

"I confess to you that I used to follow the same religion that most of my Latter Day Saints brethren continue to mistakenly follow," Aalford said, keeping his gaze fixed on White Calf. "Those who persist in following that religion have been led astray. They forget or ignore the command that the Lord gave directly to Joseph Smith, the founder of our religion. And what was that command?" He paused and pointed to one of the older children, a boy White Calf guessed to be about twelve.

"That a man should take many wives and that those wives should be obedient to him."

"Good. That's exactly what the Lord said. The non-believers have always refused to heed the command of the Lord. They made life more and more difficult for our people and we were forced to flee from place to place. Then what happened? Those who set themselves up as leaders of our people turned traitor. They lost their courage and they agreed to follow the rules of the non-believers. But some of us retained our courage and our faith. We refused to turn our backs on what the Lord said was good. And that is why some of us founded are own churches. That is why you all sit here today in The Church of the True Saints."

White Calf was aware that Aalford lived with three women and had children with all of them. He had no problem with that. As long as his boss paid him well, which was always the case when White Calf made his special deliveries, Aalford could take as many wives as he wanted. There were times when he himself grew tired of Two Bear Woman, when climbing on top of her no longer interested him. It was like eating the same food every day. He lost interest. Even when he did mount her, he imagined he was riding a beautiful young body.

When he had been working for Aalford for three years, the unexpected happened. The prophet, for that was how Aalford's family referred to him, approached him and smiled.

"I'm pleased," he said.

White Calf, stacking hay bales, looked at him impassively. Why shouldn't he be pleased? White Calf thought. I do the work of three men.

"I'm not only talking about your work," Aalford said, as if reading his thoughts. "I'm talking about your attending church whenever you're here on the farm."

"I like what you say," White Calf said. "It makes sense."

"Good. I knew the Lord would reveal the truth to you. And now, I would like to make you an offer."

White Calf looked at him suspiciously. He was already doing certain things for Aalford that could get him into big trouble, but those things were profitable and worth the risk.

"I would like to give you a gift," the prophet said, again smiling.

White Calf waited, saying nothing.

"You know Sharon."

White Calf wasn't sure if that was a statement or a question. He'd never bothered to learn the names of Aalford's children. But Sharon, he knew, was the oldest of Aalford's daughters, the one who already had the body of a mature woman.

"Sharon and her sister, Rebecca, are not my children. They were children my first wife, Constance, brought with her, children she had with a non-believer who left her." He paused for effect. "Children I was willing to accept as my own. And how has this girl, Sharon, repaid me? Has she shown me obedience?" He shook his head. "She's thirteen now, old enough for marriage. I was willing to take her as my new wife, but she refuses, wailing like a beast. Her mother has pleaded with her to obey, but the girl is obstinate. And since she refuses my kind offer, I would like to give her to you."

White Calf blinked. It was not what he had expected. "What if she refuses?"

"You've attended my church long enough to know the importance of obedience. The only thing that prevents me from beating her into obedience is the pain it would cause to Constance, her mother. You won't have to worry about that."

White Calf's thoughts turned to Two Bear Woman and the two sons he had with her. His wife would not be happy if he brought this girl to their home. But he had the other house to put the girl in. It was not like the two women would have to share the same space. Besides, why should he worry about whether or not Two Bear Woman was happy? Aalford was right. Her duty was to obey her husband.

White Calf waited in his truck when the day came to head back to his house. Aalford led Constance and both of her daughters out to him. Sharon, already as tall as Constance and even fuller-breasted, clung to her mother. Tears ran down her cheeks. Aalford stepped up to White Calf's rolled-down window.

"I have a favor to ask of you. My wife would like you to take Rebecca, too. She says Sharon would be happier that way, and I agree. Rebecca is only nine, but she knows how to take care of a home. She can help your wife."

White Calf didn't know whether he was referring to Sharon or to Two Bear Woman, but he acquiesced. Having the younger one living with her sister would make it easier for him.

White Calf had been mistaken about things being easier for him. In the four years that had passed since he brought the two girls to his place, Sharon had, for the most part, shown obedience to him and given him three children. But the younger one was nothing but trouble. When she turned thirteen, the same age Sharon was when White Calf took her as a wife, Rebecca had fought his attempts to make her his new wife. In the end, he'd succeeded in penetrating her, but he had almost had to strangle her to make her comply. And every time after that she lay like a stone when he mounted her, until his disgust outweighed his lust for her. Her disobedience extended beyond the bedroom. She fought him on everything, conniving with her sister behind his back and refusing to obey his commands. White Calf tried to keep his anger in check, but the little bitch knew which buttons to press.

White Calf put his truck into gear and drove away from the phone booth, following the road back to the rez. She won't disobey me any more, he thought.

17

On Sunday evening, Raymond pondered the information given to him by Bobby Dubois. He'd thanked his old friend for being a big help, but now he wondered if that wasn't stretching the truth a bit. The bear claw had struck a chord in both Raymond and his cousin, Standing Bear, but Raymond didn't know anyone named White Calf and he was willing to bet his cousin didn't either. Just because White Calf wore a griz claw didn't mean he was the man they were looking for. There had to be someone else, someone older who he and Standing Bear did know, but who?

Raymond was almost too distracted to think about dinner, but it was getting late. He hunted in the fridge for a steak and removed a package of frozen french fries from the freezer. Standing in front of the grill as the steak cooked, he thought again about his conversation with Bobby. That was when he remembered what Homer had told him about hay being found on the girl's clothes by the lab in Missoula. White Calf delivered hay, Bobby said. Maybe it meant something, maybe it didn't.

Raymond sat at the kitchen table, half of his steak and fries uneaten. He was draining his second can of *Coca Cola* when he realized he was getting a caffeine rush. He wrapped the leftovers on his plate in aluminum foil and stuck them in the fridge. Eyeing his telephone, he thought of calling Mary but decided it was too late. He turned on the TV but couldn't concentrate on anything. Every few minutes he jumped up to wander into the kitchen or bathroom, forgetting what he was doing. By the time he crawled into bed near midnight, he was so hopped up from soda he tossed and turned for hours before falling into a fitful sleep.

He awoke suddenly, surprised to see it was seven-thirty. He'd overslept. He dressed quickly and drove to the *Red Crow* café, where he ordered a coffee to go. Perkins was sitting on the bench in the waiting room reading a newspaper when Raymond arrived at the Tribal Police building.

"Good morning," Perkins said, lowering his paper. "How was your weekend?"

Raymond muttered something inaudible and walked up to Leonard Nye, who was manning the desk. "Chief in?" he asked.

Leonard nodded and Raymond knocked on Homer's door.

"Perkins is waiting outside for you," Homer said.

"Yeah, I saw him."

"You look like you've got something on your mind."

"I met with an old friend yesterday. He gave me the name of a guy who wears a griz claw."

Homer looked at him in surprise. "Who is he?"

"Someone named White Calf. Ever heard of him?"

"Can't say that I have."

"He lives on the rez, south of the Two Medicine, and delivers hay."

"Hay?" Homer said, leaning forward.

"Half the people in this state are around hay," Raymond said, reading the chief's mind. "So you never heard of White Calf?"

"Doesn't ring a bell. You sure he lives on the rez?"

"That's what my friend said."

"He's done a damn good job of hiding himself in that case. Maybe he has reasons."

"I went through the files. Nothing on him, but we better check him out."

"I guess you better."

Raymond gestured with his thumb toward the door. "Do I have to take my shadow with me?"

"Yes, you do. Dammit, Raymond, lose that attitude about Perkins. Now get out of here. And come see me as soon as you get back."

"Let's go," Raymond said, walking up to Perkins and startling him. "The chief wants us to check something out."

"Go where?"

"I'll tell you on the way there. That your Subaru hatchback parked outside?"

Perkins nodded.

"Good. You can drive. I'm tired."

"So where are we going?" Perkins asked when they were seated in his car.

"I don't know exactly, but it's about fifteen miles northwest of Valier."

"You want me to drive to Valier first?"

"No, toward Cutbank. We'll head down from there. When we get south of the Two Medicine River, we'll try to find the place."

"What place?"

"We're going to see a man about a bear claw."

"Who is he?"

"Name's White Calf. Delivers hay to ranches all over the state. That's all I know about him."

"And he wears a bear claw?"

"That's what I've been told."

"Care to go into any more detail?"

"Jesus, if I knew any more I'd tell you."

"Calm down. It's your show. I'm just playing chauffeur."

"Yeah, right. Don't go blowing smoke up my ass. You federal agents think we're just a bunch of dumb Indians running around with our heads up our asses."

"Raymond, you've got yourself one hell of an attitude problem."

Raymond glowered at him. "So what did you come up with over the weekend? You think there's something better we should be doing?"

"I never said that. I think we should follow up on any lead we get."

Perkins took the Highway Two turnoff out of Browning heading east. Both men reached up simultaneously to lower their visors as the morning sun streamed into the car. Perkins chuckled to himself.

"What's so funny?" Raymond asked.

"I was just thinking. Do you have to work extra hard to be obnoxious or does it just come naturally to you?"

"*Ee mah tusk kee,*" Raymond said softly.

"What's that, fuck you in Blackfeet?"

"Close."

18

"**S**hit, we've gone too far," Raymond said. "We're leaving the rez. Another few miles we'll be in Valier."

"I haven't seen anybody we can ask," Perkins said.

"Let's try those guys," Raymond said, pointing out two white men hovering over a tractor on the edge of the road. A white pickup was parked behind the tractor.

Perkins drove slowly until they were alongside the men. Raymond lowered his window.

"You fellas know where we can find a guy named White Calf?"

The taller of the two, a crewcut man in a denim jacket kneeling alongside the tractor, stood up and stared at Raymond. His gaze went from his uniform to his face. The other man, short, burly, and wearing a grease-stained jacket, stepped in front of Perkins' car and looked down at the license plate before joining his companion.

"Where are you from?" asked the tall man, coming closer.

"Browning," said Raymond.

"I never would have guessed."

The short man grinned as if he'd heard a good joke. Perkins, sensing Raymond's anger, leaned toward the open passenger window.

"Do you know White Calf?" he asked.

"Why do want to see him?"

Raymond glanced at Perkins. "Let's go," he said.

Perkins drove further down the road. "Friendly folk around here," he said.

"If we'd stayed there a minute longer I would have gotten out of the car."

"That temper is going to get you in trouble some day."

"I don't like putting up with shit. Especially from whites."

"So what now?" Perkins asked, driving slowly in the direction of Valier.

"Make a U-turn. We'll go back to the rez. Maybe we'll spot someone who can direct us."

They drove slowly back toward the tractor, where the two men stood watching them.

"Assholes," Raymond grumbled softly.

"Lot of those in the world," Perkins smiled.

Raymond, looking in his side-view mirror, twisted around in his seat.

A white pickup, driving quickly, followed closely behind, then passed on Perkins' left and pulled up sharply in front of him. Perkins stopped and opened his door as the driver of the truck stepped out of the cab. It was the tall man who'd been with the tractor.

"You didn't answer my question. Why do want to see White Calf?"

"He a friend of yours?" Perkins asked.

The man studied Perkins as if an Indian wearing a suit and tie was beyond his comprehension. "What if he is? What's that to you?" He swaggered toward Perkins, opening and closing his fists as he got closer.

Perkins reached for his wallet and flashed it in the man's face. "FBI. Does that answer your question?"

The man stopped in his tracks, stared open-mouthed at the wallet, then at Perkins. He appeared to grow visibly shorter as his shoulders hunched forward. He pointed down the road to the rez. "About five miles ahead of you there's a dirt track off to the right. It's easy to miss. There's no sign. Follow that for about two miles. You'll come to a dip in the road. Just past it, there's another track heading left. Maybe a half-mile down that you'll come to White Calf's place."

"Thanks," said Perkins, getting back into his car.

"He doesn't like visitors," the man called to him.

Perkins drove on without acknowledging the man's remark.

"That's the second time I've heard that," Raymond said.

"What do you mean?"

"The guy who told me about White Calf said he wasn't a friendly type. He also said he was big."

"You're big, too," said Perkins, "so why worry."

White Calf's cabin of hand-hewn logs came into view when they were still almost a quarter mile away. Smoke curled from the chimney. A late model GMC diesel 4X4 truck with a flatbed hitched behind was parked to one side. On a small hillock to the rear of the cabin, an outhouse was visible. As they drew closer and passed a wooded rise on the right, a second house, small and wood-shingled, came into view on the southeast side of the property. Three storage sheds, the larger one tin and the other two rough pine and plywood, were spaced out on ground between the two houses. Prominently displayed on a post just ahead of them was a NO TRESPASSING sign.

Raymond and Perkins stepped out of the car and approached the cabin. Before they could knock, the door opened and a stocky buxom Indian woman confronted them. She stared at them sullenly.

"Excuse me," Perkins said, "we're looking for White Calf."

"Who is it?" said a man's voice from inside the cabin.

"Two men looking for you."

The woman stepped back as White Calf pushed past her. He stopped just outside the doorway and studied the two men, his eyes darting from one to the other.

Bobby Dubois was right, Raymond thought. White Calf was a big son of a bitch, deep chested and at least six-five. An aquiline nose and piercing eyes gave him a raptor's appearance. Long black hair, worn loosely at shoulder length, accentuated his size. His clothes, jeans and flannel shirt, were nondescript, but there was nothing nondescript about the twelve gauge Remington shotgun resting across his left hand. White Calf's right hand encircled the stock just behind the trigger guard. It wasn't only the weapon that disconcerted Raymond. There was something familiar about White Calf's face, something that reminded him of someone.

"What do you want?" White Calf said, his voice rough, unfriendly. "Didn't you see the sign? You're trespassing."

"I'm a federal agent," Perkins said, flashing his identification. "Officer Two Teeth is with the Blackfeet Tribal Police."

White Calf ignored Perkins and stared at Raymond long enough to make him nervous.

"We're conducting an investigation," Perkins said, "and we'd like to ask you a few questions."

"About what?"

"Do you own a grizzly bear claw?" Raymond asked.

White Calf's head snapped sharply toward Raymond. The question had caught him off guard. "You think I've been hunting grizzly bear? That's illegal."

"Officer Two Teeth is asking if you wear a grizzly claw," Perkins said, watching White Calf's eyes.

"A lot of people wear claws."

"Do you?" Perkins persisted.

White Calf kept his gaze focused on Raymond. The truculent look in his eyes sent a chill through the tribal cop. He watched the shotgun, expecting White Calf to point it at him at any moment.

"Come to think of it, I used to wear a bear claw," White Calf said slowly, turning his face toward Perkins. "A long time ago. But I lost it."

"What's a long time?" Perkins asked.

"Years."

"You sure about that?"

"What's so special about a bear claw?"

"Someone told us you wear one," said Raymond.

"If it was someone who saw me years ago, maybe he's right. But that claw's been gone a long time."

The three men turned toward the wood frame house as its front door flew open. A white woman wearing a faded housecoat and carrying an infant came toward them. White Calf intercepted her before she could approach them. He planted himself in front of her.

"Where the fuck do you think you're going?" he said sharply, trying to keep his voice down.

"I saw the man's uniform. I thought he had news about my sister."

"This has nothing to do with your sister. Get back in the house and stay there. Now!" he hissed as she hesitated.

Raymond and Perkins hadn't recovered from their astonishment when White Calf came back to them.

"Anything else I can help you with?" he said.

"Who was that woman?" Perkins asked.

"None of your business," White Calf said. "Now get off my land." He maneuvered the barrel of the shotgun toward the two men and moved his finger into the trigger guard.

"Let's go," Perkins said to Raymond, who kept staring at the house a hundred feet away.

"Did you get a good look at that woman?" Raymond said as Perkins backed his car up. "I thought I'd seen a ghost."

"You know her?"

"Didn't she look familiar to you?"

Perkins hesitated.

"Check out that picture in your jacket pocket."

Perkins crept slowly down the dirt track He withdrew the photo of the murdered girl from his pocket and placed it on the steering wheel. His foot rested lightly on the accelerator, the car inching its way along as he studied the picture. "There is a resemblance."

"Resemblance! That woman back there could pass for this girl's older sister." Raymond tapped his forefinger on the photo for emphasis. "And she was trying to tell us something before White Calf stopped her."

Raymond twisted in his seat and stared out the rear window as the cabin faded into the distance. The last thing he saw was White Calf, standing in the same spot where they'd left him, the shotgun now held loosely in his right hand.

19

irk Aalford, stepping out of his house, was surprised to see his flatbed parked out in the pasture and half-loaded. In the afternoon's fading light, White Calf pulled down bales and stacked them. He looked up as the prophet approached but continued working.

"I didn't expect you until tomorrow or Thursday," Aalford said. "What's the big rush? You're not leaving until Friday. You have all day tomorrow or Thursday to load."

"I'd rather deliver it today. You can give your customer a call."

"That makes no sense. Hingham is on your way Friday."

"I have some personal stuff to take care of. It's better this way."

Aalford's eyes narrowed. "What's going on? You in some kind of trouble?"

"It's just more convenient for me to deliver the hay today."

"It'll be getting dark by the time you get there."

"That's okay. I'll finish loading while you call your customer."

Aalford, annoyed, said nothing.

"I'll come up to the house when I'm finished."

"Don't bother. I'll come back after I talk to him."

His employee's taciturnity ordinarily didn't bother Aalford, but it was obvious that something was on White Calf's mind. During the seven years White Calf had worked for him, Aalford had found him to be reliable. The Indian didn't shirk work and he abstained from alcohol, qualities that had led the prophet to trust him implicitly. Now, however, he found White Calf's behavior troubling. Why the sudden rush to make the delivery? And what did he mean about "personal stuff?"

Maybe Constance's daughters are giving him problems, Aalford thought as he walked toward the house. Or maybe his Indian wife isn't happy with the situation. But that didn't make sense. Indian women were obedient and White Calf had told him that she helped Sharon with each of her deliveries. If White Calf's women were the cause of his moodiness, White Calf would have to deal with it. But given his business arrangement with the Indian, if it was something else Aalford wanted to know about it.

White Calf wiped the sweat from his brow with his arm. He had fastened down the bales with straps, tugging on them to make certain the bales were secure. Aalford approached him carrying a plastic bottle filled with water.

"Thought you might be getting thirsty."

White Calf nodded his appreciation. He downed the water with greedy swallows.

"Here are the driving directions for your delivery. Man's name is Gustafson. He should be easy to find. I just talked to him so he knows you're on your way. He'll have a check for you."

"And the Friday delivery?"

"It'll be after midnight, which makes it Saturday."

"After midnight when?"

"1:30 in the morning, with Miguel."

"Where?"

"You know the roadside park just outside of Belknap Agency?"

"Yeah."

"Miguel will be waiting for you."

"Why Fort Belknap? Couldn't he make it closer?"

"I don't give them orders. They tell me. The stuff will be safe until Friday?"

"Don't worry about it."

"When will I see you back here? Saturday afternoon?"

White Calf nodded.

Aalford cocked his head and regarded White Calf closely. "How are Sharon and Rebecca?"

"Why do you ask?"

"I was wondering if they were annoying you."

"They're fine."

"Two Bear Woman still okay with it?"

White Calf, opening the cab door, turned to him. "What's with all the questions?"

"You seem distracted. Troubled. I just want to make sure everything's all right."

"There's nothing wrong."

"That's good because I don't want anything to go wrong. The Belknap delivery is our biggest of the year."

"You don't have to worry," White Calf said, hoisting himself into his seat.

Aalford watched the truck and flatbed bounce their way slowly out of the field and onto the dirt road. A cloud of dust obscured White Calf's rig as he drove back to Sunburst. Aalford remained in the pasture, watching the disappearing swirl of dust. In spite of White Calf's reassurances, the prophet was troubled.

20

"I feel like we've wasted an entire day," Raymond said.

"Not a complete waste," said Perkins, driving the Subaru. "That's a search warrant you're holding. And look what else we learned. We know White Calf's first name is Arlow and we know he did a year in the Marines before he was dishonorably discharged."

"Big deal. How's that going to help us? What if our visit spooked him? He could have taken off already and we won't know that until we get there. Waiting until tomorrow is crazy. I think we should head out there right now before it gets dark."

"Why would he take off? We didn't lead him to believe we wanted him for anything. Anyway, it took some doing to get that paper you're holding. I didn't exactly have a very persuasive argument."

"You had enough. A guy greets us with a shotgun in his hands. He may be involved in a murder. And he's holding a white woman against her will."

"Jesus, Raymond, we don't know that for a fact."

"You saw how frightened she was. And she just happens to look like a girl who's been murdered and mutilated. What about that fancy new pickup? Guy lives in a shack and has that kind of vehicle? And what about those cuts?"

"A lot of people go into debt for fancy wheels. And what cuts are you talking about?"

"Across the knuckles of his right hand. You didn't notice?"

"I was too busy watching the shotgun."

"Remember what that doc, Hartman, said? The dead girl had her front teeth knocked loose? Whoever did it might have cuts on his hand? Well, White Calf had cuts on his hand. And that bullshit about losing the bearclaw years ago. You know he was lying."

"I'm not disagreeing with you. That's why we have a search warrant. But we're not going out there by ourselves. We'll exercise this warrant after we get more backup."

"Why didn't you bring one of your men with you today?"

"I'm investigative specialist on call for this week. The other two agents have enough to do. I'll discuss it with them this evening. In the meantime let's talk to Homer if he's still in the office."

"He'll be there. He's always the last one out."

"We missed lunch. Want to grab a burger?"

"I'm not hungry."

"What's bugging you, Raymond?"

"I feel like we're dragging our feet on this case. We've got one good suspect and we're acting like we have all the time in the world."

"I want to get this guy as much as you do. Maybe more."

"What do you mean, *more*?"

"I can't get that dead girl out of my mind since I got those photos. I keep seeing her in my dreams, but she always looks like one of my daughters."

"Yeah," Raymond said, "I can't get her out of my mind either. Don't forget, I found her. I didn't only see her in photos. All the waiting pisses me off. I wish we could have gotten something from White Calf to match against those hairs the lab in Missoula found on the girl's clothes."

"You could have asked White Calf for a saliva specimen. He looked about ready to spit in your face. And while you were at it you could have asked him for his boots to match against that print we have."

"Very funny. Was it my imagination or did something about me bug him? I didn't see him giving you looks like he gave me."

"It wasn't your imagination. I noticed it, too. I don't think I've ever seen so much hate on a man's face. You sure you never met him? Maybe you arrested him years ago, when he was younger."

"I know I never met him. And yet—" Raymond fumbled for words. "There *was* something familiar about his face even though I know I never saw him before. Does that make sense?"

"Well, he looked at you like he knew who you were."

"Maybe I arrested someone in his family a long time ago. Who the hell knows?"

"We'll be at headquarters in about twenty minutes. What are your plans after we talk to Homer? You going to your girlfriend's house?"

"How the hell do you know I have a girlfriend?"

"Everyone at Tribal Police Headquarters knows. What do you want me to do, plug my ears? Why are you so touchy?"

Raymond sat in sullen silence.

"This suit and tie really get to you, don't they?" Perkins said.

"So how'd you manage to get out of South Dakota and go to college and law school?"

"You're going to hold that against me, too?"

"No, I'm just wondering. Fifty percent of our kids on the rez don't finish high school. It can't be any better in Pine Ridge."

"Probably worse. The answer is I can run."

"What does that mean?"

"I got an athletic scholarship to University of Nebraska."

"In track?"

"Football."

"Football! You're not big enough. I mean your height's okay, but you don't carry the weight."

"Not for playing the line, but I was a hell of an offensive end."

"No shit? I'm impressed."

"But like you say, I don't have the weight for the pros. So, since I had to do something, I went to law school."

Raymond lapsed into silence. "I don't get it," he said after a few minutes had gone by.

"What don't you get?"

"You came out of Pine Ridge, right?"

"So?"

"Didn't some heavy-duty shit go down on the rez there about thirty years ago? Wounded Knee and all that. I remember hearing about it in school."

"You mean the AIM business?"

"What's AIM?"

"American Indian Movement. I was a kid when all that happened. I remember some of the people who were involved—Russell Means, Leonard Peltier. FBI was all over the rez. My mother was so scared she wouldn't let me go to school unless my father took me."

"See, that's what I mean."

"What are you talking about?"

"After all that shit with the FBI, how could you go to work for them? I heard they tried to frame a bunch of the Lakotas. Didn't they send that guy, Peltier, away for life?"

"Yeah, I see where you're going with this. It is ironic."

"Ironic? I think it stinks."

Perkins laughed. "Yeah, I can see where you would. But if you want an answer to your question, I'll tell you. By the time I was in my last year of law school, I still didn't have a clue about what I wanted to do. Private practice didn't appeal to me, which was just as well. Not many firms interested in hiring red men. But around that time the FBI was actively recruiting minorities. You know— blacks, Spanish. I think it surprised them when I walked in. They don't get many Indian applicants."

"I still don't get why you wanted to work with the feds. Especially after the shit they pulled on your rez."

"The pay was decent, and there was the whole status thing, like—" He dropped into a deep bass. "I'm with the FBI."

Raymond suppressed a smile.

"But it was more than that. I figured if I went to work for them, it might change some of their ideas about Indians."

Raymond snorted through his nose. "So you were going to get rid of all their prejudices single-handed, just by being Mr. Nice Guy."

"I wasn't that naive. I don't know what I really thought. Maybe I just wanted to show them that an Indian could do the job as competently as a white man. Then, the next time an opening came along, maybe they wouldn't pay so much attention to the applicant's skin color."

"So how do you find it?"

"Boring sometimes. Other times, good. Like everything else."

"They accept you?"

"I can't speak for everyone, but the guys I work with are great. What about you? Any college?"

"Community college for a while. I got married after the first year, then took what work I could find until I landed the job with the Tribal Police. That was twenty years ago."

"The marriage didn't work out, huh?"

"Being married to a cop isn't the easiest thing, and I didn't like getting nagged all the time."

"No kids?"

Raymond shook his head. "We spent too much time fighting."

"So what does your girlfriend do?"

"Mary has two jobs. She works for Head Start and for the Piegan Institute."

"Piegan Institute? What's that?"

"Piegan Institute tries to keep the Blackfeet language alive. They run a school for kids and teach everything in Blackfeet."

"That's neat."

Raymond looked at him suspiciously, as if he were listening for any hint of sarcasm.

"I've lost touch with friends in Pine Ridge. I wonder if the Lakotas have a program like that."

"No family there?"

Perkins frowned. Talking about family was a sore subject with him. He shook his head.

"Your folks still alive?"

"Both dead."

"Mine, too," Raymond said.

"Well, we're here," Perkins said, driving into the Tribal Police Headquarters parking lot. Let's go make arrangements for our reinforcements."

21

"Hey, Ed, what's up?" John Hartman called as Ed Rule, the emergency room physician on duty, stepped out of an examining room.

"Hi, John. Beth asked me to page you. She's got a mother and her infant in exam room two and wants you to see the baby. I've got a guy with liver failure in here so I can't help her."

John opened the door and found his wife starting an IV on an unconscious Blackfeet woman. The feeble cries of a baby came from a corner of the room. Lucy, the ER nurse, was weighing the infant.

Beth glanced up after adjusting the IV drip.

"Looks like you've got your hands full," John said.

"Twenty-two years old," Beth said. "Uses *Oxycontin* and is heavily into meth. She's smoking more than a gram a day." Beth spread the unconscious woman's lips with gloved fingers. "Look at her teeth."

John grimaced at the sight of the woman's rotted teeth. Beth moved a loose front incisor with her fingers, dislodging the tooth from the gum.

"Looks like she's got 'meth bugs,' too," John said, pointing to the scratches and scars on the woman's face and arms.

He walked over to the fussing baby as Lucy tried to comfort it. The infant writhed in her arms, curling up its legs. "Seems to be colicky," John said, "but we've been fooled before."

"I took its pacifier away," Beth said. "No sense taking chances."

John nodded. A few weeks after they'd arrived in Browning, he had seen a screaming infant in the ER with what appeared to be classic colic. After two days of unsuccessful treatment, the baby convulsed. John learned that the floors and rugs of the baby's apartment were saturated with meth dust. Each time the pacifier fell on the floor, the baby's grandmother placed it back in its mouth. The dose of meth received by the infant had almost killed it.

"Baby's underweight, probably anemic," John said to his wife. "Vitals are good. I'll admit him and watch for signs of meth toxicity. We'll get Social Services involved."

Beth's patient groaned and clawed at her chest. "She's coming around," Beth said. "I thought we were going to lose her when she came in. That meth-Oxycontin combo can be a killer."

"Who brought her in?"

"A guy who could barely speak English. Said he was her husband, but took off before we could talk to him."

"Blackfeet?"

Beth shook her head. "Mexican."

During their four months in Browning, John and Beth had encountered a growing number of Blackfeet women married to Mexican men. It went hand in hand with the increasing meth problem on the rez. Mexican illegals married Blackfeet women as a means of remaining in the country. It also facilitated meth distribution on the rez.

John ran his fingers over the woman's arm, tracing its scarred veins. "Looks like she's shooting up, too."

"The sites are old," Beth said. "I guess she found out she could get as big a bang for the buck by smoking it."

"A gram must be costing her almost two hundred bucks a day," John mused.

"One of the orderlies recognized the husband. Cops brought him here to be checked out last year after he was stopped for speeding. They thought he was drunk or stoned. The police found three 'eight-balls' in his car. He claimed it wasn't his car and he had no idea that there was meth in the vehicle. Somehow he managed to convince the judge."

"Well, if it was his meth and he's bringing in that much on a regular basis, he's scoring a thousand dollars on each delivery."

Beth placed her stethoscope on the woman's chest and listened as she watched the monitor. "Heck of a lot better than when she came in. I'll get her admitted."

"Take the baby up to Peds, Lucy," John told the nurse. "I'll be up to write orders."

"Thanks for coming down," Beth called as John held the door for the nurse.

He turned. "Do you know what I was just thinking? Remember when we drove here from Gallup, some of the motels we stopped at had those pig-tail light bulbs? They'd gotten tired of replacing the regular kind because meth users were heating their drug in the bulbs?"

"How can I forget? It means any room we stayed in could have seen its share of meth users."

"It also means any guests using those rooms could have been breathing in meth dust."

Beth frowned. "That's a horrible thought, John. Especially now." She patted her abdomen.

22

It was night when White Calf returned home and disconnected the flatbed from the truck hitch. He had unloaded his ten tons of hay in Hingham and wouldn't be needing the flatbed for his delivery in Fort Belknap Saturday morning. The bed of his truck would be sufficient for the bales he planned to carry.

The glow of a kerosene lamp came through the cabin window. He entered to find Two Bear Woman sitting at the table with his two sons. Each of the boys held a pencil and wrote his answers to the arithmetic problems their mother posed. The only education they received was from Two Bear Woman. White Calf refused to allow them to attend school. As far as he was concerned, the fact that they could read and write and do simple arithmetic was education enough. His wife was always pestering him to bring home books for the boys. Whenever he passed a secondhand book store in his travels through the state, White Calf, if he remembered, bought ten or twelve books at a time, explaining to the proprietor that they were for children seven and ten. Having no interest in what his sons were reading, he paid no attention to the titles. The boys always reacted as if he'd brought them a valuable gift. If months went by and he bought no books, Two Bear Woman would complain that the boys had to read the same books over and over.

"I saved some stew for you," Two Bear Woman said, standing up to ladle it onto a dish. She set the dish and a cup of coffee in front of him. "You had a delivery?" she asked.

He nodded, not speaking until he'd finished eating. "I have to load a little more in the truck tonight and leave here early tomorrow. I may be gone for a while."

The boys looked up from their papers.

"You kids can go to bed now," Two Bear Woman said. "We'll do more tomorrow."

Once or twice a month White Calf loaded a dozen bales from one of the sheds into the bed of his pickup truck. To Two Bear Woman it made no sense. Why keep the hay in the shed and why waste his time on such a small delivery? But she knew better than to ask him any questions.

"You have enough food here for a few days?" he asked her before going out.

"We'll need things by the weekend."

He left without replying and headed to his truck. He drove it to the storage shed closest to Sharon's house and left the headlights on to illuminate the interior. The bales had been ready to go for days, but he'd had to wait until Aalford gave him the word. Ordinarily, knowing that his meeting with Miguel was to be after midnight Friday, he would have sat tight until Friday evening. But the arrival of the two cops had spooked him. What if they decided to come back? They might want to search the property. It would be better for him to leave early the next morning. That would also give him plenty of time to make sure at least one of those cops would never come back again.

After loading the bales in his truck, White Calf opened the glove compartment. He removed the check Gustafson, the rancher, had given to him. It was made out to Aalford Farm for a thousand dollars. Chickenfeed compared to the real money Aalford received, White Calf thought, tucking the check in his shirt pocket.

He turned off the headlights. It was dark in the house. Sharon and the children must already be asleep, he thought. Leaving the truck where it was, he pushed open the door of the house. His son's harsh breathing came from the sofa. White Calf's three-year-old daughter coughed and moaned in the bedroom, where she slept on a cot. Sharon was in bed with the baby, who had fallen asleep while nursing. She trembled as White Calf slid in next to her. He knew she expected him to be all over her, but he was in no mood. He hadn't slept for days and he had too much on his mind. His thoughts tumbled over one another. It wasn't until he heard Sharon's rhythmic breathing that White Calf, too, drifted into sleep. Minutes later, his snores filled the room.

Sharon slipped out of bed as morning's first light filtered through the window. She started a fire and made the coffee. White Calf, who'd followed her from the bedroom, lit the kerosene lamp on the table.

"How many slices of toast?" she asked, placing the bread on top of the woodstove.

"Three."

She set the toast and margarine in front of him, then poured his coffee. A bruise on her left cheek, and a swollen lip, were clearly visible in the glow cast by the lamp. White Calf had given her those on Monday, after the visit by the cops. "Don't you ever step out of this house when people are around," he'd said menacingly, standing over her while she lay sobbing on the floor. The two older children were in the room at the time. The three-year-old huddled terror-stricken in one corner, too frightened to cry, while the younger boy sniffled and covered his eyes.

After breakfast, White Calf put on his hooded sweatshirt while Sharon sat down to nurse the baby. He paused at the door.

"I'll be away for a while. You need any food, ask Two Bear Woman. And if any visitors come, remember—keep your mouth shut."

He got into the truck and drove slowly toward Valier. The wheat stubble in the fields on either side of the dirt road glowed in the early morning sunlight. It was cold, but it promised to be a nice day and he had all the time in the world. White Calf didn't want to arrive in Browning until late in the afternoon.

He stopped in Valier and bought a take-out coffee. Sitting in his truck, he fished a small cellophane packet out of his shirt pocket. He emptied the powder into his coffee and took a sip. He could imagine the prophet's reaction if he knew White Calf was using meth. Aalford had told him early on in their relationship that the main reason he'd hired him was because White Calf abstained from alcohol. Well, he still abstained from alcohol, but after all the years of delivering meth for Aalford, wasn't it normal for White Calf to have become curious? Besides, he wasn't addicted, he rationalized. And he wasn't breaking into Aalford's packages. He wasn't that stupid. Miguel would have caught on immediately. Instead, whenever he made a delivery to Miguel, he'd buy an 'eight-ball' for his personal use. "For you, amigo, special sale price," Miguel always said.

White Calf used it whenever he had the need. Times like now when he had to be alert and sleep was out of the question. Afraid to get hooked, he avoided snorting it or smoking it. He simply dropped his quarter-gram into his coffee and waited for it to kick in. And when it did, his energy was inexhaustible. Loading and unloading tons of hay was child's play. He found he could go days without sleep.

As his coffee cooled, White Calf took bigger swallows. He was starting to feel the drug's effects. Unconsciously, he flexed his biceps. There was only one problem with Miguel's meth. When he used it for a few days in a row, his fuse grew shorter. He found it difficult to control his temper. That bitch, Rebecca, had learned about his anger the hard way. She had it coming, he thought. Just like someone else does.

White Calf checked his watch. Early. Plenty of time to do some fishing on Lake Frances. The hunting would come that evening in Browning.

23

"Isn't this overkill?" Oliver Briggs said. "I'm swamped with paperwork and you drag me out of the office to serve a goddamn warrant?" Perkin's fellow federal agent had a fireplug's shape. Dressed in a flannel shirt, jeans, and workboots, his attire was in marked contrast to Perkins' customary suit and tie. Briggs glanced at Bill Jameson, the supervisor of the Browning FBI office, hoping his boss would back him up.

"Don't look at me, Ollie," Jameson said. "Perkins met the guy, I didn't. I'd take his word if I were you. If he says he needs backup to serve the warrant, trust the man."

"But he's already got three Blackfeet cops to go with him. What is this White Calf, a friggin' army of one?"

"Look at it this way," Perkins smiled, "you'll be out in the fresh air, seeing new parts of the rez and getting a little exercise, instead of sitting behind your desk and getting fatter."

"Hey, watch it, Mister," Briggs said, "that's muscle, not fat."

"Whatever it is, it's grown in the past month," Jameson laughed.

"You have a wife to cook for you. I have to rely on the local pizza joints for my sustenance."

"No one says you have to eat the entire pie at one sitting," Jameson said.

"Hey, no fair the two of you ganging up on me."

"We better go," Perkins said, glancing at his watch. "I told Raymond we'd meet him at Tribal Police Headquarters at ten."

Briggs adjusted his shoulder holster and slipped on his *Carhart* jacket.

"I'll hold down the fort," Jameson said. "Good luck. And watch yourselves."

"So who's going with us besides your pal, Raymond?" Briggs asked as he slipped into the passenger seat of Perkins' car.

"If all my pals were like Raymond, I'd feel sorry for myself."

"He still ragging your ass?"

"A red man in a suit is too much for him."

"So dress like me. Make the man happy."

"When it gets cold enough, I might. In the meantime, Raymond can get a grip. To answer your question though, I don't know who else is coming along. That'll be up to Homer Whitecloud."

The chief greeted them when they walked into Tribal Police Headquarters. He introduced Leonard Nye and Ira Sands. "And you know, Raymond Two Teeth, don't you?" he said to Briggs.

"No, but I've heard a lot about him from Perkins," Briggs said, shaking Raymond's hand.

"I'll bet you have," Homer laughed. "Raymond knows the way so you might as well follow him."

"I remember how to get there in case Raymond tries to give us the slip," Perkins said, winking at Homer.

"Be careful," the chief cautioned. "If White Calf is the man we're looking for, you know what he's capable of."

"I'm always careful when I'm looking at the wrong end of a shotgun," Perkins said.

24

"Truck's gone," Perkins said to Briggs as he followed Raymond's cruiser onto White Calf's property.

"There's a flatbed parked there, but you're right. No sign of another vehicle."

"Maybe we spooked him."

Raymond came up to them as they stepped out of their car. "Flatbed's here so we know he's not making a hay delivery. Place looks deserted."

"Only one way to find out," Perkins said, walking up to the cabin door.

It opened before he could knock. Two Bear Woman stepped outside, closing the door behind her. She looked impassively at the men.

"Is White Calf here?" Perkins asked.

She shook her head. "He went out early."

"Did he say when he was coming back?"

"He said he'd be away for a few days."

"Did he happen to say where he was going?"

She shook her head.

"Are you his wife?"

She nodded. "I am Two Bear Woman."

"We have a search warrant," Perkins said, holding out the document.

She ignored the paper and opened the door.

In spite of the light filtering through the windows, the interior was gloomy. Two Bear Woman's sons sat at the table reading by the light of the kerosene lantern.

"These your boys?" Perkins asked.

She nodded.

"White Calf's their father?"

"Yes."

"How come they're not in school?"

"White Calf doesn't want them in school. I give them their lessons."

While Perkins questioned the woman, Briggs, Ira, and Leonard searched the bedroom. They looked in drawers and closets, peered under the mattress and bed, and examined the floor for loose boards. Raymond poked around in the main living area of the cabin while listening to Perkins' conversation with Two Bear Woman. He flicked the light switch several times. Nothing happened.

"Don't you have power?" he asked Two Bear Woman.

"It got turned off. White Calf won't pay the bills."

"Who lives in the other house?" Perkins asked.

Stone-faced, the Indian woman regarded him in silence

"The other house?" Perkins persisted.

"Sharon and her sister, and Sharon's kids."

"Who's Sharon?"

The two boys at the table looked up from their books. They watched their mother closely, as if interested to hear how she would answer Perkins' question. Two Bear Woman gave them a sharp look and they returned to their reading.

"White Calf's boss believes men should have more than one wife. He gave Sharon and her sister to White Calf."

Perkins and Raymond looked at one another.

"Do you know the name of White Calf's boss?" Perkins asked.

"He calls himself the prophet, but his name is Aalford."

"Where does he live?" Raymond asked.

"Up near the border somewhere. Not on the reservation. White Calf never told me where."

"Can't find anything," Briggs said, coming back into the room with the two tribal cops.

"We'll have to search the other woman's house, too," Perkins said.

"Go ahead," Two Bear Woman said. "It wasn't my idea for him to bring those two here."

"Thank you for your cooperation," Perkins said. "Sorry to have bothered you."

"Is White Calf in trouble?" she called to them as they headed for the door.

Perkins paused and stepped up to her. He extracted the photo from inside his jacket and held it up for her. "Have you ever seen this girl?"

Two Bear Woman walked toward the window and studied the picture. "That's Rebecca, Sharon's sister. I haven't seen her for a while. I thought she was sick or something. What happened to her face?"

Perkins took back the photo. "White Calf wears a bear claw, doesn't he?" he said.

"He did. Until a week or two ago. I asked him what happened to it and he said he lost it. Why?"

"If we have any more questions, we'll come back after we talk to Sharon," Perkins said.

The men walked slowly toward the other house.

"So White Calf and his boss are polygs," Briggs said.

"What's that?" Raymond asked.

"Polygamists. Guys who have more than one wife. I knew there were a few of them around here, but they don't advertise it."

They stopped in front of the wood frame house. Perkins turned to look at the three sheds between the cabin and house. "We'll have to check those out, too," he said before knocking on the door.

"Yes?" said a woman's voice.

"FBI," Perkins said. "We have a warrant to search your house."

Sharon, holding her baby, opened the door a crack. "My kids are sick," she said.

A child coughed inside the house, as if to confirm what she said.

"We'll try not to inconvenience you, but we do have to search the house."

Sharon poked her head out and looked around nervously.

"If it's White Calf you're worried about," Perkins said, "he's not here."

She opened the door for them.

The interior of the house was darker and colder than Two Bear Woman's cabin. A kerosene lamp sat on the table in a room that served as kitchen and living room. Residual heat from a small wood-burning stove whose fire had gone out earlier provided little warmth. A young child, his upper lip encrusted with mucous, sat propped against a cushion on the sofa. He regarded the visitors apathetically. Persistent coughing came from an adjoining room.

"Who's in there?" Raymond asked.

"My daughter."

The house had a musty odor. Raymond decided it was as poor as any hovel he'd seen on the rez.

Sharon, wearing a flowered cotton dress that was too large for her and a moth-eaten sweater, sat down on the sofa next to her son. She followed the movements of the men while her baby rooted for her breast.

Perkins wandered into the bedroom, where twin beds filled most of the space, leaving barely enough room for a small dresser in one corner. On one of the beds lay a young girl, her face flushed and feverish. Saliva dribbled from her mouth, soaking the sheet alongside her head. After each paroxysm of coughing, she had difficulty catching her breath.

Perkins searched through the dresser drawers, finding only a few items of worn clothing. Peering under the beds he found only a dust crop. Raymond, leaning over a pillow on the empty bed, called to him. "What do you see here?" he asked.

Perkins placed his face inches away from the pillow, then looked up at Raymond. "A couple of long hairs."

"Dark hairs, right?"

Perkins nodded.

"Sharon's a blond. So was her sister. We can compare these with the hairs the lab found on the dead girl's sweater."

"A match won't mean much now that we know White Calf lives here."

"Let's take 'em anyway," Raymond said.

Perkins withdrew a plastic bag from his jacket pocket and carefully placed the hairs inside.

"Do your children need a doctor?" Perkins asked Sharon when they returned to the living room.

"My husband doesn't believe in doctors."

"Is White Calf your husband?"

"In God's eyes."

"He's the father of your three children?"

She nodded.

"How old are you?"

"White Calf told me not to talk to anyone."

"White Calf's not here. We won't let him hurt you. You can talk to us."

Sharon regarded him warily, as if uncertain whether to believe him. "I'm seventeen," she said softly.

Perkins and Raymond exchanged glances.

"The woman we talked to in the cabin, Two Bear Woman, told us she's White Calf's wife, too."

"Yes."

"She says your sister lives here with you."

"She does, but she ran away."

"When was that?"

"More than a week ago. My husband looked for her but he couldn't find her."

"Do you know why she ran away?"

"Rebecca found a kitten and hid it in the shed. None of us is supposed to go into White Calf's sheds. He told me he yelled at her and she ran away."

"You didn't call anyone to help you find her?"

"We have no phone. White Calf says she'll come back when she's ready."

"How old is your sister?"

"Thirteen."

"Is your sister White Calf's wife, too?" Raymond interrupted.

"In God's eyes, but she isn't obedient. White Calf gets angry with her."

"Did White Calf do that to you?" Perkins asked, pointing at her cheek and lip.

Sharon looked down without replying. Perkins saw she was on the verge of tears. "White Calf will be angry if he learns I was talking to you."

"You remember me from the last time I was here, don't you? You came out of the house while I was talking to White Calf."

Sharon nodded.

"Is that why White Calf beat you? Because you came out of the house?"

"I thought you were here about my sister," she said, tears welling in her eyes.

"Would you like us to take you away from here?"

"White Calf would be furious," she said, her eyes dilating with fear. "He says he'll kill us if we ever try to run away."

"Don't worry, he's not going to hurt you anymore."

"Two Bear Woman told us a man named Aalford gave you to White Calf," Raymond said.

"The prophet is my stepfather. I didn't want to be his wife so he gave me to White Calf."

"Your mother is married to Aalford?"

"Yes, she's one of his three wives."

Raymond turned away, mumbling to himself. Briggs and the other two tribal cops stood just within the door, listening to Sharon's replies in silence.

"Why didn't your mother stop Aalford from giving you to White Calf?" Raymond asked, unable to hide his anger.

"My mother couldn't do anything. My stepfather is the prophet." She spoke slowly, as if explaining things to a child.

"You're Mormons?" Perkins asked.

"We have our own church. The Church of the True Saints."

"Did White Calf ever beat Rebecca?"

Sharon's frightened look returned. She shook her head forcefully.

"What about when he found out she'd hidden the kitten in the shed?" Perkins asked.

"I don't know. He told me she'd run away." She buried her face in her hands.

The front door suddenly opened and Two Bear Woman stepped into the room. "Have you shown it to her?" she asked Perkins.

"Not yet."

Sharon looked in confusion from one to the other. "Shown me what?"

"Come to the window where there's light," Perkins said gently. "I'd like you to look at a photograph."

"I'll hold the baby for you," Two Bear Woman said.

Sharon looked at Perkins uncertainly.

"Is this your sister?" He handed her the same photo he'd shown Two Bear Woman.

Sharon stared at the picture. Her arm dropped to her side. Still holding the photograph, she staggered unsteadily to the sofa, where she collapsed. She raised her tear-stained face to Perkins and began to keen loudly, rocking back and forth in her grief.

"I'm sorry," Perkins said, sitting down next to her.

"He beat her," she wailed. "White Calf beat her. How is she?"

Perkins lowered his head.

Sharon's scream startled all of them. The boy on the sofa and the baby held by Two Bear Woman began to cry.

"Where is she? Where is she?" Sharon yelled.

"Her body was found in Browning," Perkins said.

"He's evil, he's the devil!" she wailed.

"We're going to take you and the children away from here," Raymond said. "We'll make sure White Calf pays for what he's done."

"You'll all be taken care of," Perkins interjected. "White Calf won't bother you anymore." Perkins turned to Ira and Leonard, standing immobilized like statues near the front door. "Put them all in the car and stay with them."

Sharon, moaning, paid no attention to what he said.

"I'll go check the sheds," Perkins said.

"What about you?" Raymond asked Two Bear Woman, still holding the baby. "Would you like us to take you and your children away from here?"

"This is our home. We'll stay."

"When we find White Calf, we'll have to arrest him. You'll be here by yourselves."

"We'll stay," she repeated.

"It's not a good idea. He may come back here. There's no telling what he'll do."

"I don't think he'll come back. If he does, I don't think he'll hurt us."

"You've seen what he's capable of. He's dangerous. And you're isolated here. Not even a phone to call for help."

"I'm not afraid."

Exasperated, Raymond left the house.

25

"Find anything in there?" Briggs asked as Perkins came out of the metal shed.

"It's just a storeroom for tools and farm equipment."

"How are the woman and kids doing?" Perkins asked Raymond as he approached them.

"Ira and Leonard are staying with them by the car. She's still hysterical and the kids are all upset. I can't believe this shit."

"What about Two Bear Woman? Did you convince her to leave?"

"Stubborn like a mule. Says she's not afraid of him."

"She ought to be."

"I told her that. Didn't do much good."

"Maybe it'd be better if Ira and Leonard took Sharon and her kids to Browning now," Perkins said to Raymond. "You can ride back with us."

Raymond nodded. "That's a good idea. I don't think there's much chance of White Calf showing up." He walked off to talk to his fellow tribal cops.

"When you get to Browning," he told Leonard Nye, "drop the woman and kids off at the hospital. Social Services will find them a place to stay after the doctor examines the kids."

As the police cruiser carrying Sharon and the children drove away, Perkins pushed on the plywood door of the shed closest to Sharon's house. Raymond and Briggs stood on either side of him. A smell of decay assaulted them as the door swung open. Scraps of hay covered wooden palettes set on the dirt floor.

"Why the hell would he put hay in here?" Raymond asked.

Perkins aimed his flashlight beam toward the rear wall. A small, indistinct mass lay on one of the palettes.

"What is that?" Briggs asked.

The smell grew stronger as they approached.

"It's a dead animal," Briggs said. "Packrat maybe?"

Raymond nudged the small, gray furry mound with his boot. "It's the girl's kitten."

"Yeah," Perkins said, kneeling next to it. "Head's bashed in."

"How can somebody get that angry about a kitten?" Briggs said, talking to himself.

Perkins, his feet on the slats of the palettes, scanned the floor with his light. "Something set him off when he found the girl in here," he said, talking to himself.

Raymond squatted in the middle of the shed and brushed away alfalfa stems with his hand. "Let me have your light," he said to Perkins. He aimed the beam toward the floor. A one-inch long curled strip of plastic protruded from a space between two slats. Raymond stepped aside and reached down to lift the wooden palette. He rested it on the adjoining palette and moved the flashlight beam back and forth around the plastic strip.

"What is that, broken glass?" Perkins asked, crouching next to Raymond.

"Look again," Raymond said.

Perkins got on his knees. His face was no more than a foot above the dank ground. Slowly, he raised his head and looked at Raymond. The tribal cop nodded.

"Ollie," Perkins said to Briggs, who hovered over them, "I've got some plastic bags and spoons in the glove compartment."

"What is it?" Briggs asked.

"It looks like White Calf is running meth."

"Maybe he's using it, too," Briggs said. "That would account for what he did to that girl."

"What do you think?" Perkins asked Raymond while Briggs went to the car.

Raymond shrugged. "Seems that every violent crime on the rez these days involves meth. I was talking to Darrell Walks Alone at the Chemical Dependency Center the other day. He often gets called in on domestic abuse cases. Darrell says everyone blames the abuse on alcohol, but when you ask about meth use you find out the truth. As for White Calf, who the hell knows? I haven't met any meth users who cut the eyes and tongue out on little girls."

Before Perkins could reply, Briggs returned. Perkins used a spoon to pick up the small shards of methamphetamine and the piece of plastic. He placed them in a Ziploc bag.

"You think White Calf might come back here?" Briggs asked.

Perkins looked at Raymond.

"What are you lookin' at me for? You think because he and I are Blackfeet I know the bastard's next move? You're an Indian. What do you think?"

Perkins shook his head and turned to Briggs. "See what I have to put up with from this clown. No, I don't think he'll come back any time soon."

"But he left his women and kids here," Briggs said.

"Somehow I don't think they're high on his priority list."

"Now you're thinking," Raymond said, turning away to hide his grin.

"I still don't understand these people," Briggs said as they drove back to Browning.

"What people?"

"White Calf. Aalford. Polygamists."

"What you call polygamy," Perkins said, "I call abuse of women and children. That girl, Sharon, couldn't have been more than thirteen when White Calf made her pregnant for the first time. And then he tried to do the same with her sister."

"No argument," Briggs said. "I know there are pockets of them around—Idaho, Utah, Montana, Canada—but this is the first time I've encountered them."

"Most of them were Mormons originally," Perkins said. "Then they broke away when the LDS church came out against polygamy."

"That shows how sick they are," Raymond said from the back seat. "Any sane man knows it's hard enough to put up with one wife."

Briggs turned in his seat. "I gather you speak from experience."

Raymond ignored him. "So when are you going to check out this so-called prophet?" he asked Perkins.

"I was just thinking about that. We should be able to locate him without too much difficulty. But let's ship the hair from the pillow, and the crystals, down to the Crime Lab in Missoula first. Then we can plan a visit to Mr. Aalford."

26

"How are the children?" Beth asked her husband as he came out of the ER examining room.

"The little girl has pertussis. It'll be touch and go for a while. I started her on antibiotics and admitted her."

"I'll bet none of these kids has had immunizations."

"You're probably right."

"How are the two younger ones?"

"The boy and the infant are anemic and have colds. We'll have to hope they don't come down with whooping cough. Did Lucas finish his workup on their mother?"

"I don't know if he was able to examine her. She was screaming hysterically and Lucas had to get her out of the ER."

"So that was the commotion I heard while I was examining the kids."

"The mutilated girl you saw in the ER the other day was her sister."

"What? Are you sure?"

"That's what the tribal cops who brought the family in told me. They have a suspect, too— the husband."

"Jesus! Why would he kill a kid?"

"Do you know how old that girl is?"

"Which girl?"

"The mother of the kids you just examined. Seventeen."

"Seventeen! That means he's been having sex with her since—"

"Yeah, probably since she hit puberty. Maybe it's not such a big leap from raping children to killing them.

"Anyway, Lucas couldn't get her calmed down so he had to sedate her. She's in a private room on the ward and Lucas requested a psych evaluation. He has her under a suicide watch."

"Poor kid."

"Lucas says she blames herself for her sister's death. She kept screaming her sister's name —Rebecca—and the name White Calf. Kept calling him the devil."

"What could she have done to prevent it? She's just a kid herself."

"Yeah, a kid with three children of her own. Does the social worker know you're not admitting the two younger ones?"

"Yeah. Ramona found a family for them to stay with. Unfortunately it'll mean taking the baby off breast milk, but in the condition the mother's in . . . " John made a helpless gesture with his hands.

"John, do you think Sharon's husband might come to the hospital when he finds out she's here?"

"I can't see that happening. You said he's a suspect in the girl's murder. If the cops are looking for him he won't show himself."

"But what if he doesn't know the police are looking for him?"

"How could he not know?"

"The cops said he wasn't there when they went out to the house. They don't know where he is. They told me, too, that he has another wife who lives at the house—a Blackfeet woman."

"She's still there?"

"With her two kids. She didn't want to leave."

"He'll know the cops are after him if he goes back to his house. The Indian woman will tell him. But I still don't see him coming here. If anything, he'd try to get as far away as he can from the reservation. Why didn't this Blackfeet woman report what was going on? She knew her husband was having sex with a minor."

"Maybe she was too scared. If White Calf did those terrible things to Sharon's sister, we know what he's capable of."

"Let's hope they find this guy soon and put him away."

"Sharon probably won't rest easy until they do."

"Did the police tell you anything else?"

"No, but here's a man who might know something," Beth said, indicating Raymond Two Teeth, who had just entered the ER waiting room.

Raymond waved when he spotted them. "Just thought I'd drop by to see how they're all doing," he said.

John gave him an update and gestured toward Beth. "My wife is worried that White Calf might come to the hospital if he learns his wife is here."

"I don't see that happening. He's probably far away from here by now."

"Is he really a suspect in that girl's murder?"

"Until we get some tests back, let's say he's a person of interest."

John grew pensive. "It's a big jump from bigamy to murder."

"I don't know if bigamy is the right word. White Calf never married that girl, Sharon. Given her age, statutory rape describes it better."

"Do you have a photo of him that we can post in the hospital?" Beth asked. "That way, if anyone spots him we can alert the police."

"Not yet, but in the meantime we can alert everyone to call us if someone comes in asking for Sharon or her kids."

"If he's really on the run and far away from here, like you think, the police might not be able to find him for a long time. And the border is so close . . . "

"You have to have more faith than that, Doc. We'll find him. You can count on it," Raymond said, surprising himself at his certainty.

27

R aymond was tired and looking forward to dinner at Mary's. He'd caught up with his paperwork, and the specimens Perkins had collected at White Calf's place were on the way to Missoula. He'd briefed Homer, and "be on the lookout" orders had been issued for White Calf. He'd done enough for one day. Even Perkins, who Raymond thought of as a workaholic, seemed glad to be heading home for the evening.

Both men had parted in sour moods from Tribal Police Headquarters.

"What's going on between you and Perkins?" Homer asked Raymond after Perkins and Briggs left his office.

"Nothing," Raymond said. "I'll see you in the morning, Chief."

"Nothing, huh. That's why you look at one another with daggers in your eyes?"

Raymond didn't answer.

"Perkins say what his next move will be?" Homer asked, unable to keep his annoyance from his voice.

"I know he's going to try to locate Aalford, White Calf's boss. After that, I don't know."

The chief regarded his sullen cop with exasperation. "Raymond, I don't know what I'm going to do with you. Go on, get out of here."

As he drove to Mary's, Raymond thought about what had transpired between him and Perkins that day.

"I still think you blew it," Raymond had said in the car on the drive back to Browning.

"What do you mean?"

"We should have taken White Calf back to Browning for questioning when we first went out there. It was obvious he was lying about the bear claw. Once you had him back in Browning, you could have leaned on him and gotten a specimen for DNA comparison with the hairs on the girl's sweater."

"On the basis of a bear claw that may or may not have belonged to him?"

"We know now that it did."

"We didn't know anything then. A lawyer would have had him out in no time. Even now the bear claw isn't enough to pin the murder on him. Is his name on it? His fingerprints? And the hairs on the sweater don't prove anything either. He lived in the same house, for Christ's sake. Everything we have is circumstantial, including the meth. White Calf could deny knowing anything about it. A lawyer would claim the crystals could have been on the ground for years."

"Circumstantial, huh? We have his hairs on the dead girl's sweater, the girl's dead kitten, traces of meth, Sharon's bruises from the pounding he gave her, and his wife's testimony that he was lying about the bear claw. You don't think a jury would put all that together?"

"Raymond, I feel the same way you do. I believe he's the one responsible. I'm only pointing out that a defense lawyer could make some good arguments.

And before you start blaming me for not bringing him in when we were at his place, I'd like to remind you that the entire time we were there he was holding a shotgun."

"Goddammit, there were two of us. Did you really think he was going to shoot us?"

"Knowing what we know now, I wouldn't have wanted to test him. I want to nail him as much as you do, but we still have to play by the rules. And that means making sure we have enough evidence to convict him."

"Sometimes you have to bend the rules, especially when dealing with a scumbag like White Calf."

"I don't know about that."

"Oh, right, I forgot. The FBI always plays by the rules. I seem to recall some directors of the Bureau getting in trouble, but I'm probably imagining it. I'm sure you never step out of line. You remind me of a guy I grew up with. His old man was a minister in Heart Butte, but the kid converted and became a Catholic. Really pissed off his father. The kid was so Catholic he was practically tripping on his beads. Kind of like you. You joined the white man's club so now you're whiter than white."

Perkins slowed down and stared at Raymond in the rear-view mirror. "Raymond," he said, "go fuck yourself. You're getting tiresome."

Briggs, who until then had stayed out of it, intervened. "Hey, guys, we're all on the same side, remember?"

That had ended their conversation.

It was rapidly getting dark. Gray clouds obliterated the peaks of the Rocky Mountain front and the sky over Browning took on a leaden cast. Raymond wondered if they'd get some snow. He also wondered what Mary was cooking for dinner. Preoccupied with his altercation with Perkins, and anticipating the evening with Mary, he never noticed the truck that pulled out behind him as he left the Tribal Police parking lot.

28

"What's bothering you, Will?" Liz Perkins asked as her husband slid into bed next to her.

"Is it that obvious?" he said, surprised by her remark.

"Even the girls picked up on it. When I went to Christine to kiss her goodnight, she whispered in my ear 'doesn't Daddy feel well, Mom?'"

"It's this case I've been working on."

"The one with the murdered girl?"

"Yeah. I've never been involved in a case with so many ramifications—the murder and mutilation of a child, polygamy, drug running, sexual abuse of children."

"You've made no progress on it?"

"Some. We're pretty sure we know who killed the girl, even though we have no idea where he is now. And we have a lead on the meth distribution."

"Then you've made a lot of progress. A week ago you didn't know anything."

Perkins smiled and kissed her. "That's one of the reasons I love you. You know how to look on the bright side."

"Are you insinuating I only know how to look at the world through rose-colored glasses?"

"Of course not. It's just that given my personality, I need someone like you. You know what I'm trying to say. Someone who can see the glass half-full rather than half-empty."

"Buy you're still not telling me everything, are you?"

Liz Perkins could read her husband like a book. They had met at the University of Nebraska, where Liz was a sociology major. She and Will Perkins had been assigned a project that required them to work together. By the end of the semester, they knew they were in love. Liz Mehrens was the first white girl Will had dated. When things got serious, he had no idea how Liz's family in Cleveland would react to their daughter's involvement with an Indian.

"My parents have invited us for Thanksgiving," Liz told him when they were in their senior year. Seeing his hesitation, she smiled and kissed his cheek. "You'll have to meet them sometime," she said. "It might as well be now."

Nervous was not an adequate word to describe Will's emotional state as they stepped off the plane. He was close to panic. A few hours later he knew he needn't have worried. Sitting at the table with Liz's family in Shaker Heights, Will felt as comfortable as if he'd known them for years. Family was what had been missing from his life since the death of his own parents when he was twelve. After the fiery car crash that had claimed their lives, he'd been shunted from relative to relative, never feeling really wanted by any of them. What his experiences had taught him was to guard his feelings, to build a wall around himself. Liz and her family had torn down that wall brick by brick.

They were married in Cleveland a year later. While Will was in law school, Liz had some success in selling the articles she wrote on women's issues to magazines. She continued to write even while raising their two daughters. Thanks to the financial help provided by Liz's generous parents, they had managed to survive the lean periods between sales of her articles.

"You haven't answered my question," Liz persisted.

Will sighed. "It's not just the case, it's the tribal cop working it with me."

"What about him?"

"Raymond Two Teeth is probably the most difficult person I've ever been around. The guy walks around with a huge chip on his shoulder, and for some reason he's taken an intense dislike to me."

Liz pursed her lips. "I may be off base on this, but could it have something to do with your working for the federal government? The Indians have had some bad experiences with BIA and the FBI."

"But I'm an Indian myself, for Christ's sake."

"Even more reason for him to be distrustful. Maybe the way he looks at it, you've sold out."

"Is that the way you see it?"

"You know better than that. And it's not like you to feel sorry for yourself."

"I don't. Sometimes I think it has nothing to do with me. Maybe it's just Raymond's personality. Homer Whitecloud, the Tribal Police chief, and I, get along just fine."

"I don't know Raymond so I don't know how much I have to offer. It could just be his personality, as you say, but you were always laid back no matter who you had to work with. Keep in mind though that none of your previous assignments were on a reservation. You never worked with an Indian cop. This is different for you. And maybe for him, too."

"I'm beginning to wonder if my getting assigned to Browning was punitive on the Bureau's part."

"Why, because you're an Indian? Then how do you explain Ollie and Bill Jameson being here? You're the one who told me they're two of the best agents you've ever worked with."

"I know, I know. Damned Raymond has me tied up in knots even though I try not to show it when I'm around him."

"How is he as a cop?"

"That's another thing that drives me up the wall. He's impetuous, wants to act before thinking things through. But I have to admit, he is good. Raymond was the one who found the clue that led us to White Calf."

"White Calf?"

"He's the one we think murdered the girl."

"So Raymond has some good points?"

Perkins laughed. "Yeah, he has some good points. He doesn't miss much. The funny thing is what happened the one time Raymond and I met White Calf. I shouldn't be telling you this. You know I hate to bring casework home."

"Sometimes talking things out makes them clearer."

Perkins nodded. "Anyway, White Calf seemed to know who Raymond was. If looks could kill, Raymond would have been dead."

"Raymond hadn't seen him before?"

"Nope. Not that he remembers anyway."

"Maybe White Calf has something against tribal cops."

"What am I doing talking about Raymond Two Teeth and White Calf when I'm lying here next to the most beautiful woman in the world?"

"You're not getting off that easily, Will Perkins. But I do believe that things will work themselves out between you and Raymond."

"I sure hope you're right. Being in the same car with him isn't my idea of fun." Perkins chuckled. "He even calls me names in the Blackfeet language. Can you believe it?"

"So. You must know a few of your own in Lakota."

Perkins laughed. "What is this, the modern day version of counting coup?"

29

Raymond parked in front of Mary's house and stretched after closing his truck door. The pickup following him parked a hundred feet away on the same side of the street. The driver stepped out of the cab, leaving his door ajar. Except for the muted bass of a rock song coming from a trailer further down the block, the street was quiet. As Raymond reached Mary's door, a sixth sense made him turn. Instinctively, he raised his arm and leaned back to ward off the shadowy figure moving like a blur behind him. His assailant's weapon caught him on the side of the chest just below the left armpit. Raymond stumbled back against Mary's door and fell to the walkway, the pain in his ribs excruciating. He gasped for air, every inhalation intensifying the pain. The door swung open. Mary screamed when she saw Raymond on the ground, the huge stranger standing above him. The man swung around, raising his shotgun. Mary slammed the door, dropping to the floor as White Calf squeezed the trigger of his weapon. The impact of the blast shattered the wood. Lights flickered on up and down the block and front doors opened. Raymond struggled to his knees. White Calf, regarding him calmly, reached into his pocket for another shell.

"Hey, what the fuck's going on?" a man called from two houses away.

White Calf turned as a burly man in a tee shirt approached. He hesitated for a moment, then jogged toward his pickup, tossing the shotgun in first and leaping into the driver's seat. The burly man and three people from adjoining trailers converged on Mary's house as White Calf's truck roared to life.

Two men helped Raymond to his feet. Doubled over in pain, he clutched at his chest. "Mary!" he gasped. Calling out her name aggravated the pain in his ribs and he fell heavily against the men supporting him.

Slowly the splintered door opened and Mary staggered out. Her cardigan was bloodied where pellets had penetrated her right shoulder and upper arm.

"Oh, Jesus, are you all right?" Raymond asked, every word requiring an effort.

Before she could answer, a Tribal Police cruiser, lights flashing, screeched to a stop. Ira Sands leaped from the vehicle, his hand on his open holster.

"Shit, Raymond," he said, recognizing his fellow officer. "What happened? Are you okay?"

"Help Mary," Raymond said. "She's been shot."

"Henry, Big Moose," Ira yelled, recognizing two of the men in the crowd gathering outside Mary's house. "Help me get them into my car."

The shorter of the two men assisted Mary toward the police cruiser, while Big Moose and Ira supported Raymond. Ira turned on his lights and siren when they were in the car and drove to the Blackfoot Community Hospital. He careened into the driveway and stopped abruptly at the Emergency Room entrance. "I need two stretchers," Ira yelled when an orderly stuck his head out the door.

Ira helped Mary and Raymond from the car as a doctor, a nurse, and two orderlies raced up to them, the orderlies pushing gurneys. Silently, they helped Raymond and Mary onto them, covering them with blankets.

Ira watched them disappear behind the glass doors before calling the Tribal Police dispatcher. "This is Officer Sands," he said. "I'm at the Community Hospital. Notify the chief that Officer Two Teeth is hurt and we have a gunshot victim. I'll wait for him here at the hospital."

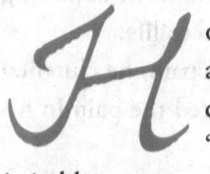 30

omer Whitecloud paced back and forth by the Emergency Room admissions desk, waiting for Doctor Ferguson, the physician on duty, to come out of the examining room.

"What did the people at the scene tell you?" Homer asked Ira irritably.

"I was too busy with Raymond and Mary to question anyone. Big Moose helped me get Raymond into the cruiser. He said he'd heard a gunshot, came out of his house, and saw Raymond on the ground. An Indian, a big guy with hair down to his shoulders, was standing over him holding a shotgun. When he saw

Big Moose coming he ran to his truck. Mary came out of the house bleeding from a gunshot wound. You think some jealous—"

"Hell, no!" Homer snapped. "Call that FBI man, Perkins. Tell him we're at the hospital, that Raymond's been hurt."

Ten minutes later tires squealed as Perkins' Subaru swerved into the hospital parking lot.

"What happened?" Perkins shouted when he spotted Homer in the ER waiting room.

"Raymond was attacked. The same guy fired his shotgun at Raymond's girlfriend and she was wounded."

"Who was it? Did you get him?"

"He got away. The description we have is an Indian, a big guy with shoulder-length hair. He was driving a GMC *Sierra*. Sound familiar?"

"White Calf!"

"That's what I figure," Homer said.

"But why? Why would he do something so stupid?"

"Good question. If he's pissed off about your visit, why did he go after Raymond first and not you? Unless he's saving you for later."

"Chief, it makes no sense. Maybe we rattled his cage by asking him about the bear claw, but he must know that if we had anything on him we would have taken him into custody. And if we did spook him, why isn't he running instead of attacking a tribal cop right in the middle of Browning?"

"All I know is that now we do have something on him. Assault and attempted murder. We're alerting all towns on the rez and the sheriffs in surrounding counties. Ira's checking with DMV for the plate number of the truck."

"I don't get it," Perkins was still repeating to himself when the ER physician appeared behind the registration desk.

"I've given him something for pain," Doctor Ferguson told them as he led Homer and Perkins to the exam room. "The X-Rays show fractures of two ribs. Fortunately there was no damage to the lung. I'd like to keep him here overnight, but he insists on leaving. He'll need lots of rest. I've given him a rib belt and a prescription for a pain-killer. He'll be mighty sore for a while."

Raymond lay on the exam table, his eyes half-closed, a dreamy expression on his face.

"How you doin'?" Homer asked, placing his hand on Raymond's shoulder.

Raymond opened his eyes and stared at Homer, Perkins, and the doctor for a moment before he recognized them. He raised his hand in a weak greeting.

"What did you give me, Doc? I'm so tired."

"Good. The medicine will help you rest."

"The pain's not bad now unless I take a deep breath. Where's Mary? Can I see her?"

"She's in the next room and she's okay. We're going to keep her in the hospital. The surgeon will have to pick out the buckshot and splinters in her shoulder and arm. Fortunately, no bones were involved. It's a good thing she had the presence of mind to dive to the floor before that lunatic fired at the door."

Raymond struggled to a sitting position, pushing away the doctor's hands as Ferguson tried to restrain him. "I want to see her," he said.

"You're going to be wobbly on your feet because of the painkiller. I still think you should spend the night in the hospital."

Raymond shook his head.

Ferguson looked helplessly at Homer and Perkins.

"Raymond, don't be such a stubborn ass," the chief said. "Stay here tonight."

"I want to see Mary. Then I'm out of here."

Homer shrugged and nodded to the doctor.

"Okay then, we'll give you some pills to take home with you tonight and someone can fill the prescription for you in the morning."

Raymond leaned heavily against Homer as he slid off the table. "How'd you know I was here?" he asked, turning to Perkins.

"Ira called me."

"Take me to Mary," Raymond said, turning back to Doctor Ferguson.

The doctor held his arm and led him into the adjoining exam room.

"We'll wait for you outside," Homer said as the door closed.

Mary, wearing a hospital johnny and covered by a blanket, struggled to sit up on the examining table when she saw Raymond.

"Are you okay?" she asked.

"I should be asking you that."

"I thought he'd killed you when I saw you on the ground."

"He'll wish he had when I find him."

"Your voice is funny," Mary said. "Like you've been drinking."

"It's the medicine I gave him," Doctor Ferguson said. "He's got two broken ribs."

Mary reached out to Raymond with her hand. "The doctor says I have to stay here."

"I know," he said, taking her fingers in his. "Want me to pick up Delia?"

"I don't think you're in shape to pick up anyone. Besides, it'd only scare her. I'll tell her tomorrow when she gets home from school."

"You sure you're okay?" Raymond said.

She nodded. "I'll be all right. The doctor says the wound is superficial. Who did this, Raymond? I only saw him for a moment, but I didn't recognize him."

"I don't know. I never got a good look at him."

"I think it's time for you to go home before the pain killer wears off," Doctor Ferguson said. "I'm sure the chief will give you a ride."

"I'll see you tomorrow," Raymond said, squeezing Mary's hand.

"Be careful, Raymond," she called as he reached the door.

"How is she?" Homer asked when Raymond stepped into the hallway.

"She seems okay. If she hadn't been on the floor when he fired . . ."

"Listen," Perkins said, "why don't I drive you home. That okay with you, Chief?"

"Doesn't matter to me," said Homer. "My dinner's on the table and it can't get any colder. And Raymond, I'm putting you on sick leave. Don't think about coming to work tomorrow."

Raymond brushed away Perkin's hand as the agent tried to assist him into the passenger seat of the Subaru. He rested his head against the back of the seat as Perkins turned out of the hospital lot. Driving slowly, Perkins threw concerned looks at his passenger.

"Oh shit!" Raymond groaned when the car hit a pothole.

"Sorry."

"The stuff he gave me must be wearing off."

"You have enough medicine to get you through the night?"

"The doc gave me four tablets to take home with me."

"Let me have the prescription. I'll pick up the rest for you in the morning."

"I'll drive down and get it."

"Well, just in case you don't feel like driving tomorrow."

Raymond closed his eyes and lapsed back into silence.

"You never saw him come up behind you?" Perkins asked after a few minutes.

"Not till the last second," Raymond said, his speech slurred. "I was right at Mary's door when something made me turn. All I saw was a dark shape swinging something at me. I got my arm up just before it hit me."

"He wasn't trying to hurt you, Raymond. He wanted to kill you."

"How do you know that?"

"If you hadn't raised your arm, that blow probably would have caught you in the side of the head. We'd be having your funeral tomorrow."

"I've made some enemies over the years, but this makes no sense. The guy must have been drunk or on drugs."

"He was stalking you, Raymond."

"Bullshit."

"Bullshit, huh? One of the neighbors gave a description of him and the vehicle he was driving. He was an Indian, big guy with shoulder length hair, and he carried a shotgun. He was driving a GMC *Sierra*."

Raymond's eyes opened wide. He leaned forward and looked at Perkins incredulously. "Why?"

"That's what I'm trying to figure out."

31

"John, did you hear about the shooting?" Beth asked as they sat down for lunch in the cafeteria.

"Somebody mentioned something about a cop getting attacked in town last night."

"The cop was Raymond Two Teeth."

"Raymond? Is he okay?"

"He had fractured ribs. Ferguson wanted to admit him but Raymond insisted on going home. His lady friend had shotgun pellets taken out of her shoulder this morning."

"You mean someone beat him and shot his girlfriend? Was it a love triangle?"

"Men," Beth said, shaking her head. "Always jumping to conclusions. The ER nurse told me the suspect is someone we're already familiar with."

"Who?"

"Sharon's husband. White Calf. The FBI and Tribal Police are looking for him."

"This is crazy. If he knows the cops suspect him of murdering Sharon's sister, why would he come to Browning? He must be completely mad."

"So I was right to worry about him coming to the hospital, wasn't I?"

"But he didn't come to the hospital. He went after a Tribal Police officer. It makes no sense."

"Why don't you talk to Dr. Ferguson since he took care of Raymond in the ER. Maybe he knows something."

The ER nurse, a young Blackfeet woman, had a puzzled expression when John Hartman walked in.

"We didn't call you, Dr. Hartman. Do you have a patient coming in?"

"No, I was looking for Dr. Ferguson."

"He has an asthmatic in the exam room. Shall I tell him you're here?"

"No, I'll wait for him to come out. Were you working last night?"

"No, Margaret was. They had some excitement. You heard about the attack on a police officer?"

"Yes. Raymond Two Teeth. I know him."

She smiled. "Everyone knows Raymond. He's a fixture in town. From what Margaret told me, both Raymond and his friend are lucky to be alive."

"Do you know why they were attacked?"

"I guess policemen have enemies."

"But why would this person shoot at Raymond's friend?"

The nurse shrugged. "Maybe because she happened to be there? I don't— oh, here's Dr. Ferguson now."

"Hi, Doug," John said, greeting the emergency room physician. "A little excitement yesterday, I understand."

"Yeah. I'm glad we don't see cops getting attacked too often. What's up? You have a patient coming in?"

"No, I was just curious about what happened with the police officer. My wife and I know him."

"Raymond took a good wallop, hard enough to fracture two ribs. The guy probably hit him with the same shotgun he used to fire at Raymond's friend. She was lucky—if she hadn't hit the deck, it might have killed her."

"Any idea why it happened?"

"Not really. There was an FBI man here with Homer Whitecloud, the police chief. I overheard some talk about a suspect."

"If Raymond had two broken ribs, how come you didn't admit him? Weren't you worried about lung damage?"

"Don't think I didn't try. He insisted on going home, and he wasn't taking no for an answer." Ferguson chuckled. "I got the impression Officer Two Teeth doesn't like being told what to do. I heard Homer tell him he better not show up for work today. But you know something? It wouldn't surprise me if he did."

32

erkins waited at the pharmacy counter as the druggist filled Raymond's prescription for pain pills.

"Tell Raymond to take them only when he absolutely needs them," the pharmacist said. "We don't want it to become a habit."

"I'll tell him."

On the way to Raymond's, Perkins stopped at Tribal Police Headquarters to see if there was any word on White Calf's whereabouts. Merle Wagner, the officer at the front desk, shook his head. "No one's spotted the truck. We got the license number from DMV this morning." He scribbled it on a piece of paper for Perkins. "I've passed it on to the sheriffs in all the surrounding counties. And I know the chief has the address where White Calf works."

"Is Homer in?"

"No. He said he was going to do a little looking around. I can radio him if you want to talk to him."

"No, don't bother. But he really should have someone with him. White Calf is armed and we know he's dangerous."

"Don't worry about Homer. He'd call for help before trying to apprehend him. Some of the other men are out looking, too. If he's on the rez, someone is bound to spot the truck."

Perkins was surprised to find Raymond dressed and standing by the stove, a coffee cup in his hand. He wore a flannel shirt, down vest, and jeans.

"About time you got here," Raymond said.

"Hey, I had to wait till the pharmacy opened to get your prescription."

"Coffee's fresh. Sit down and I'll pour you a cup before we head out."

"Head out where? Aren't you supposed to be in bed? You heard Homer last night. You're on sick leave."

"You didn't hear him say I'm quarantined, did you?"

"The chief's got it covered. We know the license plate number on the truck and his office contacted the sheriffs in all the counties around here. Homer and some of the other men are already out looking for White Calf. If he's still on the rez, they'll find him."

"Nobody knows the rez better than me. We can take some back roads even Homer doesn't know. Maybe we'll spot the truck."

"What the hell are you talking about? You're in no condition to go driving around."

"Let me have my pills."

Perkins handed him the bottle. "The pharmacist said you can pay him next time you're in the store. And that you should take them only when you really need them."

Raymond scrutinized the label on the bottle. "*Oxycontin*, huh? I could make a lot of money on these. Forty bucks a tablet if I sold them on the street." He washed down a tablet with his coffee.

"Yeah, I can really see you doing that."

"Don't let my honest face fool you."

Perkins made a dismissive motion with his hand. "Did you talk to Mary this morning?"

"They were picking out pellets when I called. The nurse said she was doing okay."

"Good. Well, get yourself some rest. I'm heading out. I'll stop by later to see how you're doing."

"You won't have to," Raymond said, following him to the door.

"You sure you're okay?" Perkins asked as his car bounced down a dirt track along the Cut Bank River. "This can't be doing your ribs much good."

"I'm okay," Raymond said, taking his prescription bottle out of his pocket.

"You don't want those to become a habit. Listen, this is stupid. Let me drive you home."

"Hold it," Raymond said, raising his arm.

"Want me to turn around?"

Raymond, gazing out across a dry creekbed ignored him. "No, I thought I saw something. It's just a whitetail. Keep driving."

"We can't spend the day doing this. These roads are bad enough to put you back in the hospital."

"Stop worrying about me."

"White Calf had all night to get away. He could be anywhere."

"Maybe that's what he wants us to think, that he's headed far away from Browning. There are plenty of places to hide on the rez."

"For a man maybe, not for a truck."

"There are scattered homesites everywhere. Back in 1912 every Blackfeet was allotted a half-section of land, but many sold off pieces of their ground. What's to stop him from forcing his way into someone's place and hiding his truck in their barn or garage? We might not know about it for days or weeks, if the person was alive to tell us."

"Then what are we doing out here?"

"Maybe we'll get lucky."

"What I still can't figure out is why White Calf attacked you. He could be far away from here by now if he hadn't come back to Browning."

"Maybe he's just a psycho and our going to his place set him off."

"Yeah, but he went after you, not me."

"Maybe you're next on his list."

"I still say it makes no sense. Unless he is crazy, like you say. But he didn't strike me that way when we talked to him."

"We were only with the guy for a few minutes. You think a sane person does what he did to that little girl?"

"I don't know what to think. Oh, I forgot to tell you. Homer has Aalford's address."

Raymond gave him a sly look. "There's a place called Santa Rita directly ahead. Turn off to the south there and we'll pick up the road from Cut Bank to Shelby. Then we can get on Fifteen and head up to Sunburst."

"Sunburst? Where the hell is that?"

"About ten miles south of the Canadian border."

"Why do you want to go there?"

"Because that's where Aalford is."

"How the hell do you know that?"

Raymond smiled at Perkins' consternation. "Two Bear Woman said Aalford's place was near the border. I figured it had to be close to the rez so I called the Toole County Sheriff's office this morning. They knew exactly where Aalford was."

"You've been busy."

"I can't just sit at home feeling sorry for myself."

"You've done enough for one day. Why don't you let me drop you at your place. I'll pick up Briggs at my office and he and I will head up there. Homer won't be very happy if he knows you're doing this."

"We're closer to Sunburst now than we are to Browning."

"You're sure you're up to it?"

"I'm fine. Working takes my mind off the pain. Do you have your cell phone with you? I want to call Mary."

Perkins passed it to him.

"Hey, it's me," Raymond said when Mary picked up the phone in her room. He listened for a minute. "I'm with Perkins," he said.

Perkins heard Mary's voice increase in volume but he couldn't make out what she was saying. Raymond held the phone away from his ear. "I gotta go," he said. "We'll pick you up at the hospital later and drive you home."

"Pissed off with you, right?" Perkins said when Raymond handed him the phone.

"She says I should be home resting."

"She's right."

"They're letting her go home later today. They got all the pellets out. You mind if we pick her up when we're back in Browning?"

"That's fine. Now give Homer a call. He ought to know where we're going, and then I'll call my office."

Raymond passed him the phone. "You can call your office. I'll call Homer, but after we see Aalford."

33

*T*wenty-six miles north of Shelby, Perkins left the highway at the Sunburst exit. He stopped at the Prairie Market and asked for directions to Aalford's farm.

"Did they know?" Raymond asked as Perkins slid into his seat.

He nodded and drove slowly, peering off to his right. "There's the road we take," he said, indicating a dirt road sandwiched between two vacant stores. Fields of yellow stubble stretched out on both sides of the track.

"You know this country?" Perkins asked.

"Those are the Sweetgrass Hills in the distance," Raymond said. "The border of the rez is ten or fifteen miles west of here, off to your left. The Canadian border's even closer. My cousin and I once went fishing on a small lake just south of us. Hay Lake, it's called."

Perkins checked his odometer and pointed to the right. "That must be it. They said it was two and a half miles from town."

A dirt driveway led to a sprawling white frame house with a garage off to its right. The late morning sun reflected off a green Ford F-150 parked in front of the garage. Its right front fender was crushed. Ninety-five model, Raymond said to himself, storing the information away. When it came to recovering stolen cars and trucks, Raymond had no peer on the Tribal Police force. Another vehicle, obscured by shadows, was parked inside the garage.

A barn, its raw pine boards weathered and stained, came into view north of the house. An overhang, built to create a storage area, projected from the building's western side. Beneath it a tractor and baler were parked.

The hay fields of Aalford's farm, stubbled at this time of year, spread in all directions, their uniform monotony broken only by giant rolls of hay weathering in a distant meadow and a rectangular stack of bales covered by tarps. Off to the northwest, a white building capped by a pointed spire was situated incongruously at the edge of a hayfield.

Perkins parked near the garage. Raymond, holding his taped ribs with one hand, eased himself out of the car.

"You okay?" Perkins asked.

Raymond ignored him. "Looks peaceful enough," he said. "No sign of White Calf's rig."

High-pitched voices drifted across the fields. A parade of children, twelve by Perkins' count, filed out of the white building in the distance. "Must be a school," Perkins said.

The children, ranging in age from four or five to a boy who appeared to be in his early teens, headed in Raymond and Perkins' direction. A slender man brought up the rear of the procession. The children fell silent as they marched past Perkins and Raymond, ignoring the two men as if they didn't exist.

"Go inside and get ready for lunch," the man shepherding them said. "Tell your mothers I'll be along shortly for prayers."

Raymond and Perkins studied the weathered face of the thin man as he approached. They each guessed him to be in his early forties but were perplexed by his appearance. He wore a white shirt, pressed slacks, and an expensive sports jacket. Neither of them was accustomed to seeing a farmer as well dressed as Aalford.

"Can I help you gentlemen?" Aalford asked, smiling.

Raymond watched Aalford's eyes, paying no attention to his smile or his words. He could tell more from a man's eyes. There was nothing friendly or welcoming in Aalford's greeting.

"Are you Mister Aalford?" Perkins asked.

"I am. And you are?"

"FBI," Perkins said, flashing his identification. "This is Officer Two Teeth of the Blackfeet Tribal Police. We understand a man named White Calf works for you."

"Yes. He delivers hay for me. Is he in some kind of trouble?"

"When did you last see him?"

"Tuesday. He loaded up ten tons of hay for delivery. We don't get many calls for hay this late in the year, but a rancher in Hingham needed some for his horses."

"When do you expect him back?"

"He said he was taking a few days off and would be back on the weekend. What's this all about?"

"How do you get in touch with White Calf when you need him?"

"He doesn't have a phone. I have to depend on him calling me."

"Isn't that a little unusual? An employee you can't reach?"

"We manage. Besides, White Calf stays up here when we're really busy."

"We'd like to talk to him if you have any idea where we might find him," Raymond said.

"He lives on the reservation, but you probably know that."

Raymond nodded. He pointed to the building with a spire on its roof. "Pretty convenient having a schoolhouse on your own ground. Are you the teacher?"

"Actually that's a church."

"Really? What denomination?"

Aalford's eyes flicked warily from Raymond to Perkins, who stood off to the side as if he were bored by the conversation.

"The Church of the True Saints."

"I'm not familiar with that one. Are you the pastor?"

"Well, pastor may not be the right word, but yes, I'm the head of the church."

"Where do the children go to school? We didn't pass one on the way here."

"We home school, Officer—Two Teeth, is it?"

"Uh huh. I don't mean to pry, but are all these kids yours?"

"I don't see where my family is any of your business." Aalford's smile had disappeared. He regarded Raymond with a cold stare.

"Well, it isn't, of course. I just noticed some of the kids were about the same age and I thought I heard you say the word mothers to the children. Do you have more than one wife?"

"You're out of your jurisdiction here. The reservation is that way, in case you forgot." Aalford jerked his thumb toward the west.

"So you haven't heard from White Calf since he left?" Perkins asked, stepping in front of him.

"I told you I didn't expect him until the weekend."

"Yes, you did tell us. And you don't know of any way we can get in touch with him?"

"That's right. You still haven't told me what this is all about. Did he have an accident with my flatbed?"

"No, no accident. Do you know this girl?" Perkins held up the photo of Rebecca taken by Dr. Hartman.

Aalford blinked several times, but his face remained impassive. "It looks like Rebecca, my stepdaughter. Her sister is White Calf's wife. Rebecca lives with them. Did something happen to her?"

Perkins regarded him closely. "She doesn't live with them anymore," he said. "She's dead."

A flush of color appeared on Aalford's cheeks.

"I don't understand. What happened to her?"

"That's what we want to talk to White Calf about."

Aalford opened his mouth to say something, then frowned. "This is very distressing news."

"Yeah," Raymond said, "we can see that."

"If you gentlemen will excuse me, I have to inform Rebecca's mother. You don't have any more details you can give me? Had she been ill?"

"As long as I'm here, why don't I speak to Rebecca's mother," Perkins said.

"I'd prefer that you don't. It would be better if I give her the news."

Perkins nodded slowly, as if mulling over Aalford's response. "Here's my card," he said. "It has my cell phone number on it. Tell Rebecca's mother she can call me. Well, we don't want to keep you from your family. Do you mind if we look around?"

"Yes, as a matter of fact I do. This is going to be a difficult time for us. I must ask you to leave."

"You'll call if White Calf contacts you?" Raymond asked.

"Of course. But you know how unreliable Indians are."

Raymond locked eyes with him. "Like some whites, you mean. But he's worked for you for a long time. Why would you keep a worker who's unreliable?"

"You're trespassing," Aalford said. "Now get out of here." He wheeled around and walked stiffly toward the house without looking back.

"He's all broken up about his stepdaughter's death, isn't he?" Raymond said. "I get the feeling we're not very popular."

"No, we're not. And we're going to be a lot more unpopular before we're through with Mr. Aalford. You heard the man. 'This is going to be a difficult time,' he said. He doesn't know how difficult."

"You gave Aalford your card for the dead girl's mother. Do you really think she'll contact you?" Raymond asked as they drove back to Browning.

"She'll probably never see that card. In fact, it wouldn't surprise me if Aalford never told her anything. Even if he does, I'd be surprised if she called. Remember what Sharon called Aalford? The prophet? My guess is no one in Aalford's house does anything without his permission. Prophets like to run the show."

"You think Aalford is involved with White Calf's running meth?"

"You mean you think his religious scruples would prevent him from doing it?" Perkins teased.

"Am I supposed to laugh now?"

"You have a great sense of humor, Raymond. It's one of the things I like about you."

"*Ee mah tusk kee,*" Raymond grumbled under his breath.

"Someday you'll have to tell me what that means."

"Someday I will."

"Okay, you want to know what I think about Aalford? The particles of meth in White Calf's shed had to come from somewhere. I can't believe White Calf killed the girl because of a kitten. She must have seen something in that shed he didn't want her to see. Like packages of meth. Aalford's got the perfect front for distributing it. A hay business. And he's a religious man, head of whatever the hell cult he professes to lead."

"I just wanted to make sure we're on the same wavelength," Raymond said.

"Maybe when we catch up to White Calf we'll get some answers about Aalford. I don't think much of pedophiles and exploiters of women. I'd like to put him away for a long time."

"I'll bet the sheriff whose office gave me Aalford's address knows he has multiple wives."

Perkins glanced at him. "So why don't they go after him?"

"You know how law enforcement operates in rural areas. They take a 'don't make waves' approach to things. As long as no complaints are filed, everything is above board."

"Even when the so-called wives are minors?"

"We don't know how old Aalford's women are, or how old they were when he made them pregnant. Can you believe it? Twelve kids.

"Listen, do me a favor. Call Homer and tell him we've been to see Aalford. Just in case he called my house to see how I was doing. I don't want him worrying and going out there for nothing."

"After you call me names like *ee mah* whatever it is, you want me to do you a favor? You call him," Perkins grinned. "Besides, you're the one who insisted on going with me."

"I don't want him busting my chops. Come on, I took you to Aalford, didn't I?"

Perkins laughed. "You took me? I love it. You're too much, Raymond." He dialed the number and turned to Raymond. "Ira's putting him on. Sure you don't want to talk to him?"

Raymond shook his head.

"Hey, Chief, just wondering if anyone's spotted White Calf or his truck. No luck, huh." He glanced at Raymond. "Yeah, he's with me. Insisted on coming along. We've been up to see Aalford. I'll tell you all about it when I get back." Perkins listened. He smiled. "Okay, I'll tell him." He listened again, nodding. Raymond, uncomfortable as the seconds passed, fidgeted in his seat. "Thanks," Perkins said. "I'll see you this afternoon."

"What was all that about?" Raymond asked as Perkins tucked his cell phone into his jacket pocket.

"A couple of developments. The lab in Missoula set a speed record in getting the results back. We have the DNA from the hair on the girl's sweater and the hair on the pillow. As we suspected, they're a match. And the crystals were definitely meth."

"So that confirms what we already knew."

"We still want all the evidence we can get for the day we have White Calf in a court room."

"What was it Homer said you should tell me?"

"Oh yeah," Perkins said, laughing. "Homer said to tell you you're an asshole."

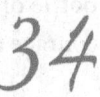

aymond sat at his desk and tried to concentrate on the reports in front of him. Walking into Tribal Police Headquarters the morning after his trip to Sunburst with Perkins, he had encountered an angry Homer Whitecloud.

"Since when do you go off the reservation with the FBI without clearing it with me? You were placed on sick leave. Did I say anything about sick leave including a trip with Perkins to Sunburst?"

"Chief, you don't expect me to sit around and do nothing when there's a guy out there who tried to kill me."

"Don't tell me what I expect. Is that supposed to be an apology?"

"Okay. You're right, I should have cleared it with you."

"You damn well should have. And since you feel well enough to run around with busted ribs, I'm taking you off sick leave. But you work at your desk until I say otherwise. No outside patrols. Is that understood?"

Hoping the chief would relent in a day or two, Raymond meekly assented. Sitting at his desk seemed to aggravate the pain in his ribs. If he could get out of the office and actively work the case, he knew it would take his mind off the pain, but there was no sense trying to use that argument on Homer. As things stood, there really was no case to work. There hadn't been a sighting of White Calf's truck. And if White Calf had any close friends or associates besides Aalford, they hadn't made their presence known.

In a way, Raymond was pleased that nothing was happening. If White Calf was spotted now, the chief wouldn't allow Raymond to join the search. And if there was one thing Raymond Two Teeth wanted, it was to be in on the capture of the man who had mutilated Rebecca, wounded Mary, and caused him so much pain it hurt to breathe.

Raymond fingered the bottle of pills in his pocket. He wanted desperately to take one, but he knew *Oxycontin* wasn't to be toyed with. He'd arrested enough kids on the rez who were getting their hands on the narcotic and becoming addicted. Pushing himself back from his desk, he walked to the cabinet where a bottle of Tylenol was kept. After swallowing three of them, he summoned up his courage and knocked on Homer's door.

"Can I talk to you about the case?"

"What case?"

Raymond hated it when the chief played coy.

"I know Perkins filled you in about Aalford."

"Aalford's the FBI's problem, not ours."

"What if White Calf shows up there?"

"After what's happened? I don't think so. And if he does, the feds will have to make the arrest. In case you're forgetting, Sunburst is not on the rez."

"I can't understand why no one has spotted the truck."

"The problem with you, Raymond, is you're too impatient. We'll get him. In the meantime, why don't you clean up some of the paper work that's been accumulating on your desk. By the way, how's Mary doing?"

"We brought her home from the hospital yesterday. She's okay."

"You don't look happy about it."

"She's pissed off with me."

"That shows she has good sense."

"She's sore but hopes to be back to work in a few days."

"Uh-huh. Maybe you should take a lesson from that."

Seeing he was getting nowhere, Raymond headed back to his desk.

"Hey, Raymond," said Leonard Nye, sticking his head into the room. "You have a visitor."

Raymond suppressed a smile. Mary must have dropped by to make peace. He was surprised to see John Hartman, the pediatrician, entering the room.

"I hope I'm not intruding," John said.

"No, how are you, Doc?"

"I should be asking you that."

"I'll live." At the moment, Raymond wondered if that was true. The three Tylenol hadn't kicked in yet.

"I just wanted to see how you were doing and I wanted to ask you something."

"Shoot."

"I hear that White Calf—the man you suspect of killing the girl—was the person who attacked you. Is that true?"

"Who told you that?"

"You know how things get around in the hospital."

"It's an ongoing investigation, Doc. Right now we're looking for White Calf. That's all I can tell you."

"Why do you think he attacked you?"

"Assuming it was White Calf, I wish to hell I knew the reason. But as things stand now, I don't."

"So my wife was right to worry about him coming back here. If he went after you, how do we know he won't come after Sharon? Or Sharon's little girl? She's still in the hospital with whooping cough."

"If he was after Sharon, he would have gone to the hospital before coming after me. Something else is involved here. Tell your wife not to worry. We'll get him."

John said nothing and Raymond scrutinized him closely. "Is something else bothering you, Doc?"

"I just wish you had the murderer in custody. Maybe then there'd be some kind of closure. That poor girl's face keeps me from sleeping."

"Doc, that makes two of us. But White Calf can't hide forever."

35

Perkins was surprised to receive a call from Raymond Two Teeth inviting him and his wife to dinner at Mary's on Friday. "Are you sure?" he said. "You and Mary can't be feeling well enough to have guests."

"It'll be something simple. Nothing fancy. Mary insisted. She wants to meet you."

"Where are you now?"

"Sitting at my desk."

"Homer said you could go back to work?"

"He wasn't happy about my going up to Aalford's with you, so he took me off sick leave. But he won't let me go out on patrol."

"Hey, don't complain. You have to give those ribs a chance to heal."

"Anyway, will you and your wife come?"

"If you're sure Mary is up to it, I'll be there, but I'm afraid it'll just be me. My wife's mother is ill and she had to fly out to Omaha yesterday."

"You have two girls, right? You can bring them."

"Why, thanks, Raymond, but we may not be able to talk as freely if the kids are along. We have good neighbors. Their daughter likes to baby sit so that's no problem. If you'd rather put this off until Liz gets back—"

"No, come," Raymond said. "Mary is just getting over being angry with me for running up to Sunburst with you, so I don't want to disappoint her on this."

"We're sorry your wife couldn't come," Mary said when Perkins arrived on Friday evening. "Will her mother be all right?"

"Liz—my wife—said they operated on her yesterday for her gallbladder. I spoke to her this morning and Liz said she's doing fine. She might be discharged tomorrow so my wife may be home this weekend."

"Does her mother have anyone to care for her after she's discharged?"

"Liz's dad is there. He's in good health."

"That's good. Raymond says you have two girls."

"Christine and Lucy. They're good kids. Chris is ten and Lucy nine."

"I have a thirteen-year-old. Her name is Delia. She's staying over at her friend's house tonight.

"Why don't you and Raymond relax and have something to drink while I finish making the salad. Raymond is a teetotaler, but I have some beer if you'd like."

"That'll be fine."

"Raymond? *Coke*?"

"I'll get it," he said.

"Any news?" Raymond asked as he handed Perkins the beer.

"Nothing. It's like he disappeared off the face of the earth, but at some point he'll show himself."

"What're you doing about Aalford?"

"I don't think White Calf will be stupid enough to go there, but we're having the farm watched just in case."

"Tough to do without being noticed in a place as small as Sunburst."

"Our men know how to blend into the woodwork. Listen, are you sure Mary is well enough to have a guest for dinner? I feel guilty about putting her out."

"Hey, I'm the one grilling the steaks. She's just putting potatoes in the oven and making the salad."

"It's really nice of her. I appreciate it." He looked up as Mary came back into the room. "I told Raymond I thought it was too soon for you to have a guest."

"I'm okay. Really. Just a little stiffness in the shoulder. Besides, Raymond is the one doing the cooking." She smiled. "I have big ears and that's what I heard him tell you."

"Hey, it's the truth," Raymond said. "Just let me know when to start the grill."

"You and Raymond are a pair," Perkins said. "The walking wounded."

"It's better than being the lying-down dead," Raymond said.

"You're both lucky, that's for sure."

"Raymond, you can start the grill now. How do you like your steak, Mr. Perkins?"

"Please, call me Will."

"No, call him Little Crow," Raymond said. "That's his Lakota name."

"You're Sioux?"

"Yeah, he's from Pine Ridge," Raymond said.

"I think Mr. Per—Will—can talk for himself, Raymond. Go start the grill."

"Okay, I'm going."

"Raymond tells me one of your jobs is at the Piegan Institute," Perkins said. "I think it's great that you're trying to keep the old language alive."

"I've been working with the Institute for four years, but it was founded fifteen years ago. For the past hundred years BIA forced our children into English-only boarding schools. The kids weren't allowed to speak their own language. Only old people still spoke it and it was in danger of disappearing. I'm sure the same thing is true of the Lakota language."

Perkins nodded. "I heard recently that half of the Indian languages spoken in this country when the whites arrived have disappeared."

"That's true," Mary said. "You know how the idea of immersing kids in their native language came about? The Maoris in New Zealand and native Hawaiians created language nests, total immersion centers. Students listened to and spoke the native tongue all day. We do the same thing. We built a school, the Real Speak school. The parents pay a modest tuition and the kids have all their classes in the Blackfeet language."

"You were a Blackfeet speaker when you went to work for them?"

Mary laughed. "I spoke a little, but I attended classes with the children for a year. That's how I learned it and now I'm a teacher."

"That's impressive."

"It's really rewarding for me and it makes the kids proud of their heritage." She turned to Raymond when he came back into the room. "You'll have to bring Will to our school. The children will be impressed to meet a real FBI man."

"Especially one that looks like them," Raymond said.

"I hate to get off the topic, but perhaps you have some ideas about why that man, White Calf, attacked Raymond and shot at me."

"He doesn't know any more than I do," Raymond interrupted.

"Raymond, I'm losing patience. Will you let the man speak."

"I wish I could think of a reason," Perkins said quickly, wanting to head off an argument. "Raymond told you that we went out to his place before all this happened to ask him some questions?"

She nodded. "Raymond said you found a bear claw near where the girl was murdered."

"That's right, Raymond found it. I don't usually talk about ongoing cases, but since Raymond's already told you—"

"Hey, you think it's easy keeping anything from this woman?"

"Anyway, Raymond found out that White Calf wore a bear claw. When we questioned him, he lied to us, said he'd lost it years ago. Maybe our questioning set him off. He might have thought we suspected him of being implicated in the girl's murder."

"It still makes no sense. You didn't arrest him. And what good does it do to kill people working on the case? That wouldn't stop the investigation."

"You're right," Perkins said. "It makes no sense at all. That's the conclusion we've all come to."

"Doesn't your wife worry about you?" Mary said. "White Calf went after Raymond. How do we know he won't go after you next?"

Perkins smiled, trying to assuage her concern. "My wife always worries about me. She just tries not to show it. Did Raymond tell you everything that happened when we went out to White Calf's place?"

"Hey," Raymond said, "spare us the melodramatics."

"No, I think Mary should know this. Especially in view of what's happened. Something strange went on between White Calf and Raymond. It was as if White Calf knew who Raymond was. You know the old saying, 'if looks could kill'? Well, that's how White Calf looked at Raymond."

"Hey, Perkins, what the hell do you think you're doing? She's been through enough without this bullshit."

"He came after you once, Raymond. Whatever is going on is between you and him, at least in his mind. And there's no way to know if he'll make another try. Mary should know that."

"He'd have to be crazy," Raymond said.

Perkins pursed his lips. "Call him crazy or call him a psychopath, Mary still has to be alerted to what he might do. I'm convinced that the only reason he shot at her was because she saw him. It was you he was after, Raymond."

"Let him come. There's nothing I'd like better."

"Raymond, please . . . " Mary said, rolling her eyes.

"Nobody doubts your bravery," Perkins said, "but White Calf isn't looking for a fair fight. He wants you dead, even if it's from a bullet in the back."

"I'm not going to hide," Raymond said angrily.

"Nobody expects you to hide," said Mary. "Will is just saying that you have to be cautious."

"Okay, I'll watch my back. And so will he," Raymond said, jerking his thumb at Perkins while talking to Mary. "Homer will be very upset if he lets anything happen to me."

"It's not a joke," Mary said.

"Look," Raymond said placatingly, "I'll be careful. I promise. But I still don't believe this is anything personal between White Calf and me. I never met the guy till we went out to his place."

"Are you sure you didn't put someone in his family away?" Perkins asked.

"I checked," Raymond said. "I went through all my old cases and his name never popped up. And outside of his problems in the military, White Calf has no criminal record. So let's just drop this and enjoy our dinner. Are you ready for me to put the steaks on?"

Later that evening, as Perkins prepared to leave, Mary asked him to wait a moment. She returned holding a colorful belt and held it out to him. "My great-grandmother made this," she said. "I'd like you to have it."

Perkins studied the belt under the hallway's overhead light. "The beadwork is beautiful," he said.

Mary smiled. "There is some beadwork, but most of it is quillwork."

Perkins gave her a puzzled look. "Quills as in porcupine?"

She nodded. "Blackfeet don't do quillwork anymore, but my great-grandmother was an old Piegan lady who believed it was sacred to work with quills. This piece is unusual because she combined some beadwork with it. I think originally it was meant to be a decoration for a buffalo robe, but I made a belt out of it. I was going to have Raymond wear it, but—" She laughed. "He outgrew it."

Raymond, standing behind them, frowned. "She feeds me too much, then she complains about my weight."

"How did she fasten the quills to the leather?" Perkins asked, ignoring Raymond.

"My mother told me her grandmother held the quills in her mouth to soften them. Then she flattened them between her teeth and put them in place. She passed two sinew threads through the leather and folded the ends of the quills under the threads. Finally, she flattened the quills some more by pressing them with a bone. Anyway, it's a lost art now."

"Thank you for offering, but really, I can't take it. It's probably very valuable and it belongs in your family."

"I'd like you to have it. For keeping an eye on Raymond, you know, for watching out for him."

"Listen to her," Raymond said, irritated. "I'm the one who has to watch out for this Lakota kid. He's not on home ground and I don't want him to get his suit dirty."

Mary looked at Raymond, annoyed, but Perkins simply smiled at her.

"You must have extraordinary patience, Mary, to put up with this guy. I always like it when he shows his nicer side. It's the Raymond I've grown to know and love."

36

It was past midnight when a GMC *Sierra* drove east along the Hi-Line. White Calf hadn't seen another vehicle in the past half-hour. He was glad to be on the move. Since the fiasco in Browning Wednesday evening, he'd camped at Lake Elwell. He was sure the neighbors of the woman he'd fired at had given the cops his description and that of his truck. It was best to get off the rez and camp in the woods for a few days, he'd decided, rather than take a chance on having the truck spotted.

His headlight beams picked up an occasional coyote darting across the road, or mule deer grazing along the edge of the highway. He sipped the coffee he'd bought at a diner in Havre. He'd added the last quarter gram of his meth to it. Since his botched attempt to kill the cop, he'd been using meth twice a day. He hadn't slept in two nights but he wasn't tired. Only one thing mattered now—his meeting with Miguel. In a little over an hour, he'd be able to score another eight-ball. And his money worries would be over.

White Calf drove carefully, staying at the speed limit. "Stupid bitch," he said aloud. If the cop's lady friend hadn't opened the door, he would have finished off Two Teeth before the neighbors could interfere.

He thought of the day Two Teeth and the fed had shown up at his place. He knew immediately they were there because of the body he'd dumped near the old factory in Browning. Someone obviously had found it, but even so, he couldn't imagine how they'd traced it to him. When Two Teeth mentioned the grizzly claw, he knew. White Calf thought it had torn loose from his neck up at Aalford's while he was loading hay, but the cops must have found it where he'd left the girl. Someone must have told them he wore one. He couldn't think of any other reason for them to end up at his door.

White Calf angrily clenched the steering wheel. If Rebecca hadn't found the kitten and tried to hide it in his shed, none of this would have happened. He wasn't sure what she'd seen or not seen in the shed. And if she spotted the bags of meth, did she know what she was looking at? It didn't matter. Sharon, Rebecca and the kids had been told never to go into his sheds. The moment White Calf saw Rebecca crouched in a corner next to his bales with that mangy kitten no bigger than a rat in her arms, he'd lost it. Aalford's words flashed through his head. 'Women must be taught to obey.' This little bitch had never obeyed. Even when he was on top of her, she lay as if she was made of stone, as if her body was there but she wasn't. She cowered in the shed, shaking her head from side to side as he came nearer, protecting the kitten with her arms. Seeing her like that intensified his rage. White Calf remembered how the bones of her face had crunched under the blow from his fist. After that he'd killed the kitten, smashing its skull against the corner of a wooden palette. He wrapped the unconscious girl in a tarp and placed her in the bed of his truck. No definite plan came to his mind as he drove toward Valier, but he left the road before reaching town. He found a spot where he couldn't be seen by passing vehicles and took the girl out of the tarp. Her eyelids were fluttering and she was moaning. White Calf knew what he had to do. He hit her again, the bones of her cheek rolling like marbles under his knuckles. Her moaning stopped before he'd removed his knife from the sheath strapped to his leg. White Calf used his thumbs on her eyes and his knife on her tongue. Blood soaked the ground around her head. He wrapped her in the tarp again and tossed her into the bed of his pickup. Then he headed to Browning. He wasn't sure she was dead when he dumped her by the abandoned factory. If she wasn't, he knew she soon would be.

White Calf thought about Two Bear Woman, Sharon, and the kids. There hadn't been much food in the house or cabin when he pulled out. That's their headache, he decided. If they got desperate, one of them could hitch a ride to Valier. When Aalford had given him Sharon to be his wife, White Calf should have refused to take Rebecca. But the prophet had insisted he take her, too. Aalford didn't give a damn for either girl. They weren't his blood. He had twelve more children of his own. White Calf hadn't stood his ground and now he was paying for it.

Gradually, he relaxed his grip on the steering wheel. His worries would soon be over. He was already more than two hundred miles from Browning and soon he'd have money in his pocket—lots of money. Aalford had told him to collect fifty thousand from Miguel for each pound. That was a hundred fifty thousand dollars. It was the biggest shipment of meth he'd ever transported for the prophet. That amount of meth was worth a hell of a lot more than a hundred fifty thousand on the streets. Miguel would probably make a hundred percent profit on the deal, but he'd also have to take all the risks.

A hundred fifty thousand is fine with me, White Calf thought. It was money Aalford would never see. What was he going to do about it, complain to the cops? He'd be getting a visit from them soon enough if they suspected White Calf was involved in the girl's murder and the attack in Browning. They were bound to find out he worked for Aalford. Was the prophet, that fine religious gentleman, going to tell them he'd given White Calf three pounds of crank to deliver? Aalford would be furious, but he'd have to seethe in silence.

In all the years he'd worked for the prophet, White Calf had never stiffed him. He'd brought the man every dollar of every transaction and never taken even a quarter-gram of the man's meth. But things had changed. Thanks to Aalford's stepdaughter, that cunt, Rebecca, White Calf was a man on the run. Aalford's suppliers in Spokane would be unhappy, too. When they learned White Calf had taken off with the money from Miguel, White Calf would be a marked man. He wasn't worried about Aalford, but the Mexicans were a different matter. They'd kill him slowly if they caught him. He tried to reassure himself that they'd be more pissed off with Aalford than with him. White Calf was just the delivery boy, one chosen by Aalford. Aalford was their middle man, so it was his problem. White Calf had no idea who the prophet's suppliers in Spokane were. In case the feds or the cops ever caught him making a delivery, he figured the less he knew, the better.

White Calf pondered his next move. As soon as he collected the money from Miguel, he'd get out of Montana. Gillette would be his first stop. His cousin, Black Moon, had been working in Wyoming for three years. He could hole up with Black Moon for a couple of days while he decided where to go. Yeah, with a hundred fifty thousand in his pocket, the whole country was his.

37

Raymond and Mary greeted the morning with groans.

"My shoulder hurts more today than yesterday," Mary said.

"I feel like I've been kicked by a mule," Raymond complained.

"There's Tylenol in the medicine chest," Mary said. "I'll bring you some." She slowly assumed a sitting position. "I'll take some, too."

Raymond rolled over on his uninjured side while Mary used the bathroom. He dozed off, awakening when the aroma of breakfast drifted into the room. He yawned, got up, and dressed slowly. Mary had left the bottle of Tylenol on the nightstand, along with a glass of water . He swallowed three of them. I feel like an invalid, he thought, as he leaned on the wall for support and made his way to the kitchen.

"Smells good," Raymond said, sitting down at the table. He watched Mary in silence for a few minutes. "I thought your shoulder was hurting," he said finally.

"We still have to eat," she said, tossing him a smile. "The eggs and toast won't cook themselves. The eggs are almost done. Pour us some coffee."

Raymond laughed softly as Mary set a plate of toast, hashbrowns, bacon, and scrambled eggs in front of him.

"What's funny?"

"What a pair of lovebirds we are, snoring our way through the night."

"Who snores?" she said.

"I must have been dreaming," Raymond said, winking at her.

"If you weren't an injured man, I'd hit you with this frying pan."

"If I wasn't an injured man and you weren't an injured woman, I'd jump your bones."

"That's the furthest thing from my mind right now. Teaching next week won't be much fun if I still feel like this."

"Why don't you take sick leave?"

"What about you? You're the one who should've been in bed instead of wandering all over creation with Perkins. And what did it get you? Homer terminated your sick leave and made you sit at a desk."

"You know how hard it is for me to stay home and do nothing. So what did you think of him?"

"Who, Homer?"

"No, Perkins."

"He seemed nice."

"Nice, huh. For a Sioux in a suit?" Raymond smiled.

"Better get beyond the suit, Raymond. He really seemed like a nice guy. I liked him."

"Why'd you have to give him that fancy belt?"

"Don't tell me you're jealous."

Raymond made a dismissive gesture with his hand.

"I just want him to look after you."

"Come off it."

"Is there something about him you don't like?"

Raymond shrugged.

"That's not an answer."

"Ah, he's okay, I guess," Raymond said, pushing back from the table. "I better get myself down to headquarters. See if there have been any new developments."

"You should have stayed on sick leave. Homer was just watching out for you."

"Like you want Perkins to do, right? How come no one understands I can watch out for myself?"

"Don't be so grumpy. Go home and get some rest."

"I told you, I'm going to my office."

"You're a stubborn man, Raymond Two Teeth."

Raymond clutched at his chest as he bent over to get behind the steering wheel. "Sonofabitchin' ribs!" he said aloud. Mary's right, he thought. Maybe it was better for him to head home. If he rested over the weekend, he might be in better shape by the time Monday rolled around. He might even be able to persuade the chief to let him go out on patrol.

Raymond had almost arrived at his trailer when he spotted a familiar vehicle in his rear view mirror. The driver followed him down the driveway and pulled up alongside as Raymond parked. Stale cigarette smoke wafted from Standing Bear's truck as his cousin stepped out of the cab.

"You following me?" Raymond asked.

"I was on my way to the garage when I spotted your truck. I heard about the excitement at your lady friend's the other night. You okay? You're not standing up straight."

"Sore ribs. I'll live."

"I've got some frozen venison steaks at home for you. I can drop them by this weekend."

"Thanks. Want to come in for some coffee?"

Standing Bear shook his head. "I've had two cups already. I have a couple of things to finish up at the garage, then I'm heading down to Great Falls to see my mother. I was going to ask you if you'd like to come along, but it doesn't look like you're in shape to go anywhere."

"Not on a ride to Great Falls, that's for sure. I'll have to take a raincheck. You give my aunt a hug for me."

"She asked about you when I spoke to her. It's been a long time since you last visited."

"Don't make me feel bad. How is she?" Raymond gestured to his head.

"She's clear most of the time. Not bad for almost eighty. Listen, I hope you don't mind but while talking to her on the phone I asked her if she remembered anyone who wore a bear claw."

"What did she say?"

"She asked me if it was something you wanted to know. That surprised me. I told her it was something we were both wondering about."

"Why'd she ask that, I wonder?"

"Beats me."

"What else did she say?"

"Nothing. She just let it drop. Maybe when I'm down there I'll ask her about it."

"Yeah, do that. And give her my best. Tell her I'll come see her as soon as I can."

"You mean as soon as you can stand up straight again?" Standing Bear's rumbling laugh accompanied him into his truck.

Raymond gave a half-hearted wave as his cousin drove off.

38

White Calf was getting close to Fort Belknap Agency. Aalford had arranged for him to meet Miguel by the roadside park at one-thirty in the morning. Miguel was the only contact White Calf had dealt with during his years working for the prophet, but he still knew nothing about him. He was probably Mexican but White Calf didn't even know that for sure. Their meetings never lasted more than five minutes. White Calf would give Miguel the plastic-wrapped packages of meth stored in one of his hay bales and receive a cheap suitcase or duffel bag of cash in return. If White Calf wanted to make a meth buy for his personal use, it only prolonged their meeting by another minute or so. End of story.

A nighthawk swooped down in front of the truck, startling him. He leaned forward to catch another glimpse of it, but it had disappeared into the cold blackness of the fall night. As he rounded a curve between Zurich and Fort Belknap Agency, the red tail lights of a vehicle parked up ahead on the edge of the road startled him. Automatically, his hand reached toward the passenger seat and his loaded shotgun. He checked his odometer in case it was a cop. The cruise control was still on and was right at the speed limit. If it was a motorist with car problems, there was no way he was going to stop, not with three pounds of meth in the bed of his truck and Miguel waiting for him.

White Calf caught a glimpse of the Montana Highway Patrol logo as he drove past the idling vehicle. The trooper swung onto the road and followed him, keeping six or seven car lengths behind. He hadn't turned on his flashing lights, which White Calf took as a good sign. But why the fuck was he following him? Was he just checking him out because it was a quiet night and he had nothing better to do? When the cop passed the turnoff to Harlem, the last exit before Fort Belknap Agency, White Calf knew he was stuck with him. There was no way he could stop at the roadside park where Miguel was waiting with a cop on his tail.

"Oh, shit," he said aloud. He had suddenly realized that the Highway Patrol must have the license plate of his truck. They knew, too, that he had a shotgun. The cop, alone in his car, wasn't about to pull him over. He was probably radioing for help. If White Calf didn't conclude his meeting with Miguel in a hurry, the cops might have enough time to get a couple of cars to the intersection of Highway Two and Route Sixty-six where it cut off to the south, the route he intended to follow after getting his money from Miguel.

He grasped for a solution. There was only one thing to do. He eased his truck onto the shoulder and waited. Maybe the cop would keep going. The police cruiser pulled off the road and parked thirty feet behind him, its lights on and the engine running. White Calf couldn't wait any longer. He lunged for the handle of the passenger door. Grasping his shotgun, he opened the door just enough to slither out headfirst. Hidden behind the side of the truck, White Calf crouched, edging his way toward the rear bumper. He leaped out of the shadows, raised the barrel of his shotgun, and fired.

The windshield of the cruiser disintegrated. The figure behind the steering wheel was hurled back against the seat by the impact of the blast. White Calf loaded another shell and approached closer, his weapon raised. The shattered windshield was covered with blood. The cop wasn't moving. White Calf raced back to close his passenger door and climbed into the driver's seat. Moments later he sped down the road with his window open, listening for approaching sirens. The cold wind burned the skin of his face and hands and penetrated his jacket. He drove for a couple of minutes, until he spotted the turnoff to the roadside park where Miguel's Toyota was parked, the engine idling and the car's lights turned off.

White Calf jumped from the driver's seat as the door of the parked car opened and a slim, wiry figure wearing a baseball cap emerged. He was visible for only a second in the glare of the vehicle's roof light, then lost in the shadows after he'd closed the door.

"Miguel?" White Calf called.

"Yeah. You got it?"

"Let's do it." White Calf clambered over the tailgate and dug his hands into a hollowed-out hay bale. He ignored the needle pricks of sharp stems of hay and removed the three bags of meth.

Miguel reached for the plastic-wrapped packages White Calf passed down to him. Climbing down from the truck bed, White Calf followed Miguel to his Toyota, where the Mexican stored the three packages in his trunk.

"I heard a gunshot back there," Miguel said, turning his face toward White Calf. "Seemed mighty close. It had me worried, amigo."

"I heard it, too. Some guy jacking deer probably."

"He must have been using a cannon."

Miguel extracted a grease-covered suitcase from the trunk and passed it to White Calf. "A hundred fify thousand. Want to count it?"

White Calf knew the Mexican was grinning even though he couldn't see his face.

"I trust you," White Calf said. He was about to ask Miguel to sell him an eight-ball of meth when a thought came to him. He stared at the Mexican's car. The cops were looking for his *Sierra*, not for a Toyota. They'd be crawling all over the roads, setting up roadblocks, once they found the cop's body. "Hey, Miguel," he called, "before you go, there's something I want to show you."

He walked quickly back to the truck, Miguel a few steps behind.

"What you got? It's getting late, man."

"Just this," White Calf said, opening the passenger door and removing the shotgun. He slid the bolt and raised the muzzle toward Miguel.

"You crazy, man?"

The noise of the blast had barely subsided when White Calf tossed the suitcase back into Miguel's trunk. He threw the shotgun onto the passenger seat and slid in behind the wheel.

White Calf headed west on Highway Two, back in the direction from which he'd come. He passed the Highway Patrol car, still idling on the other side of the road. No other vehicle was in sight, but since the cop had probably radioed his position, it wouldn't be long before the road was swarming with police. He hoped the cops would be expecting him to continue east toward Glasgow or to turn off south on the road to Billings. It doesn't matter, he thought. They're looking for a pickup, not a Toyota. Confirming what he was thinking, a police cruiser, its blue light flashing, sped past him in the direction of Fort Belknap. If White Calf was lucky the cops wouldn't spot his truck and the body in the roadside park until daylight. I should have taken Miguel's wallet, he told himself.

Once they ID him, they'll learn what kind of car he drove.

For now, he had to make a decision. Just past Havre he could either continue west on the Hi-Line toward Shelby and Cut Bank or take the southwest turnoff toward Great Falls. Without giving it a second thought, White Calf continued driving west. The cops, he decided, wouldn't expect that. Besides, he'd changed his mind about going to Gilette. Another plan was taking shape

39

Will Perkins embraced his wife as she stepped out of the car Saturday evening. "I can't believe you're home so soon."

"My flight got in a few minutes early and the highway from Great Falls was clear."

"No, I mean with your mom having had surgery Thursday."

They were interrupted by their two daughters dashing out of the house to greet their mother.

"Hi, darlings," she said, scooping each one up for a kiss. "What are you doing outside without a jacket? It's freezing."

"How's Grandma?" Christine, the ten-year-old, asked, as her mother shepherded her into the house.

"She's doing fine. And how are my girls? Taking good care of Daddy?"

Lucy, the nine-year-old, nodded. "We baked Daddy a chocolate cake yesterday. The babysitter helped us."

"You did?" She looked at her husband for confirmation.

Perkins nodded. "They sure did."

"How did it come out?"

Christine laughed. "It was lopsided, Mom."

"But it was sure good," Lucy said. "Can we cut Mom a piece?"

"Later, kiddo. Dinner's almost ready." Perkins stored his wife's suitcase in the hall and helped her out of her coat. "Sauce is made and I just have to add the spaghetti to the pot."

"Hey, I like being spoiled," Liz Perkins said. "Maybe I should go away more often."

"So, tell me about your mother. You said they did the surgery through a scope?"

"It's amazing, Will. She looks great and has hardly any discomfort. She was discharged Friday after I spoke to you."

"Wow. I thought you had to be in the hospital for at least a week after that surgery."

"That was in the old days."

Their daughters sat at the table, their chins resting on their hands as they took in every word.

"You girls can go wash up," Perkins said. "Dinner will be ready in a few minutes."

The pasta water had just come to a boil when the phone rang.

"I'll get it," Liz said. "Now I know I'm home." She held the receiver to her ear and listened, glancing at her watch. "I'll tell him," she said.

"What was that about?"

"That was Chief Whitecloud. He's called a meeting in his office at eight o'clock this evening. He hopes you'll be able to attend."

"On a Saturday night? Something must have happened."

"Any new developments on that case you're working on while I was gone?"

"White Calf's disappeared. No one has spotted him or his truck."

"How are Raymond and his girlfriend doing?"

"They're still sore, but otherwise okay. Raymond's so crazy he insisted on going with me to see White Calf's boss. That was the day after he was attacked."

"He must think he's Superman. You didn't give me too many details on the phone. They got all the pellets out on his girlfriend?"

"Yeah. I had a nice evening with them yesterday. They were sorry you couldn't be there."

"I'm surprised they wanted company so soon after the attack."

"Me, too. I think Mary's just nervous about what happened. She thinks White Calf may try again if he's carrying some kind of grudge against Raymond. Anyway, she wanted me to keep an eye on Raymond, make sure nothing happens to him."

Liz laughed. "Raymond must have loved that."

"I think he was ready to strangle her. Look what she gave me." He stood up to let her see the belt.

"That's beautiful," she said, running her fingers over it.

"Her great-grandmother made it. Those are porcupine quills."

"How come she gave it to you instead of to Raymond?"

"It doesn't fit him." He chuckled. "Raymond's nose was out of joint."

"I'm glad you're going to keep an eye on Raymond, but who's going to keep an eye on you?"

Perkins and Liz ended the conversation when the two girls reappeared. Perkins served the spaghetti and ladled out the sauce.

"Good spaghetti, Dad," Lucy said.

"Thanks, sweetheart."

Fifteen minutes later, Perkins pushed himself away from the table. "I hate to run, Liz, but it's almost eight. I'd better go see what Homer wants."

Perkins had never seen so many officers gathered at Tribal Police Headquarters. At least thirty filled the office. "Glad you could make it," Homer said.

"I figured it was important."

"It is."

Perkins spotted Raymond in a corner of the room. The two men nodded to one another.

"Gentlemen," Homer said, raising his voice above the din in the room. He stepped behind one of the desks and looked out at them. "I asked you all to come in tonight because of some developments related to the case of our murdered girl. Early this morning, sometime between one and two AM, a highway patrolman was killed on the outskirts of Fort Belknap Agency."

A ripple of conversation spread through the room and Homer held up his hands. "No one likes to hear that a fellow law enforcement officer has been killed, but that's not the only reason why I called you down here. "The officer was killed by a shotgun blast." Perkins and Raymond exchanged looks. "Later this morning troopers found a GMC *Sierra* at a roadside park about two miles from the shooting. The pickup belonged to the man we're looking for, White Calf. They also found another body, killed with a shotgun. The murdered man's driver's license gave his name as Miguel Torres, with an address in Great Falls. Miguel has a sheet. Two arrests for drug possession. Served six months the second time for intent to sell. Highway Patrol traced his vehicle through DMV. It's a Toyota

Camry and they figure White Calf is now driving it."

"Anything in the truck?" Perkins asked.

Homer nodded. "The bed was filled with hay bales. One of them had a hollow center. Whatever had been in there was gone. And the officers found a tarp with old blood stains under the hay."

"He must have wrapped the girl's body in that," Raymond said.

"And we have a pretty good idea what was in the hay," Perkins added.

"The truck and everything in it are now down in Missoula at the Crime Lab. Now, everyone write this down. We're looking for a blue Toyota Camry, Montana license 2C4352. You all have descriptions of White Calf and you know he's armed and dangerous. "

"Those crimes were two hundred miles from here, Chief," Ben Red Leaf said. "Why do you think he might be coming back here?"

"We don't know where he is. But he does know this area and he attacked one of our officers during the past week."

The men glanced at Raymond, who self-consciously stared at the floor.

"You think he's really crazy enough to come back and try it again?" one man asked.

"It doesn't make sense," Leonard Nye called out. "If White Calf met this Miguel for a drug and cash exchange, he must have a lot of money on him now. He's probably headed anywhere but here."

"Like I said, we don't know. He was heading east when he shot the trooper, but another cop speeding to the scene remembered a car passing him heading west. It could have been a Camry, but he wasn't sure. Anyway, if you were White Calf and wanted to throw the police off your trail, what would you do? You might head back to the rez because no one would expect you to do that.

"As far as the money is concerned, you're probably right. He's got enough to keep him going for quite a while is my guess. In fact, Miguel had a hundred twenty bucks in his wallet that White Calf didn't bother to take.

"All I'm saying is, keep your eyes open and watch yourselves. We're dealing with a cop killer. From here on, we're assigning two men to a cruiser. All vacations and leaves are cancelled as of now. And beginning tomorrow some of you may be working double shifts until we get this guy. I don't want to hear any complaints. That's all I have to say. Thanks for coming down and get your rest tonight. You'll need it."

The men filed out, talking among themselves. Only Perkins and Raymond remained behind.

"So we don't really know where he's heading," Perkins said.

The chief shrugged his shoulders. "All guesswork at this point."

"Something tells me you're right when you said he might come back here. Not only because we wouldn't expect him to do that, but because it would give him another crack at Raymond."

"Don't worry about me," Raymond said. "I hope the bastard does come back. I'm just concerned about Mary."

"Can Mary stay with a friend or relative until we get White Calf?" Perkins asked.

"Forget it," Raymond said. "She'll never go for that. I'll talk to her about staying at my house."

"Much as you might like that," Homer said, "it's not a great idea. It's only a matter of time till he finds out where you live. If he doesn't know already."

"Homer's right," Perkins said. "There's a good chance, too, White Calf will switch cars. He knows by now that we're looking for that *Camry*. He can follow you without you knowing."

"White Calf may head up to Aalford's to hide out for a while," Raymond said, trying to deflect attention away from him.

"No way," Perkins said. "We're still watching Aalford, and White Calf isn't stupid. He sure as hell doesn't want to have to turn over the money he got from Miguel. He'll need it to keep running."

"Well, Aalford's the Bureau's headache," Homer interjected. "Keeping an eye on Raymond and apprehending White Calf is mine."

"Forget it, Chief," Raymond said. "I can take care of myself."

"How are your ribs?"

"Fine."

"Then how come you're walking like Frankenstein? But if you feel that good, you and Merle Wagner can share a cruiser as of tomorrow. The town's been going to hell without you, Raymond," he said, grinning. "Now go home and get some rest."

"I know you have your own priorities," Homer said to Perkins after Raymond had gone, "but I do have a favor to ask. I am worried about Raymond. White Calf's made one attempt on his life. I'm not sure he's done."

"What would you like me to do about it?"

"Raymond needs someone to keep close watch on him."

"That's what his girlfriend told me. But I can't just follow him around. Besides, he wouldn't stand for it." Perkins smiled. "He gets pissed off just by being in the same car with me. What do you think he'd do if he knew I was watching his every move?"

"I'm not asking for that. But whenever you're out and about, especially evenings, maybe you can swing by Raymond's place, and Mary's, too. My men will do the same while on patrol. I can't spare men to sit in a cruiser outside their houses. I wish I could but I can't. Damn it, I won't rest easy until we get White Calf."

"Incidentally," Perkins said, "we should have White Calf's driver's license photo by Monday or Tuesday. DMV is sending it to my office. We'll get the newspapers to publish it and get it posted all over the state. That'll turn up the heat on our man."

"It'll be a big help."

They left the building together, surprised to find snowflakes drifting down.

"We might be getting a storm tonight," Homer said.

40

The ringing of the phone jerked Perkins out of a sound sleep. He groped for it, trying to get it on one ring so Liz wouldn't be awakened.

"Sorry to bother you," Homer Whitecloud said.

"Don't you ever sleep?" Perkins grumbled.

"My men found the car about two hours ago."

"The *Camry*?"

"Yeah."

Perkins pressed the light on his alarm clock. Two-twenty AM. "Where?" he asked.

"On a dirt road south of Cut Bank. It's snowing heavily. In case you haven't looked out the window, we already have three or four inches down. White Calf skidded off the road and cracked his axle in a ditch. The bastard had put Oregon plates on the car."

"So he's back on the rez. Nothing in the car?"

"No."

"How far was this from here?"

"No more than fifteen miles."

"He'll head here."

"Not tonight he won't. There probably won't be much traffic, if any, on the Cut Bank road tonight."

"So no chance he'll find another set of wheels?"

"There are scattered farms in the area where he can get a car, but I don't think he'll try it tonight with the snow coming down. We'll call everyone in the area with a phone to warn them. He'll probably try to find a place to hole up. It's too bad the snow will wipe out his tracks. My men will go out there at first light to begin the search."

"He won't get far if it's snowing as hard as you say."

"The problem is he knows this country. My guess is he'll look for an abandoned cabin or barn for now."

"He could try to make it back to his place."

"That's ten miles. Too far in the snow. Anyway, I just wanted to keep you posted. Sorry about waking you up."

"No, I appreciate your letting me know. Have you called Raymond? I can't think of any other reason for White Calf to be heading this way. He's obsessed."

"I have men riding past Raymond's trailer at regular intervals. I'll talk to him in the morning."

"What about Mary and her daughter?"

"We're keeping an eye on her house, too. If we're lucky, that bastard, White Calf, will freeze to death tonight."

"I have a feeling that's too much to hope for."

Perkins checked with Tribal Police Headquarters in the morning as soon as he woke up. There had been no new developments. White Calf was still on the loose. The agent tried to mask his frustration when he spoke to the chief. Knowing the rez as well as the Tribal Police did, why hadn't they been able to find him? Had they contacted every homestead in the area? Checked every vacant building? Looked in abandoned vehicles?

"My men have been on the ground since six AM," Homer said testily. "The snow obliterated any prints he might have left. We're checking every structure where he might hide in a three-mile radius. If we don't find him, we'll expand that to a six-mile radius. And we'll keep going till we get the sonofabitch. The snow is really hampering us. There are ten inches on the ground in some places. But if he's on the rez, we'll find him."

"Is Raymond out there, too?"

"He wanted to go but I wouldn't let him. I don't think he's in any shape to go trudging through the snow."

"I'm amazed you were able to convince him."

"Convince him, hell. I had to order him to stay in Browning. I told him I'd shackle him to his desk or put him in a cell if I had to."

41

White Calf had been lucky. After the Toyota slid into the ditch, snapping the rear axle, he'd found a perfect hiding place for the meth. No more than a hundred feet from the road, his sharp eyes had spotted the shadowy form of a coyote sniffing at the ground. It disappeared into the darkness as White Calf approached. He found the ground hole that had caught the coyote's interest and widened it with his hands. At that point White Calf hesitated. He'd used up his own stash of meth. If there was ever a time he needed it, it was now. Every cop and fed in the state, both on and off the rez, must be looking for him. He wrapped two of the packages in an old sweater he found in Miguel's trunk and placed them in the depression he'd excavated. After scooping earth and snow over the sweater, he covered the area with deadfall. Stomping off to a nearby pine whose bark had been stripped away by porcupines, White Calf etched a slashmark just above the point where the bark had been peeled.

The light snow that had begun falling earlier was coming down heavier. White Calf smiled to himself. There'd be no footprints leading from the car. He unzipped the suitcase and ran his fingers over the wads of bills. Bending over the bag, he inhaled deeply. Money had its own smell. White Calf had carried as much as seventy-five thousand back to Aalford, but he now had twice that amount in his possession. The remaining plastic-wrapped package of meth went into the suitcase with the money. He lifted the bag from the car and slammed the trunk lid. He had to cover as much ground as possible before anyone spotted the car.

Turning in a slow circle, he tried to decide in which direction to head. Three miles to the west, the road he was on would almost meet a bend of the Two Medicine River. If he cut north from there on a rough track for a mile, he'd come to a homestead occupied by an old couple, two whites who'd lived on the rez forever. He brought them hay every year for their cows and two old nags. When he reached their place, he'd be able to spend the remaining hours of darkness in their barn. Then, at first light, he'd . . . No need to think that far ahead, he decided. The old man had a pickup truck. That was the important thing.

Another half-inch of snow had fallen in the short time that elapsed since he went into the ditch. White Calf balanced the bag on his shoulder and set off down the road at a gentle lope, his free hand holding his shotgun. The moon, partially obscured by falling snow, still gave off enough light for him to see his way. He knew this part of the rez as well as he knew the fingers of his right hand. Getting to his turnoff spot near the river would be no problem. It would take him forty-five minutes at most, then another twenty to the homestead.

White Calf had broken into a sweat by the time he turned off to the north. The snow was now a solid white curtain, making it virtually impossible to see the track. Three more inches of powder had accumulated. The temperature had fallen and his ungloved hands ached in the cold. He had stupidly left his gloves at Gustafson's place in Hingham.

He moved by instinct toward the Gilson farm, his suitcase held securely on his shoulder. He released and retightened his grip on the shotgun, trying to stimulate circulation in his numbed fingers.

Ahead of him White Calf heard a dog barking. Moments later he made out the hazy silhouettes of the Gilson house and barn. A dim light burned in a window of the house. He made his way to the rear of the barn and peered out to make sure no one was awake. The dog was no longer barking. Moving quickly, he slipped along the side of the barn. A horse kicked the stall boards as he passed. The front doors of the barn were closed. White Calf slid one door open just enough to squeeze through with his bag, then closed it behind him. It was cold in the barn, but not as bad as outside. The rich aroma of hay and manure filled the air. Gilson's cows contentedly chewed their cud. The horses, aware of his presence, fidgeted in their stalls.

White Calf, feeling his way, clambered up to the hay loft. He squeezed between bales, far enough back so anyone entering with a light would not be able to see him. Slashing the twine around one bale, he kicked the hay into a cushion. Reclining, the shotgun at his side, he used his suitcase as a pillow and closed his eyes.

The lowing of a cow awakened him. He was sure he hadn't slept more than a few minutes, but the luminous hands of his watch showed it was almost six-thirty. Gilson must be coming to milk the cows. White Calf climbed down from the loft and stationed himself to the side of the front doors. He placed his bag and shotgun on the floor behind him and withdrew his knife from the sheath fastened to his leg. A dog barked and pawed at the door. "What is it, boy?" old man Gilson's voice asked. One door slid open and the dog, a black lab, bounded in. Gilson, a shrunken figure wearing a stained barn jacket and an old wool cap, slipped into the barn behind the dog. Snow covered his cap and shoulders. He stamped his boots, unaware of the figure only a few feet away, and turned to pull the door shut. The dog barked hysterically as White Calf jerked the old man's head back with his arm and slid the knife across his throat. A short grunt and a hissing noise, like air leaving a tire, were the only sounds to come from Gilson. Warm blood spurted onto White Calf's hand as he lifted his knife. The old man slid to the floor, his head flopping awkwardly. Severed arteries pumped bright red streams that spattered the door and floorboards, while dark venous blood pooled beneath him. The dog paused in his frantic barking to sniff at his owner and the blood flowing from his body, then growled and snapped at White Calf's legs. White Calf launched a fierce kick, his boot driving the dog against the barn door. Before the animal could recover, White Calf, with an upward thrust, plunged his knife into its chest. The dog emitted a short plaintive cry, collapsing next to its owner.

White Calf searched Gilson's pockets for his keys, then slid the door back and peered out into the murky dawn light. It was still snowing, but not as heavy as earlier. All was quiet by the house. He lifted his suitcase and shotgun and tramped through the snow toward the car port. Protected by the house from the storm blowing off the mountains, Gilson's old Ford pickup had only an inch or two of snow on its windshield. White Calf hesitated, debating his next move. If he drove off, the old lady might hear and come out to look for her husband. She'd call the police and they'd follow his tire tracks right to Browning. Leaving the suitcase and shotgun next to the truck, he slipped his knife from its sheath and opened the door of the house.

42

"Beth, listen to this," John Hartman said to his wife as they were finishing breakfast. "Front page in the *Great Falls Tribune*. 'Blackfeet Tribal Police and the FBI are conducting a search for Arlow White Calf, a suspect in three homicides and a criminal assault. White Calf is wanted for questioning in the murder of a young girl whose body was found in Browning and in the killing of two men near Fort Belknap early Saturday morning, one of them a highway patrolman. Authorities believe he may be hiding out on the Blackfeet reservation. White Calf is six feet five, weighs over two hundred pounds, and is considered armed and dangerous.' And there's a photo of him from his driver's license."

He passed the newspaper to Beth, who stared at the photo for a long time. "Let's hope they catch him before he hurts anyone else," she said finally.

"Judging from that description, White Calf shouldn't be too hard to spot. He's a big boy."

Beth pushed the newspaper aside and sipped her coffee in silence.

"You look thoughtful," John said.

"It makes me nervous knowing he's out there. He could be anywhere, even right here in Browning."

"I would think he's anywhere but here. Those last two killings were in Fort Belknap."

"Yes, but the article said he's believed to be on the reservation."

"If he is, maybe he'll try to slip across the border into Canada."

Beth shrugged. "I just have a feeling—oh, never mind."

"What is it? You still think he might come to the hospital?"

"I'm just uneasy. And so are you, John. You haven't slept well since they brought that girl into the ER. You toss and turn half the night."

"I'm sorry. I didn't realize I was keeping you up. I can't get that poor girl's face out of my mind."

Beth sighed. "Maybe I'm just being foolish. Next thing you know, I'll be putting a row of locks on our front door."

"At least now there's a picture of White Calf in the paper. Maybe someone will spot him."

"I'm sure the police will get him," Beth said, trying to sound optimistic.

John pushed back his chair. "I better get going." He stood up and grabbed his jacket. "Rounds will take me a while this morning. I've got about ten sick kids on the ward."

"I'll take care of the dishes," Beth said. "I have an hour until clinic starts."

"Lunch?" John asked, giving her a peck on the cheek.

"Let's try for one o'clock. I'll call you if anything comes up."

John carried the image of the worried look in her eyes out the door with him.

43

"Well, this is a surprise," Mary said. "What are you doing up so early?"

"I'm sorry to barge in without calling," Raymond said, scuffing his feet on her welcome mat.

"That's okay. Come on in. Delia's still asleep, but the coffee is on. You're just in time for pancakes."

"Don't go out of your way for me."

"What's wrong, Raymond?"

He sat down heavily at the kitchen table and Mary poured them each a cup of coffee. "Tell me. You're beginning to worry me."

"You haven't heard the news then."

She gave him a perplexed look. "What news? I spent most of Sunday preparing lessons for Real Speak school. I never saw a newspaper."

"White Calf killed two more people."

"What!"

"He killed a highway patrolman and a drug dealer he was doing business with. It happened early Saturday morning near Fort Belknap."

"Does Perkins know?"

"Yeah, he knows. Homer called a meeting at Tribal Headquarters Saturday night. Perkins was there."

"What did Homer say at the meeting?"

"Until we catch him, we'll have two men in every cruiser."

"Raymond, maybe you should stay here. I don't think he'd dare come back to my place."

Raymond shook his head. "I almost got you killed once. I'm not going to take a chance on doing it again."

"Then what are you going to do?"

"I'm not going to hide from him, that's for sure."

Delia, Mary's daughter, appeared in the doorway in her pajamas. She rubbed her eyes with her fists and smiled at Raymond.

"Another early bird," Mary said. "Usually I have to drag her out of bed on a Monday morning."

"I heard Raymond's voice and I thought I was dreaming."

"I'm sorry if I woke you," Raymond said.

"Well, now that you are awake, how about some pancakes for breakfast?"

"Sounds good." She yawned. "I'll go get dressed."

"I'm some pain in the ass, aren't I?" Raymond said when Delia was out of the room. "Barge in at six in the morning, wake everybody up . . . "

"You know I'm always up early. And I'd be waking Delia around now or she'd miss her schoolbus. It always makes her happy to see you. Let's finish our talk before she comes back. I don't want anything to happen to you. You have vacation time coming and you have busted ribs that need to heal. Why not take some time off?"

"I can't do that, Mary. Not while he's out there. I'd have a young girl's face haunting me wherever I went. When White Calf is dead or in prison, that's when I'll take time off."

"I wish you weren't so stubborn."

"You make good coffee," he said, holding his cup to his lips.

"Stop changing the subject. I happen to agree with Perkins. You're like a magnet for that lunatic. If you weren't here, maybe he'd know that and stay out of Browning."

"I may be stubborn but I'm not a coward." He grinned as Delia entered the room. "Do you know what your mother just called me?"

"What?" she said, surprised.

"Bait."

Delia gave him a puzzled look.

"Ignore him," Mary said. "He's just teasing."

44

The truck engine started easily and White Calf drove slowly away from the Gilson farmhouse. He had stayed off meth and slept for most of two days, waking up only to take advantage of the Gilsons' ample food supply. A few more inches of snow had fallen while he sheltered in the house. He felt better than he had in a week, well rested and with a full stomach.

White Calf peered in the rearview mirror, watching the Gilson farmhouse recede into the distance. It might be days or weeks before anyone found the bodies of the old couple. By then he'd have taken care of his business and be far away from the rez and from Montana.

The fuel gauge showed a quarter-tank, more than enough to get him into Browning. The truck bounced its way through the snow over the rough track Gilson had worn into the ground over the years. The path forged by White Calf through the snow a few nights earlier had been obliterated by the fresh powder. Anyone approaching the property would see only the tracks of Gilson's truck and figure the old man had headed into town. In minutes White Calf was back on the dirt road running along the Two Medicine River. Snow covered the branches of the cottonwoods on the banks of the river and formed an unmarred blanket on the paved section of the road just ahead of him.

He had only three miles to cover before reaching Eighty-nine, the main highway into Browning. Over the years, White Calf had avoided Browning if at all possible. He knew the town as well as he knew the rest of the rez, like the back of his hand, but that didn't mean he had to like it. White Calf and his father had never lived on the rez while his father was alive. Valier was as close as they'd come. It was only after he was kicked out of the Marines that White Calf moved onto the rez. An uncle, his father's brother, had died. He left no heirs and his place was sitting empty. Not having anywhere else to go, White Calf moved in. A few years later he took Two Bear Woman as his wife and had children with her.

White Calf's ground was close enough to Valier so he didn't feel trapped on the rez. Many Indians found it impossible to break away but White Calf wasn't one of them. For most Blackfeet, the reservation provided the comfort of being with their own people, hearing the old people speak the Blackfeet tongue, pretending that nothing had changed and the land was still theirs. White Calf had never felt that way. To him, the rez was a prison, a symbol of the enslavement of the Blackfeet by their white masters. White Calf hated all whites. He also hated those Indians who placed themselves at the mercy of the white man, those who took his welfare money and food stamps and commodities, and who collaborated with the Bureau of Indian Affairs.

His contempt for whites included Aalford, the man for whom he'd worked for years. In Aalford's case, he hated not only the man but his hypocrisy. The prophet was always spouting religion, but that didn't prevent him from trafficking in meth. Money was Aalford's real god. In spite of his antipathy, White Calf had to admit Aalford paid him well for his meth runs. And there were elements of the man's religious creed that were in line with White Calf's own thinking. Making money *was* a good thing, as was teaching women to be obedient. Aalford had given him two white women to use as wives, but generosity hadn't entered into it. He hadn't been able to control his stepdaughters and wanted to get rid of them. White Calf hadn't asked for the women, but he wasn't about to turn down Aalford's offer. Sharon, at least, had known her place. It was only Rebecca who had proved to be a troublemaker, but her rebelliousness was over. He had seen to that.

White Calf rested his hand on the suitcase lying on the passenger seat with his shotgun. This was one collection Aalford could kiss goodbye, he said to himself, tapping his fingers on the case. The contents of the bag meant a new life in a new place for White Calf. He felt no remorse for the women and children he was leaving behind. They were already part of his past and meant nothing to him. A new life meant just what it implied. It was best to be unencumbered. Two Bear Woman, Sharon, and the brats he'd fathered would have to make their own way.

Snow plows were out on Eighty-nine and Monday's noon-hour traffic heading into Browning was moving slowly. White Calf drove cautiously, hoping no one would recognize the old man's truck. The highway evolved into Browning's main thoroughfare. One- and two-storey homes covered the low-lying hills of the town. Pawn shops and souvenir stores, symbols of Blackfeet captivity to White Calf's way of thinking, lined each side of the road.

Spotting the *Red Crow* café in the Teepee Village Shopping Center, White Calf turned into the parking lot. He'd eaten a light breakfast in the Gilsons' kitchen a few hours earlier but was hungry again. He sat with his motor idling, staring at the steamed-up window of the café and debating whether he should chance having lunch there. Several pickups were parked in front of the restaurant. White Calf was just about to turn off the ignition when a Tribal Police cruiser drove into the lot and parked near the café. White Calf reached for his shotgun, placing his hand on the stock. Two cops got out of the police car, one young and slender, the other shorter and stockier. Neither one was Raymond Two Teeth. White Calf couldn't risk going into the café. He drove slowly through the lot toward an IGA supermarket, stopping in a spot recently cleared by a snowplow. The plow continued moving slowly up and down the lot as White Calf turned off the engine and stepped out of the truck. He locked the doors and walked slowly toward the market's entrance. The snow that had fallen during the night was keeping shoppers away, the clerks and cashiers in the store outnumbering the customers.

White Calf ordered turkey and roast beef sandwiches at the deli counter, along with a large coffee. He picked up bags of potato chips, a six-pack of *Coca Cola,* and a few candy bars before getting on the checkout line.

Walking back to his truck, he glanced toward the café. The police cruiser was still there. White Calf drove slowly along Main Street, watching for a place that was relatively secluded where he could park and eat. Ahead, on his right, the Museum of the Plains Indian came into view. There were few vehicles in its vast parking lot. A couple of them were covered in snow, indicating they'd been there all night. He drove in, his truck making tracks in the new snow, and headed for a spot at the rear of the museum, a place where his truck wasn't likely to be spotted from the road.

White Calf ate slowly, pondering his next move. Once the bit of unfinished business in Browning was out of the way, he'd say goodbye to Blackfeet country for good. It was a white man's world beyond the rez, but there were still many places where he could lose himself. Places like California or Colorado. Or even Canada or Alaska. The suitcase resting on the passenger seat would take him a long way. His hunger appeased, White Calf rested his head against the seat back and closed his eyes. Moments later he was asleep.

He awoke with a start. A snow plow had finished clearing the lot at the front and sides of the building, and was now headed in his direction. White Calf turned the key in the ignition, glancing at his watch as he did so. It was a little before three, as good a time as any to put his plan into operation. As he drove past the plow, the driver waved to him.

White Calf had no idea where Raymond Two Teeth lived. Had he known that, it would have made things easier. He'd checked a telephone directory but the cop apparently had an unlisted number. More than one way to skin a buck, he thought, driving toward Blackfeet Tribal Police headquarters. He would let his quarry lead him to the house.

45

Beth Hartman shivered when she left the hospital at 3:15 and slid into her Honda *Civic*. The temperature had been dropping throughout the day and the sky was an ominous gray. More snow on the way, she thought. Snow or no snow, there was shopping to be done. This being one of the rare days when all patients in the Medical Clinic had been seen by three, she had plenty of time to do some leisurely browsing at the IGA. John wouldn't be home until five. It was also a day when he wasn't on call. She looked forward to a quiet evening together. Passing a video store reminded her that it had been ages since they'd seen a movie. She decided to rent one after she finished her shopping.

Montana was back on standard time and the days were growing noticeably shorter. The low cloud cover heralded an early dusk. Beth approached an intersection with stop signs. An old Ford pickup coming from the opposite direction stopped at the same time Beth did. Her eyes met those of the driver, an Indian who looked familiar. The newspaper photo of White Calf flashed through her mind. Her heart pounded. She tried not to look at him as she drove past, but it was too late. White Calf had seen the look of recognition, then fear, on Beth's face. In her rear view mirror, Beth saw the truck make an abrupt stop and a U-turn. She sped up. If she could make it to the main street, only two blocks away, there would be too much traffic for White Calf to attempt anything. White Calf's truck was only inches from her rear bumper. Beth pressed on the accelerator, but it was too late. The Ford truck disappeared from view only to reappear alongside her car. Moments later White Calf cut his wheel sharply to the right, causing Beth to swerve. Her right front tire jumped the curb and she braked hard to avoid hitting a tree. Leaping from her car, Beth tried to run. She felt a sharp pain in her neck as her head was jerked back by the hair.

"That's a knife in your back, bitch," White Calf said. "Don't make me use it." He gripped the back of her neck with his powerful hand and forced her toward the truck's passenger door. Opening it, he removed his suitcase and shotgun.

"Get back behind the wheel in your car," White Calf ordered. He jabbed the muzzle of the shotgun into her back. "Try anything and your brains will be splattered all over the street."

As Beth got into her Honda, White Calf opened the rear door and tossed his suitcase in. He sat down behind Beth and pressed the shotgun's muzzle into the back of her neck. "Back up," he said, "and drive around my truck."

Beth peered in the rear-view mirror as she backed up. If only a car would come or the door to one of the houses along the street would open, it might distract White Calf enough for her to get out of the car. The street remained quiet.

Beth's mind raced. If she was going to run this might be her last chance. Her eyes met White Calf's in the mirror and she knew he would kill her before she had gone ten feet.

"All you have to do is drive," White Calf said, his voice menacing. "Nice and easy. Don't attract any attention."

"Where are you taking me?"

"Shut up. I'll do the talking and ask the questions. I want you to drive to Tribal Police Headquarters. Do you know where that is?"

Beth thought she had not heard correctly. She turned in her seat.

"Keep your eyes in front of you. You know who I am, don't you?"

She nodded, keeping the back of her head toward him.

"My shotgun is pointed at the back of your head. Keep that in mind. What's your name?"

"Beth."

"What do you do?"

"I'm a nurse-practitioner at the hospital."

"You have a husband?"

"He's a doctor at the hospital."

"If you want to see him again, just do as I say."

Beth's confusion matched her fear. It all made no sense. White Calf had commandeered her car, but instead of trying to get away he had ordered her to drive to police headquarters.

"Keep your speed down," he snapped. "The building is coming up on the next block."

"What shall I do when I get there?"

"I want you to park. I'll show you where."

Beth slowed her speed even more as she eyed the headquarters building on her left.

"There," White Calf ordered, "in front of that green car. Leave the engine running."

Beth parked. For a brief second, she thought of making a dash for the headquarters building. She glanced in the rear-view mirror, only to find White Calf's gaze riveted on her. As if reading her mind, he jabbed the shotgun muzzle against the back of her seat. Beth looked away.

"Now what?" Beth asked.

White Calf looked at his watch, then turned his attention to the parking lot on the opposite side of the street. Raymond's pickup was clearly visible in the lot. White Calf had to hope that this time the cop would head to his own house, not to his girlfriend's. If he went to his girlfriend's, it would screw things up. White Calf already had one hostage and didn't need a second woman in the car. He also would have to worry that someone on the girlfriend's street might recognize him and alert the police. "Now we wait," he said.

Perkins, sitting in his office, was putting the finishing touches on a report when his phone rang. It was Homer Whitecloud.

"Hey, what's up?" Perkins said.

"I just learned an old couple named Gilson was killed this weekend. A neighbor found their bodies an hour ago. Their place is four or five miles from where White Calf went off the road. The neighbor last saw them Friday afternoon. Their truck is missing."

"You have a description of the truck?"

"Yeah. Ford pickup. I'll get the details from DMV. An ambulance is on the way to pick up the bodies and a couple of my men are right behind it."

"I thought you warned everyone in the area."

"We tried, but the snow knocked out some of the lines. The neighbor who found them lives almost a mile away. He heard their cows bawling and went over to check. Gilson and the dog were dead in the barn. The old lady was dead in her bed. Looks like White Calf used a knife on them."

"Does Raymond know?"

"Not yet. His shift ends soon and I'll tell him then."

"Get a description out on the truck as soon as you can. White Calf might be in town by now."

"I already have cruisers driving past Raymond's place and Mary's at regular intervals. If he's going to make a move, he'll probably wait until nightfall."

"One thing we've learned is that you can't second-guess him. The only thing we can depend on him for is to do the unexpected. Tell me how to get to the Gilson place."

46

C hief wants to see you, Raymond," Ben Red Leaf called from behind the desk as Raymond entered the building.

Raymond had been out all day with Merle Wagner. Only a few weeks earlier it would have been the kind of day he relished, a day without stress. Chickenshit cases, as Merle called them. Kids spraypainting graffiti, petty theft, fender benders. But those days weren't what Raymond wanted now. White Calf was out there somewhere and Raymond took it personally. He owed the sonofabitch and he meant to pay him back with interest.

"How urgent is it?" Raymond called to Ben. All he wanted at the moment was to complete his paperwork as fast as possible. During his entire shift, he'd been looking forward to a hot shower at home. Standing under the soothing spray helped him to forget about the pain in his chest and the frustration he felt about White Calf.

"Ask him yourself," Ben said, going back to his crossword puzzle.

"Anything going on?" Raymond persisted.

"Jesus, Raymond, if there is Homer'll tell you."

Frowning, Raymond rapped on Homer's door and entered the office.

"Sit down, Raymond," the chief said.

"What's up?"

"White Calf, that's what's up. You know the Gilsons?"

"Old couple who live out by the Two Medicine?"

"Make that past tense. Lived. White Calf killed them."

"When?"

"Sometime this weekend. We tried to alert them the night of the snowstorm, but the phone lines were down. Neighbor found them a little while ago. I just sent Leonard and Harvey out there. The Gilson's Ford pickup is missing."

"You have a plate number?"

"I got it five minutes ago. '87 Ford F100, plate 34T4201. I've got cars keeping an eye on your place and Mary's."

"I'd like to take a run up to the Gilson place, Chief, if it's okay with you.

Look around a bit and see if I can get some idea as to what White Calf has in mind."

"Perkins is headed out there. Your shift's over, Raymond. Why don't you go home, lock your door, and rest those ribs. Just keep your eyes open."

Ben Red Leaf looked up as Raymond passed the desk. "So?" he said.

Raymond ignored him. Gone now were any thoughts of a shower. White Calf had struck again, this time even closer to Browning. And he had a new set of wheels, wheels that might carry him into town. Or that might not. It was as if the bastard was toying with them, challenging them to figure out his next move. Maybe there was a clue at the Gilsons that would point to where White Calf was headed. The chief hadn't said yes to Raymond's request to visit the Gilson place, but on the other hand, Raymond hadn't heard the word 'no.'

———————————

Beth felt White Cloud tense in the back seat. She glanced in her mirror. His gaze was fixed on the parking lot. A heavy-set man was getting into his pickup. Beth recognized Raymond Two Teeth.

"See that truck?" White Calf said. "The one backing out of the space in the parking lot? I want you to follow it. Just stay way back so he doesn't know he's being followed. I'll tell you when to start and how far behind to stay."

"That's Officer Two Teeth," Beth said.

"So you know him, huh? Okay, start driving. Nice and slow."

"Why do you want to hurt him? What has he done to you?"

"Shut up. Just drive."

Beth stayed a half-block behind Raymond's vehicle. If she approached any closer, White Calf forced the shotgun muzzle into the back of her seat. The pressure was a reminder that death might be moments away.

They were approaching Browning's main street and Raymond's car picked up speed.

"You know where he lives?" White Calf asked.

"Officer Two Teeth? No."

"Where the fuck is he going?" White Calf said, speaking to himself.

Raymond had turned onto Highway 89 and was following it south out of town.

He can't live this far out, White Calf told himself when they were six or seven miles from the town center. Just north of the Two Medicine River, Raymond took the turnoff heading east. White Calf wondered if he was heading to the old couple's place. Someone might have found the bodies. But in that case, why hadn't he taken a Tribal Police cruiser?

"Slow down," White Calf ordered. "Take that turnoff up ahead, the one heading west. Then make a U-turn."

White Calf's mind was racing. He had no idea where the cop was going or how long he'd be away from town. Traffic was lighter this far out and he didn't want Raymond to suspect he was being followed. Once again, his plans were getting fucked up.

"What time does your husband get home?" White Calf asked.

Beth considered how best to answer. "It's an early day for him. He may be there already. He's probably wondering why I'm not home."

"Okay," White Calf said. "Drive home."

Surprised, Beth turned her head. White Calf raised his weapon just enough for her to see the muzzle. "Drive," he ordered.

"Hey, Bill," Perkins said to Jameson while heading for the door. "That was Homer Whitecloud on the line. An old couple named Gilson was found murdered about twelve miles from here. Their truck's missing."

"White Calf?"

"Sure looks that way. It's not that far from where his car went off the road."

"You heading out for a look?"

"Yeah. Homer gave me driving directions. Where's Briggs?"

"Left the office ten minutes ago. Said he's coming right back."

The ringing of the phone stopped Perkins when he was almost out the door. Jameson picked up the call and motioned for Perkins to come back. "He's right here, Chief. Hold on."

"One of my men spotted Gilson's truck," Homer said.

"Where?"

"Here in town. Here's the interesting part. While the officer was looking through the cab, an old man came out of one of the houses on the street. He said he'd seen the truck cut off a car. A woman got out of the car and the guy driving the truck grabbed her by the hair. He pushed her back behind the wheel of her car and got into the back seat. She drove away and they left the truck sitting there."

"Why the hell didn't this guy call the police?"

"He thought it was a lover's spat."

Perkins snorted with disgust.

"Did he give you anything else. A description of the woman or her car?"

"He said his eyes aren't too good, but the woman had long dark hair. The guy driving the truck was big. He said the guy took what looked like a suitcase out of the truck and some long object, a stick or a bat. He wasn't sure."

"Try a shotgun," Perkins said. "He said nothing about the car?"

"Sedan, white, maybe a foreign make. Possibly Japanese. He wasn't sure."

"Shit!" Perkins said.

"Exactly."

"Have you gotten any calls about a woman not showing up where she was expected?"

"Not yet."

"Maybe he'll force the woman to drive him to Raymond's place. Have you alerted your men?"

"I told them to stop any small white car they see near Raymond's or Mary's."

"Does Raymond know what's going on?"

"I called him but there was no answer. He wanted to go out to the Gilson place when his shift ended, but I told him to go home. Of course, with Raymond that means nothing. He's probably driving out to the Gilsons right now."

"Are your other men still out there?"

"Can't be sure. Phone at the house is still down and they're not answering the radio. Maybe they're inside the house or checking around outside."

"Okay. I'm heading out there now. If Raymond is there, I'll tell him what's going on. Call me if you get a lead on the woman."

47

John Hartman was distracted as he drove home. Sharon's daughter had barely survived her bout of pertussis. It was only in the past day or so that she seemed to have turned the corner and was now on her way to recovery. And just when Sharon's daughter appeared to be out of the woods, he was about to begin the struggle again with a new patient. His final admission of the day was a six-year-old John was convinced had whooping cough. It was a disease no child should be afflicted with in this day and age. The boy, who had been born with fetal alcohol syndrome, was being raised by his grandmother. He had never completed his immunizations. He took his place on the ward with pediatric patients suffering from dehydration secondary to severe diarrhea, pneumococcal pneumonia, worm infestations, and anemia. John had had to juggle beds so that the boy could be placed in a room by himself.

Browning was not all that dissimilar from Gallup when it came to infectious diseases. The tribe may have been different, Blackfeet rather than Navajo, but once again John was working in a third-world country. When he had first begun working with the Indian Health Service, John had been a young idealist, convinced he could really make a difference. Now, after his years in Gallup and his months in Browning, he compared himself to Sisyphus, the Corinthian king, condemned in Hades to eternally rolling a heavy stone uphill, only to have it roll down again. The only way for John to persevere was to persuade himself to think in terms of individuals. Maybe he couldn't change the results of generations of abuse and neglect on the reservation, but he could make a big difference in the life of each child under his care.

Beth's car was in the garage. She had called him earlier to tell him she might finish the clinic early. He smiled in anticipation. There weren't many days when they both arrived home in time for an early dinner. Snow left from a plowing several days earlier was piled along the curb. John backed up the driveway to the garage but left his car outside. He had told the ward nurse he'd be back after dinner to check on the boy with pertussis.

The house was quiet when John opened the door. He had expected to find

Beth bustling around the kitchen. The eerie silence made him uncomfortable.

"Beth?" he called.

"In the bedroom," she answered, her voice tremulous.

"Are you all right?" John called as he hurried down the hall.

He came to an abrupt stop in the doorway of the room. For a moment he felt lightheaded. Beth sat on the edge of the bed, her hands folded in her lap. Off to one side stood White Calf, his shotgun trained on her.

"Are you okay?" John asked, ignoring White Calf.

She nodded. "I spotted him in town and he cut me off. He forced me to drive him here."

"What do you want?" John said, locking eyes with White Calf.

"Just do what you're told and no one will get hurt."

"What do want from us? We've done nothing to you."

"It's not us he wants," Beth said softly.

"That's right," White Calf said.

John looked from White Calf back to his wife.

"He wants Raymond Two Teeth."

"We barely know the man," John told White Calf.

"I want you to call the tribal cops and tell whoever answers that it's important that you speak to Two Teeth, that he should call you here. Say you have information for him about a case he's working on."

"What do I say when he calls?"

"When the phone rings your wife can answer it." He moved in front of Beth, keeping his shotgun trained on her. Although his remarks were meant for Beth, he never took his eyes off John. "You'll tell him your husband's in the shower but wants to talk to him. Say it's urgent and ask him to come over. And make it believable. Try anything funny and he'll find two dead bodies when he gets here."

Beth leafed through the phone book in the drawer of the night table. She found the Tribal Police Headquarters listing and handed the book to John. He picked up the phone and dialed the number.

"This is Doctor Hartman," he said. "Would you give Officer Two Teeth a message for me please."

"He's not there," John said, covering the mouthpiece with his hand.

"You know what to say."

"I have important information for him about a case he's working on," John said. "Would you ask him to call me as soon as you reach him. Here's my number."

"What are you going to do when he gets here?" John asked after hanging up.

White Calf glared at him. "That's not your business. Sit down next to your wife and shut up. Remember," he cautioned Beth, "when the phone rings you answer it."

———

Raymond parked his truck next to the Tribal Police car and ambulance in front of the Gilson farmhouse. Leonard Nye poked his head out of the barn to see who had just arrived. He waved a greeting.

"Hey, Raymond," Harvey called, coming out of the house, "what are you doing here? You're not on duty."

"Thought I'd come see our friend's handiwork."

"It ain't pretty. The woman's in the bedroom. Old man Gilson is in the barn. Along with his dog."

The two ambulance attendants stood by impassively, waiting for the cops to give them the signal for loading the bodies.

Raymond entered the house and followed Harvey to the bedroom. He swallowed his nausea as he looked down at the thin gray-haired woman in the blood-soaked bed. Her head was twisted awkwardly to one side, almost completely severed from her body.

"Bastard used his knife this time," Harvey said. "Guess he didn't want to take a chance on anyone hearing the shotgun."

"Find anything in the house?"

"Nah. Let's see if Leonard came up with anything in the barn."

A car was coming down the road as they stepped out of the house. Leonard emerged from the barn with his hand on his holster.

"It's Perkins, the FBI man," Raymond called to him, recognizing the *Subaru*.

"You're supposed to be resting," Perkins said to Raymond as he stepped out of his car. He nodded a greeting to Harvey and Leonard.

Raymond grunted but said nothing. Perkins accompanied Raymond, Leonard, and Harvey into the barn. Gilson's body was crumpled on the floor. Blood had soaked into the floorboards. Next to the old man was the torn body of his dog.

Perkins knelt and gently tried to turn the body over. The old man's head stayed where it was, threatening to detach itself completely from the body. "Jesus," Perkins muttered.

"He killed the old lady the same way," Raymond said. "She's in her bedroom."

Perkins, still kneeling, looked up at Raymond. "They found the truck," he said.

"Where?"

"Right in town. That's not all. We believe he kidnapped a woman and commandeered her car. Description we have is a small white sedan, maybe Japanese. Not much to go on, but Homer has men watching for it near your place and Mary's. The chief thinks eventually he'll turn up at your place, maybe even tonight."

"Good. I'll be waiting for him. I hope he doesn't hurt the woman. Hasn't anyone called wondering why she didn't show up to wherever she was going?"

"Not yet," Perkins said, standing up and turning to Harvey and Leonard. "The chief told me he was trying to reach you on your radio. He figured you were either inside the house or checking things outside."

"I better call in," Harvey said.

Minutes later he stepped back into the barn. "Raymond, headquarters has a message for you. Some doctor's trying to reach you. Name is Hartman. Says he needs to talk to you about a case you're working on. Here's the phone number." He handed Raymond a slip of paper.

"What the hell can this be about?" Raymond said, looking at Perkins. "That's the doctor you and I talked to in the hospital."

"I recognized the name. Maybe he's got more information for us about the girl."

"There's a phone in the house, right?" Raymond said, looking at Harvey.

"Kitchen, but I don't know if it's working."

Perkins accompanied Raymond to the house, pausing to look at the murdered woman in the bedroom. "What a brutal bastard," Perkins said.

"I hope he gives us an excuse to shoot him when we catch up to him," Raymond said.

"Shit, it's dead," Raymond said, unable to get a dial tone on the kitchen phone. He was about to hang up when he placed the receiver back to his ear. "Hey, I got one." He dialed Hartman's number.

"This is Raymond Two Teeth," he said. "I got a message that the doctor wanted to talk to me."

"Yes," Beth said, "George is in the shower but he wants you to come over. He says it's urgent that he talk to you."

A puzzled expression crossed Raymond's face. "George? I thought your husband's name was John?"

"Yes, it is."

Raymond stared intently at Perkins. "Mrs. Hartman, are you having trouble there?"

"Yes, that's right."

"Is White Calf there?"

"Yes. Let me give you the address."

"Listen," Raymond said softly as he wrote it down, "don't do anything to antagonize him. Tell him I'm forty or fifty minutes from town and that I'm on my way."

"Yes, thank you. I'll tell him."

"White Calf's at the doctor's house?" Perkins said incredulously.

"Waiting for me," Raymond said.

48

"Whoa," Perkins said, holding up his hand as Raymond walked toward the door. "You can't go there alone. White Calf will kill you."

"If I don't go alone he'll kill the doc and his wife."

"Just stay put for a minute. I want to talk to Homer and to Jameson and let them know what's going on. Give me that address. While we're heading back to Browning they can get some surveillance set up on the house. Leonard and Harvey can follow behind us to provide more backup."

"If White Calf spots a cop near that house, the Hartmans are dead."

"It's getting dark. That'll be in our favor. Are you armed?"

"Yeah, but I'm not taking a weapon into the house with me. First thing he'll do is search me."

"Raymond, what you're planning is suicide."

"I don't know what he's planning, but I can't see him shooting me down when I come through the door. He's got something else in mind and the only way we're going to find out what it is is by my going in there."

"What can he possibly hope to accomplish by having you there? Why didn't he just take the Hartmans' car and make a run for it?"

"I'm a cop, not a psychiatrist. Maybe he wants to use all of us as hostages. One thing we do know. He hates me enough to have come back to the rez."

"That hate is clouding his judgment. It'll be his downfall."

"I hope you're right. I don't enjoy being on the receiving end of it. Make your calls. I gotta get going."

———

White Calf stood at the side of the living room window. Every few minutes he moved the curtain aside and peered out into the street. Except for the light that filtered in from a street lamp, the house was enveloped in darkness.

Huddled together on the sofa, John and Beth watched his every move. John studied White Calf's face intently. The piercing black eyes, aquiline nose, and strong chin made him a prototype for a Blackfeet warrior, a throwback to a time when the Blackfeet were feared by other tribes. That face, however, provided no explanation for the violence that seethed beneath its surface. What puzzled John was the strange feeling that the Indian was somehow familiar. He reminded John of someone and he wished he could elaborate on it with Beth. But talking about anything with his wife was out of the question. White Calf never released his grip on the shotgun. When he did glance in their direction, his eyes told John that he wouldn't hesitate for a moment to kill both of them should it become necessary.

"You sure he said forty minutes?" White Calf's voice was threatening, as if daring Beth to admit that she had lied to him.

"Forty or fifty. That's what he told me," Beth said, trying to keep her own voice steady.

"For your sakes he better come."

"Why do you hate him so much?" John asked.

White Calf spun around, his shotgun elevated. He moved slowly toward John. Beth grasped her husband's arm. John's entire universe had contracted to the black hole of the weapon's muzzle. He felt Beth's nails digging into his flesh. The terrifying moment passed as quickly as it had come. "You mind your fucking business," White Calf said. "I wasn't talking to you."

White Calf's attention was diverted by headlights moving slowly down the street, as if the driver were checking house numbers.

"Turn on the lamp by the sofa," he ordered Beth. "You just sit there, Doc, and don't move. Your wife will open the door when he knocks. And I'll be right behind her."

———————

Raymond had seen the lamp come on as he parked his pickup. He stored his holster and weapon under the seat and opened the truck door. The street was quiet. Perkins and Leonard had parked their vehicles a block away before Raymond made the turn onto the Hartmans' street. There was no way that White Calf could have spotted them. When it came to himself, however, there was no question in his mind that his every move was being followed by White Calf. He averted his eyes from the curtained windows, feigning unawareness. He calmly closed the truck door and stretched.

The Hartmans lived in one of the prefab houses built for the hospital's physicians. It was luxurious compared to most of the houses in town. Approaching the front door, Raymond's glance shifted from side to side. In spite of his relief that his backup was nowhere in sight, at the same time it caused him some trepidation. Here goes, he told himself as he knocked.

———————

As soon as they had received Perkins' call, Homer Whitecloud and Bill Jameson had sprung into action. Jameson ordered Briggs to cover any emergency that might come up while he and Perkins worked with the Tribal Police to maintain surveillance on the Hartman house. Chief Whitecloud, at home in Heart Butte, called the police dispatcher. By the time he arrived in Browning, seven of his men were waiting for him at Tribal Police Headquarters. Others, including Leonard and Harvey, were on site with Perkins. Homer distributed rifles from the gun cabinet at headquarters while he filled his men in. Each rifle was equipped with a telescopic sight. Opening two boxes of cartridges, Homer dumped them on his desk. The men loaded their clips and tucked extras into their pockets.

"We park a block away from the house. The feds and a few of our men are already there. Fan out on that street, but make sure you can't be seen from the Hartmans' windows. If White Calf comes out, he'll probably have hostages with him. Don't take a shot unless you know you can't miss. It's dark and the only light will be from the street lamp."

"What if he gets into a car with the hostages? What do we do?"

"We follow at a distance and hope he doesn't spot us. Once we know where he's heading, we can set up a roadblock."

"What if he does spot us?"

"No chase, if that's what you mean. He'll kill anyone with him. But what the hell are we talking about anyway? We have no idea what White Calf is planning in that twisted mind of his."

Beth opened the door no more than a crack and peered out.

"How you doin'?" Raymond said with a studied nonchalance. His heart pounded and he was sure his blood pressure was through the roof.

Beth's eyes flicked to the left as she stepped back. Raymond pushed the door open and entered the house.

"Close it," White Calf ordered. He stood off to the side, his shotgun leveled at Raymond. "You sit down with your husband," he snapped at Beth.

White Calf glanced at Raymond's belt. "Lose your gun, cop?"

"I don't wear a gun when I make social calls."

"Don't bullshit me. You don't look surprised to find me here."

"I thought you'd turn up sooner or later."

White Calf stepped back to the window, not lowering his weapon, and took a fast look outside.

"I'm alone," Raymond said.

"You better be."

"Like I said, I thought this was a social call. Mrs. Hartman said her husband had some important news for me. I guess you're the news, right?"

"You and I have some unfinished business. But first, you're going to be my ticket out of here. Sit down next to those two."

White Calf remained alongside the window, alternating his gaze from the street outside to his three captives on the sofa. They watched him in silence. He's waiting for it to get darker, Raymond thought. As if reading the tribal cop's mind,

White Calf fixed him with a stare that blazed hatred. Raymond had momentary visions of Rebecca's mutilated face and the slashed throats of the Gilsons. It was impossible to forget what White Calf was capable of.

If I can catch him off guard for just one moment, Raymond thought, the Hartmans might be able to get out. But finding that one moment proved impossible. White Calf never dropped his guard. His shotgun remained pointed in their direction, his index finger always in front of the trigger.

"You," White Calf ordered Beth, "pick up that suitcase behind the sofa."

Raymond's eyes settled on the suitcase. He guessed it was filled with cash, the money taken from the dead drug dealer in Fort Belknap.

"Okay, cop, stand up. You, Doc, you stay where you are. We're going to be using your car. Toss the keys to me."

John took the keys from his pocket. He momentarily envisioned himself throwing them into White Calf's face. The muzzle pointed at him drove the thought away. White Calf grabbed his underhanded toss in midair.

"You carry my bag," White Calf said, indicating Beth with a flick of his chin. "When we get to the car I'll take it from you. You slide into the front passenger seat and I'll get in right behind you. You're driving, cop. Just don't forget that the shotgun will be pointed at the back of the lady's head."

"Don't take her, take me," John said, jumping to his feet.

"Shut up and sit down. And before you go yelling for the cops, remember I have your wife. You don't want anything happening to her."

"Why don't you leave them both here?" Raymond said. "You have me."

"When I want your advice I'll ask for it. The lady is extra insurance, in case your friends don't think much of you."

John watched from the window as White Calf kept Beth directly in front of him. He tossed the suitcase onto the back seat of the Corolla. Keeping Beth close, he opened the front passenger door. "Get in," he ordered her, while he ducked inside the rear of the car. If they were being watched by police, he had eliminated any possibility of an open shot. Raymond slid behind the wheel as White Calf adjusted his bulk on the back seat.

"Remember, cop," White Calf said, "my shotgun will be pointed at the lady's head."

"Where are we headed?" Raymond asked as he turned the key in the ignition.

"Go through town and get onto the old road to Babb."

"That's probably snow-covered. If you're heading for the border, why not take 89?"

"Just do what I tell you."

Raymond rolled slowly down the driveway into the street.

"Turn right," White Calf said, as if knowing surveillance had been set up on the street to his left. "Go through town that way."

In his rear-view mirror, Raymond spotted headlights from more than one vehicle a good distance behind him. He wondered if White Calf, too, had noticed the lights. Raymond turned off onto Duck Lake Road as White Calf had ordered. He watched his mirror as he drove. The lights had disappeared. White Calf had known what he was doing when he chose the old road. Any headlights behind them would have made it obvious they were being followed.

49

John Hartman watched from the window as his car turned to the right at the end of his driveway. Raymond Two Teeth was driving and Beth was in the front passenger seat. John tore the front door open and ran after the car. Its tail lights disappeared as it made another right turn a block ahead of him. John raced down the middle of the street, his arms pumping. The cold night air cut sharply into his lungs. A cloud of vapor accompanied every exhalation. His eyes were tearing as he turned at the intersection. The tail lights were still visible but he was almost at the end of his endurance. A car screeched to a halt alongside him.

"Get in back!" Perkins barked.

"He's got my wife and Raymond," John yelled as he leaped in.

"I wish to hell you'd stayed in the house," Perkins said.

"Can't you go any faster," John said. Two blocks ahead of them the Toyota made a right turn.

Jameson, sitting in the front passenger seat, turned to him. "You want to get them both killed?"

They kept their distance, never losing sight of the Toyota's tail lights, but never getting any closer. For the first time John became aware of more lights behind them. He glanced out the rear window. Three Tribal Police cruisers were following.

The Toyota turned abruptly onto Route 464.

"He's taking the old road to Babb," Jameson said.

"Shit!" Perkins rolled to a stop at the turnoff.

"Why are you stopping?" John yelled. "He'll get away."

"If he sees lights behind him on this road, he'll know he's being followed," Perkins explained patiently, as if he were talking to a child. "We don't want him to kill his hostages."

The three Tribal Police cars pulled up while they were talking. Homer Whitecloud jumped out of the first one.

Perkins rolled down his window. "He's taking the old Babb road," he said.

"I can see that."

"There's enough new snow on it to follow his tracks, but don't let him see your lights."

"What are you going to do?"

"Jameson and I will take 89 to Babb and backtrack. Maybe we can get him between us. You have my cellphone number."

"What about him?" Homer asked, motioning toward John Hartman.

"He was running down the street after White Calf."

"I'll go with the police," John said, grasping the handle of his door.

Homer, catching Perkins' eye, shook his head.

"Sit tight, Doc," Perkins said, setting the automatic door lock. He made a sharp U-turn and headed back the way they'd come.

Through the rear window, John caught a momentary glimpse of two of the police cars making their way slowly onto 464 before they disappeared from view.

Raymond drove slowly on the snow-covered road. They were heading north toward the part of the reservation known as Hudson Bay Divide. Babb, the road's western terminus, wasn't a popular destination at this time of year. Anyone headed for the village or the border would most likely be on 89, the main highway.

He was pleased to see there were no tracks on the snow. It would make it easy for his fellow cops to follow them. He knew they were staying out of sight, not wanting White Calf to spot their headlights. From Babb, it was only ten miles to the Piegan crossing into Canada. White Calf won't attempt to cross at a border station, Raymond told himself. By now every official crossing spot in Montana had probably been alerted. If he intended to get across, he'd have to do it illegally in a remote area. And in that case, what would he do with his hostages?

The snow got deeper as they drove further north. "Follow the road?" Raymond asked, as it veered to the west.

"Go straight," White Calf commanded. The Toyota skidded slightly as Raymond turned the steering wheel to the right.

Where the hell is he taking us? Raymond wondered. They were on Whiskey Gap Road, heading into rough country. Ranches and homesteads this far north were few and far between.

"Turn off here," White Calf said after they'd driven a mile and a half.

"We'll get stuck."

White Calf jabbed the shotgun muzzle into the base of Raymond's neck. "Do it," he ordered.

Raymond dropped into a lower gear and the car struggled through at least eight inches of snow. They were gradually heading into higher country, the unimproved road deteriorating as they went. Eventually, if they weren't blocked by snow, they'd pass about a mile to the north of Goose Lake and finally come to Camp Nine Road.

Raymond glanced at the odometer. They'd managed to cover five miles on a track they never should have been on. Several times his tires had spun on slick patches beneath the snow.

"Stop the car," White Calf said. "The woman gets out."

Raymond turned his head, alarmed.

"Easy, cop," White Calf said, pointing the muzzle of his weapon at Raymond's face.

What the hell is he doing? Raymond asked himself. If White Calf turned the shotgun on the doctor's wife, he'd have to make a move. He shifted slightly in his seat, a twinge of pain reminding him of his rib injury.

"Get out!" White Calf snapped at Beth. "And kick the door shut."

Beth slipped out of the car, slamming the door behind her.

"Drive," White Calf ordered Raymond.

"This is the middle of nowhere. You can't just leave her there. She doesn't even have a jacket, for chrissake. She'll freeze to death."

"Drive, cop, or would you rather I get out and shoot her?"

Raymond drove away slowly, his eyes glued to the rearview mirror until Beth disappeared into the darkness. Six or seven miles for her to walk before she reached the old Babb road junction, he thought. It was twenty degrees out, at best, and that bastard, White Calf, hadn't let her take a coat when she left the house. Unless his fellow officers were following behind them, there was little chance of a car coming along. Hypothermia would probably kill her before she made it to the intersection. On the other hand, she was still alive, and for that he was thankful.

———————————

Beth trudged down the road, swinging her arms, trying not to think about the cold. She was more worried about Raymond Two Teeth, alone in the car with White Calf, than she was about her own predicament. What chance did he have against a madman with a shotgun?

The cold easily penetrated the light sweater she wore. Her ankle-high boots, fine for Browning's streets, were virtually useless on the snow-covered track. As powdery snow tumbled down the inside of her boots, she wondered if she'd have any feeling left in her feet by the time she came to the 464 intersection.

Beth quickened her pace, breaking into a slow jog. Although she tried not to focus on how cold she was, it was impossible to ignore it. Her feet felt as if they were encased in ice and her teeth were chattering. Suddenly, she stopped. Am I dreaming? she wondered, hearing what sounded like a car.

As headlights approached, she raced toward them. Two Tribal Police vehicles came to a sliding stop.

"Are you all right?" Homer Whitecloud asked, jumping out of the first car.

"Yes, but he still has Raymond."

"I can't spare the men to take you back to Browning. Hop in back and we'll keep going. I'll get you a blanket."

Homer removed two blankets from the rear of the vehicle and passed them to Beth as he got back in. She wrapped them around her and curled up on the back seat, her teeth chattering.

"You sure you're all right?"

"I'm okay. Do you mind turning up the heater a little more?"

"Did he say anything when he let you go?" Homer asked.

"No. Just ordered me out of the car. I thought I'd freeze to death before I got to the junction."

"We never would have been on this road if we hadn't seen his tracks. Do you have any idea where he's going?"

"He didn't tell us anything. I'm so afraid for Raymond. Isn't there anything we can do to help him?"

"The car is bound to get stuck on this road. We'll get him."

"But what about Raymond? White Calf may kill him before you reach the car."

"Raymond's not that easy to kill. You should know that by now."

Homer exchanged glances with Jim Ryder, the officer sitting next to him. He knew they were both wondering if this time Raymond's luck had run out.

50

Whatever White Calf was planning for him, Raymond knew, would have to take place soon. Twice the Toyota had almost gotten stuck. The next time it happened might be the last. Even if by some miracle he could make it as far as Camp Nine Road, White Calf would never let him continue on to the highway. He'd want to get rid of Raymond in a spot where no one would hear the gunshot. Raymond didn't doubt for a minute that White Calf intended to kill him. If he was ordered to stop and get out of the car, or if the Toyota did get stuck in the snow, Raymond would have to make his move.

He drove slowly in low gear, the Toyota struggling as the snow got deeper.

"You drive any slower and we will get stuck," White Calf said. "Move it."

Raymond glanced at the rearview mirror. White Calf was a shadowy form behind him, his face not visible in the darkness. But his presence, even his smell, filled the car. Whenever the Toyota hit a dip in the road, Raymond felt the shotgun's muzzle grazing the skin of his neck. It was as if he were taking Death for a ride.

"Stop!" White Calf ordered.

The odometer showed they'd managed to cover almost three miles since letting Beth out of the car.

"We're getting out here," White Calf said. He jabbed the shotgun between Raymond's shoulder blades. "Move!" he said.

Now or never, Raymond thought. He opened his door and dived headlong from the car, rolling toward the road's edge when he hit the ground. White Calf cursed as he struggled to extract himself from the rear seat. Stumbling to his feet, Raymond was already running when White Calf's shotgun discharged. Hot needles penetrated Raymond's left ear and the side of his neck. He'd avoided the main part of the blast, but the pellets that hit him hurt like hell.

The metallic thud of the shotgun's sliding bolt reverberated in the night's blackness as Raymond zigzagged uphill through the snow. He threw himself to the ground moments before the second blast cut through the branches above him. Panting, Raymond took off running as best as he was able, the snow cover almost up to his knees. He darted toward the shadows of trees, hoping he wouldn't impale himself or take an eye out on a pine branch. Even while slipping and sliding through deep snow, Raymond, by instinct, kept heading north. Spider Lake, he figured, was maybe a mile away. The ground wouldn't level out until he got closer to it.

The pain from his broken ribs, which he'd ignored while the adrenaline flowed, was now intense. Diving from a vehicle and running uphill through snow at five thousand feet elevation was not what the doctor had in mind when he advised Raymond to rest. Struggling to catch his breath, Raymond cursed himself for having put on weight. There was a time when he could tramp through snow for hours, barely getting winded. Tripping over a rock, Raymond plunged face first into the snow. He lay there, unable to take a deep breath because of the pain in his chest, and listened for any sound that would tell him how far behind White Calf was.

The night was quiet, too quiet. Raymond plastered a handful of snow against his ear and neck, hoping to ease the burning pain of the shotgun pellets. He lifted himself into a kneeling position and peered into the darkness. Maybe White Calf had given up the chase and headed back to the car. If he had, what did he intend doing? Take a chance on making it through the snow until he reached the highway? Try to backtrack? Raymond felt a prickling of his scalp when he thought of White Calf turning back. He'd be certain to overtake Beth Hartman trudging through the snow toward Whiskey Gap. If he did . . . Raymond didn't want to think about it.

He listened intently for the sound of the car's engine, but heard nothing. Perhaps he was too far from the road to hear it. Or maybe White Calf had no intention of driving further. As the crow flies, it was only six or seven miles to the border from where they'd left the car. White Calf might very well try to make it on foot.

Raymond lurched to his feet and looked around him, seeing only the closest snow-covered branches before the cluster of pines became a black curtain. He could backtrack with no problem, but he'd run the risk of stumbling into White Calf. His feet were already moving forward, deciding his next move for him. He'd go on until he hit the St. Mary River. Once there, he'd follow it to Camp Nine Road and try to get help.

51

*W*hite Calf kicked his way furiously through the snow as he headed back to the car. Once again he'd let the man he hated get away from him. He had to make a quick decision. Continuing on in the car to Camp Nine Road in hopes of making it to the highway was out of the question. The car would probably get stuck before he'd gone another quarter-mile. Even if it didn't, the cops or the feds might be heading east on Camp Nine to cut him off. He could turn the car around and head back toward Whiskey Gap, but the Tribal Police might have the road blocked off south of there.

He realized now how foolish he'd been to return to Browning. If he hadn't been so intent on getting rid of the cop, he'd be miles away. He could have been in Wyoming or Idaho by now. His options at this point were down to one. The border was his only possible escape route. The North Fork of the Milk River couldn't be more than a mile away. If he followed the river, it would take him to the border. Once on the Canadian side, he could make his way to Woody's Junkyard on the 501 road. Woody was the facilitator for the occasional load of meth Aalford received from Canada. The junkman stored it until his mules could get it across the line, usually in the vicinity of the North Fork. The crossing point White Calf had in mind would put him less than two miles from Woody's. It was a spot the Mounties seldom patrolled, especially at this time of year.

He hoisted his bag from the back seat. The initial part of his trek would be through some rough uphill country. But as he got closer to the border, the ground leveled out. On the Canadian side, the country was flat, making the distance to Woody's easy to cover.

Instinctively, Raymond headed northwest, clutching his side and plodding through the snow. I can't be more than a mile from the river, he told himself, but it was difficult to orient himself with certainty in the darkness. If he could make it to Camp Nine Road, he'd have a chance of finding an inhabited cabin.

Ten minutes later, he trudged up a steep incline and found himself on level ground. Pausing for a moment to catch his breath, he peered into the darkness. The moon hadn't risen enough to provide much light, but he had to keep moving. He picked up his pace, watching carefully for any interruption in the uniform whiteness of the snow. There were gullies here and he didn't want to fall into one and break a leg.

A soft thud off to his right made his heart race. He dropped to the ground and listened. Probably snow coming down from a ponderosa branch, he decided. But there was always the possibility that White Calf had done the unexpected and followed behind him. If that were the case, Raymond's only hope for survival was to hear him coming before he had a chance to use his shotgun.

When the moon finally rose, cloud cover blocked out most of its light. Raymond heard the river before he saw it. Staying close to the shore, he followed it due west. He depended on the sound of the water and the feel of the shore beneath his boots to guide him. Camp Nine Road couldn't be too far now. As if to confirm his thought, a light appeared in the darkness ahead of him. Raymond half-ran, half-walked through the snow until he saw a cabin's silhouette. A single lamp burned inside and a jeep sat in the driveway.

Raymond raised his hand to knock on the door and hesitated. He had no idea who was inside. Perhaps White Calf had reached the cabin before him and was lying in wait, figuring that sooner or later Raymond would appear.

He crouched and moved stealthily toward the window. A bearded man sat in a chair, reading by the light of a kerosene lamp. A gray cat lay curled in the man's lap. The man looked up, as if aware he was being watched. Raymond headed back toward the door and knocked.

The bearded man, holding a rifle in his hand, pulled the door open. "What the hell!" he said, his gaze settling first on Raymond's bloody ear and neck, then moving to the Tribal Police uniform.

"Do you have a phone?" Raymond asked.

The man nodded. "I've got a cell phone hooked up to a roof antenna. Did you have an accident?"

Reminded of his wounds, Raymond touched his ear, wincing at the pain. He regarded the blood stains on his fingers with a frown. It'll have to wait, he thought, as he dialed the dispatcher in Browning.

"This is Officer Two Teeth," he said. "Can you reach Chief Whitecloud for me? Tell him I'm at a cabin on Camp Nine Road. Here's the phone number." He looked inquiringly at the bearded man and repeated the cell phone number told to him. "I'll be waiting right here by the phone."

A minute later the phone rang. It was the dispatcher.

"I'm having problems with the chief's radio. It keeps cutting out. Give me your exact location."

"Tell the dispatcher where we are," Raymond said to the bearded man, handing him the phone.

"The woman said she'd call you back in a few minutes," the man said after he'd told her the location of the cabin. "My name's Pete Riley." He extended his hand.

"Raymond Two Teeth. Thanks for helping me out. You live here year round?"

"Nah. Just up doing some hunting."

The phone rang and Raymond grabbed it.

"Officer Two Teeth?" the dispatcher asked. "I reached Chief Whitecloud. He wanted me to tell you that he picked up Beth Hartman. She's fine. He's going to contact the FBI men who took 89 up to Babb. They can cut in at Camp Nine Road to pick you up. He wants to know if you have any idea where White Calf is headed."

"Tell the chief I didn't hear him start the car up again. He's probably heading for the border on foot."

"I'll tell him," she said.

"Here's some peroxide for your ear and neck," said Riley, coming up to Raymond with a plastic bottle in his hand. "I'll clean it up for you." He shifted the lantern, creating dancing patterns of light on the log walls.

"We're hunting a killer," Raymond said, as the man sponged his ear and neck with cotton balls. "His name's White Calf." Raymond pointed to his ear. "That's a souvenir from the shotgun he carries with him. Federal agents are on their way to pick me up. Do you have any weapon here besides the rifle?"

"I've got a thirty-eight."

"I don't think he'll head this way, but if he does show up, you'll only get one shot against him. Remember, he's got a shotgun. Keep your weapons handy and lock the door. Where are your car keys?"

Riley patted his pants pocket. "What's this guy look like?"

"Big. Shoulder-length hair. You can't miss him. After I leave you ought to douse the lantern. You'll be able to see anyone approaching the house."

"You're saying I should shoot first and ask questions later?"

"I leave that to your good judgment."

———

Bill Jameson's heavy wool slipover sweater and longshoreman's cap pulled down to the top of his ears gave him the appearance of a middle-aged ski enthusiast rather than a federal agent. His eyes glinted behind his wire-rimmed glasses. Perkins, driving, knew Jameson loved the adventure of a manhunt. The man came to life when he was away from his desk.

"Well, that should make you feel better, Doc," Jameson said, twisting around in his seat after they'd received Homer's cellphone call.

"Thank God he let her go," John said. "I can't believe Raymond got away from him."

"Sometimes I think Raymond has as many lives as a cat," Perkins said. "You can ask him how he did it when we pick him up."

"The chief didn't say where Beth is now. Do you think he had a car take her back to Browning?"

"I'd guess she's still with him. As soon as we pick up Raymond, I'll call Homer to find out where to meet him."

Raymond was waiting outside for the agents when the Subaru's headlights illuminated Riley's cabin. Raymond waved to Riley, who stood at the window, and slid into the car's back seat next to John Hartman. "About time you got here," Raymond said to Perkins. "What are you doing here, Doc?"

"Jesus, Raymond, look at you," Perkins said, shaking his head. "What'd you do, stick the side of your head in a meatgrinder?"

"When we catch up to that sonofabitch, I'm going to shove that shotgun of his so far up his ass he'll be looking into the muzzle with the back of his eye."

"Homer told us he let Dr. Hartman's wife go, but how the hell did you get away from him?"

"I knew he was going to kill me, so I jumped out of the car and ran."

"Not bad for a man with broken ribs," Jameson said.

They were interrupted by Perkins' cell phone ring. "Raymond with you?" Homer asked.

"We have him."

"Is he okay?"

"Handsome as ever," Perkins said, grinning.

"We found the Toyota. Two shotgun casings next to it so this must be where Raymond got away from him. We'll wait for you here. Tell Raymond to lead you to the Whiskey Gap Road and Canal Track intersection. Stay on Whiskey Gap Road. About a mile or so from the junction with 464 you'll see car tracks turning off onto a bitch of a road. Follow them for about eight miles."

"Roger. Is Dr. Hartman's wife with you?"

"She is. Tell the doc she's fine. Once you get here, we'll try to get them both back to Browning."

"I figured he'd take off on foot," Raymond said after Perkins relayed the chief's message..

"How close are we to that intersection?" Jameson asked.

"Not too far," Raymond said. "The snow'll slow us up a bit."

"You think we have any chance of catching up to White Calf?"

"Where they found the Toyota is only six or seven miles from the border, but that's only if White Calf heads due north. He won't do that."

"How do you know?"

"If you were White Calf making your way in the dark with a suitcase and shotgun to slow you down, what would you do to make sure you were heading in the right direction and that there were no obstacles in front of you?"

"Follow a river that crosses the border?" Perkins said.

"Exactly. The North Fork of the Milk. The only thing that bothers me is that he's got a good jump on us and he knows the country."

"Yeah, but there's one thing in our favor he doesn't know," Jameson said.

"What's that?"

"We already notified the Mounties. Peter Martin, the officer I talked to, said they'd have men and dogs spread out along the twenty-six miles between the Piegan and Del Bonita crossings."

"That's a lot of ground to patrol," Raymond said, "but it's better than leaving the whole border open for the bastard."

Encumbered by his suitcase, White Calf made slow progress through snow-covered fields and gullies. Dense stands of aspen and pine blocked his way as he neared the river. He cursed at the branches catching on his clothes and hacked at them with his shotgun. His night vision was good, but the cloud cover was a hindrance. He stopped only to scoop handfuls of snow into his mouth. He was hungry, but there was nothing to do about that. Thinking about Raymond trying to make his way through the woods, White Calf clenched the shotgun tighter. He had managed to get two shots off before the cop eluded him. The rounds hadn't killed him, but White Calf had seen blood on the snow. He hoped he'd wounded him badly enough to cause pain—lots of pain.

52

Two Tribal Police cruisers sat idling by the Corolla when Perkins pulled up. Homer Whitecloud stepped out of one and grimaced when he saw the dried blood on Raymond's ear and neck. "I'm glad you're still in one piece," he said.

Beth leaped from the rear seat of the chief's cruiser. Moments later she and John were in each other's arms.

"Listen," the chief said to Perkins and Raymond. "Let's see if we can get the Toyota turned around so the doc and his wife can get back to Browning. Raymond, you can go with them. We'll give you a weapon just in case White Calf is still around."

"I'm not going anywhere but with you," Raymond said.

"We'll be going after White Calf on foot from here. You don't look in shape to walk ten feet, let alone the miles we have to cover."

"Hey, I got to Camp Nine Road, didn't I? Besides, this is personal. I'm not going anywhere until we have him."

Merle Wagner, one of the cops in the other cruiser, stepped out to defuse the standoff. "Chief, I think Raymond is afraid to face Doc Ferguson in the Emergency Room. The doctor will chew his ass and tell him his ribs will never heal if he keeps running around and getting shot at."

Homer glanced at Perkins, who shrugged. "He's a glutton for punishment. What can I say?"

"We're wasting time here," Jameson said. "The Mounties are probably deployed on their side. Let's decide how to handle our end."

"I've sent a car with four men up Meriwether Road," Homer said. "They'll cut off at Boundary Road for a few miles, then start walking in. I figure White Calf will try to follow the river to the border, so we'll drive in on the Canal Track until we reach Emigrant Gap. That's where we'll start walking east."

"That's a good plan," Raymond said. "If he's following the river, we'll have him sandwiched between us."

"Glad you approve, Raymond," the chief said facetiously. "Merle, since you did so well pleading Raymond's case, why don't you go back to Browning with the Hartmans."

"Ah, Chief," Merle protested.

"We can go by ourselves," John said.

"I'm not taking any chances," Homer said. "Merle will go with you. Come on, let's turn that Toyota around. We've got to get going."

The men got behind the Corolla to push as John steered it into a U-turn.

Perkins sidled up to Raymond. "You sure your ribs are up to this?"

Ben Red Leaf, standing next to them, overheard and laughed. "His ribs are busted, he's got buckshot in his head, but this clown don't know when to call it a day."

"I'll call it a day when White Calf is dead or in jail," Raymond snapped. "Now, who's got an extra rifle for me?"

Ben passed him one from the back of his cruiser.

"Okay, back in the cars," Homer said as the Toyota's tail lights disappeared down the road. "Follow me to Emigrant Gap."

"Let's fan out," the chief said after they'd parked their vehicles on the Canal Track where it met the gap. "Use your flashlights sparingly. And remember, there are cops coming toward us. Nobody shoots unless he's positive it's White Calf."

Raymond forged ahead through the snow, the pain in his chest forgotten for the moment. Soon only the intermittent dancing beam of his flashlight was visible, then that, too, disappeared. "Moves pretty good for a guy with broken ribs," Perkins said to Homer.

"He's a man with a mission. You go next," Homer said to Ryder. "Then Red Leaf. I'll follow." He turned to Jameson and Perkins. "You two don't know this country. You can bring up the rear, but watch yourselves."

"Doesn't have much confidence in us, does he?" Perkins whispered to Jameson.

No more than a hundred fifty feet separated each of the men as they started off, but in the darkness they were invisible to one another. Only when a man caught the momentary glare of a flashlight in the distance was he aware that he wasn't alone. The only sound audible in the blackness was the steady crunch of boots on snow and the occasional snapping of a branch.

Perkins and Jameson were at a disadvantage and they knew it. They had only a general idea of where they were headed. The tribal cops knew these woods and fields intimately. They'd traipsed them since childhood. Nevertheless, Perkins refused to use his light. I'll be damned if I'm going to be the one to give our location away to White Calf, he thought. He plodded along in the dark until a branch caught him above one eye, drawing blood. Cursing under his breath, he flicked on the flashlight. As much as possible he kept it trained on the ground ahead of him, raising the beam only when he encountered a copse of trees.

In spite of the pain from his broken ribs, Raymond moved ahead at a steady pace. Knowing that every step brought him closer to White Calf was all the incentive he needed to keep moving. The discomfort from the pellets in his ear and neck had subsided to a dull ache. He aimed his flashlight beam at the ground and swept it in an arc. The only prints in the snow were made by animals. For all any of them knew, White Calf might be on the south bank of the river. No matter which side he was on, a man following the river couldn't go wrong. Ultimately the river would lead him to Canada.

Raymond stopped and listened with his light turned off. An owl hooted in the distance, but it was another sound he'd heard. It came again, the barking of a dog. If it was one of the Mounties' dogs, it meant they were closer to the border than he'd thought, perhaps only a mile or two away.

———

White Calf navigated entirely by the sound of the river. That was a constant, whereas in the darkness his acute vision was of little help. He was lucky to catch an occasional glimpse of the water where eddies formed around rocks and branches. Pausing on a gully's edge above the river, he cautiously eased his way down. Ice had begun to form along the water's edge, none of it interfering with the river's flow. There had been no rain for weeks, and the melt of the recent snows had been minimal. The river's depth was shallow enough for a man to easily walk across. Not expecting his pursuers to use dogs to track him, White Calf, for the time being, opted to stay on the north bank.

———

Perkins tried to keep his mind off the cold. It penetrated his down jacket, and his gloves bordered on being useless. The fingers of his left hand, wrapped around the rifle stock just behind the trigger guard, ached. He thought about Liz and his daughters. He'd barely spent any time with them since he started working on this case. All of them were used to his being called away at odd hours when least expected, but it never made it easier when it happened. He tried not to think about the disappointment in his daughters' eyes when he had to leave.

"Please be careful," Liz cautioned him, as she always did when he was on the hunt for a suspect.

"Yeah," he said, turning quickly away from her. Slow leave-takings only made things worse.

53

The four tribal cops closing the vise from the east had made good time. The snow wasn't as deep south of the Del Bonita crossing and they'd passed through a relatively benign landscape while heading toward the North Fork of the Milk River. Leonard Nye, ahead of the others, figured they'd covered about five miles. If his calculations were right, he'd be at the river in less than a half-hour. He hadn't spotted any footprints the few times he'd flicked on his light, but he hadn't expected any. "Head for the river and follow it to the border," was the only instruction he and the others had received from Homer Whitecloud. The chief had also cautioned them that he and his men would be approaching from the west. "Know what you're shooting at," he'd reiterated several times. With any luck they'd have White Calf sandwiched between them, but that also increased the chance of a man taking fire from his own people. Ira Sands, Harvey Duprez, and Alvin Spotted Hawk were spread out behind Leonard. Probably no more than fifty yards separated the men, but that was a guess on Leonard's part. There was no way for him to know that with certainty. Whenever he looked over his shoulder, all Leonard saw was the blackness of night. The men were being careful with their flashlights and he never caught a glimpse of a beam.

If I were a betting man, Leonard thought, I'd wager White Calf wasn't more than a mile or two in front of us, probably as close to the border as we are. I hope to hell we can cut him off. I bet the guys coming from the west are thinking the same thing. That was the last thought passing through Leonard's mind as a dark shape loomed up in front of him.

At first Leonard thought he'd stumbled right into White Calf. It took only a fraction of a second for him to realize that wasn't the case. A loud snort informed him he'd run into an animal, not a person. Whatever it was, it was too late for him to back off. He raised his rifle, but hesitated. If White Calf were close, a shot would alert him to the position of his pursuers. It would also confuse the hell out of the guys to the west. No one would know what was going on. This late in the season, most of the brown bears had denned up, but there were always stragglers who waited until the last minute. Leonard sensed more than saw that the animal, whatever it was, was charging. He felt the earth's vibration through the soles of his boots. Dropping his weapon, he threw himself into the snow. Going on the assumption that it was a bear, he covered his neck and head with his arms.

Seconds later a searing pain tore through his left axilla as he was lifted off the ground. He knew now that he wasn't dealing with a bear, but he also knew he was in big trouble. He reached down, straining to free himself from the horn or antler that had penetrated his armpit and was threatening to tear him apart. The beast shook its head and Leonard thought his left arm was being wrenched from his body. He screamed for help, unable to free himself. I'm dead, he thought.

It was only later, when he recovered consciousness in the hospital, that he remembered hearing a gunshot before he passed out. Actually, he'd heard only the first of the three rounds Ira Sands emptied into the bull. It had taken all three to kill the animal, one in the neck, one in the chest, and one in the head. For a brief instant, Ira thought he was about to become the bull's next victim, until the massive brute collapsed at his feet.

"Jesus," Ira said as he knelt next to Leonard, shining his light on him. Blood poured from a wound in the left armpit and upper chest, saturating the downed man's shirt and jacket. Now it was Ira yelling for help. Minutes later dancing flashlight beams came toward him.

Two Mounties on the Canadian side of the border, immediately to the north of where the bull had attacked Leonard Nye, had been startled by the shots. They'd been patrolling the fields of a large cattle ranch, finding nothing more exciting than an occasional steer looming up ahead of them. The reports were so close that in the darkness it was impossible to tell which side of the border the firing was on. The dog being restrained by one of the Mounties sensed the man's momentary distraction and broke away, tearing across an expanse of snow-covered field toward the place where the shot had come from. Both men took off after it, following its path through the snow with their lights.

Ira, Harvey, and Alvin hovered over Leonard, applying pressure with their gloved hands to staunch the flow of blood from his axilla and chest. Leonard, unconscious, groaned softly.

"Listen to his breathing," Harvey said. "That horn might have gotten his lung."

"Shit, he's bleeding bad," said Alvin, raising Leonard's shirt and training his flashlight on the wounds.

"How are we going to get him out of here?" Ira asked.

"We'll have to carry him."

"It's too far back to the car. He'll bleed to death."

"I think we should fire shots at regular intervals," Alvin said, "like every thirty seconds. Maybe we'll get more help."

"We might be helping White Calf to escape by pulling men off the line," Ira said.

"Right now I'm more interested in saving Leonard's life," Spotted Hawk said. Not hesitating, he stood up and fired a round into the air. Two more rounds followed at half-minute intervals.

"Stop!" Ira said. "Listen."

The barking of a dog was getting louder by the second. The German shepherd burst through a patch of scrub pine and snapped at the men in a frenzy. The dead bull distracted the dog just long enough for him to sniff at the carcass before he turned his attention back to the men.

"Shep, here, Shep!"

"We're over here," Spotted Eagle yelled. "We need help." He shined his flashlight on the red-uniformed Mountie who joined them.

"Did you get—?" The Mountie's words ended abruptly when he spotted the dead bull. He knelt next to Leonard. "My Lord!"

"What's up?" said the second Mountie, joining them.

"This man's been gored by a bull." The Canadian stood up and conferred with his colleague for a few moments. "Listen," he said, turning back to the tribal cops clustered around Leonard, "we're less than a half-mile from the border and there's a ranch house not far from there. We can call for one of our cars or get him to the hospital in the rancher's truck. Let's carry him up there."

"We have to control the bleeding better before we try," Spotted Eagle said.

The Mountie pulled a bandana from his pocket and wrapped it tightly around Leonard's axilla, tying the knot above his shoulder. He whipped off his jacket and slipped it under Leonard's shoulders and head. "We can use this as a sling for his upper body," he said to his companion, who quickly moved to the injured man's other side.

"I'll take his feet," Harvey said.

"Do you need another one of us to go with you?" Ira asked.

"No, we can manage. You men keep up the search. Good luck."

They disappeared into the darkness, the dog scampering ahead of them.

"Good luck to you," Ira said softly.

"Let's keep moving," Alvin said. "Everyone must have heard the shots. They're probably wondering what the hell's going on."

"Including White Calf."

"Wherever the bastard is," grumbled Alvin.

"What the fuck is that all about?" Raymond said softly, stopping dead in his tracks. The gun shots were close, two miles away at most. Three shots, then minutes later, three more. Maybe White Calf got across and the Mounties spotted him. Still, it didn't make sense. If he was right about how far away those shots were and the direction from which they'd come, it would place them east of the river by at least a mile. Why would White Calf have headed away from the river? He was sure every man on both sides of the border was as perplexed as he was. Maybe it was just someone on the rez jacking deer. Anyway, Raymond didn't have the luxury to stand there and think about it. Now that he'd come to the river, he had to keep following it. If the shooting had nothing to do with White Calf, he might be close, very close.

White Calf, too, heard the shots. His only response was to shift his suitcase and shotgun to opposite hands. Maybe cops are shooting at one another in the dark, he thought, his lips curling in a smile. The shots came from far enough away that he wasn't concerned. Every tribal cop in Browning could join the hunt for him and it wouldn't make a bit of difference. The Hudson Bay Divide area of the rez was too big for a police force five times the size of Browning's to cover. Neither did the weight of his bag concern him. No money can be too heavy, he thought. Imagining how he'd spend it helped to take his mind off the distance he still had to cover. He reminded himself that he also had a couple of pounds of meth sitting in a hole, but that was for another day. Getting access to it wouldn't be so easy any time soon. Once across the border, he had no intention of coming back to the States for a very long time. It wouldn't be just the cops looking for him. Miguel's people weren't going to be very happy when they heard White Calf had killed him and taken both the money and the powder. White Calf had never met any of the Mexicans Miguel worked for, but he knew what would happen if they got their hands on him. He suddenly thought of his cousin, Black Moon, in

Gillette, Wyoming. White Calf hadn't seen him in years, but Black Moon might be interested in helping him, especially if there was enough money involved. Even if White Calf had to shell out twenty-five thousand to his cousin, it would leave plenty for him. Of course, Black Moon would have to find a buyer. Time to worry about all that when I'm on the other side of the border, White Calf thought.

The gunfire provoked a string of curses from Perkins. Men were strung out over a large area on both sides of the border with no way for them to keep in touch. They had decided against the use of radios. The distances were too great and White Calf wasn't deaf. None of the men wanted to give away his location and find himself on the receiving end of a shotgun blast. It was bad enough that they had to use their flashlights at intervals in densely treed areas or on rough terrain. If White Calf was close, a flashlight beam was equivalent to a bullseye for his shotgun.

What the hell do those shots mean? Perkins asked himself. They were rifle shots, not shotgun. Maybe some of the men had spotted White Calf. But why three shots, and then another three? "Goddammit!" he cursed, pushing his way through snow in a small draw, snow deep enough to get into his boots and make him even more miserable.

54

Raymond knew he was nearing the border when he stumbled across a snow-covered track circling a small pond. The track branched off Fox Ranch Road, which meant he was about a mile from the line. The shadowy trunks of cottonwoods broke the uniform whiteness of the pasture he was crossing. Holding his rifle in front of him, using it to push branches out of the way, he made his way through the cluster of trees. The river curved around the track off to his right, its slowly moving water heard rather than seen. He stood there for several seconds, listening intently, hoping he'd hear the barking of one of the Mountie dogs. I could continue on to the border fence, he thought, but then what? He had no idea where White Calf might try to cross. If he patrolled the fence by himself he risked getting shot by his own men on one side or the Mounties on the other. His other option was to turn to the southwest in the hope that White Calf hadn't made it this far. If that was the case, Raymond could surprise him coming up along the river.

Better to head south, he decided, figuring that the Mounties had the border covered. He moved cautiously through the snow, squinting to see any branches poking through the white blanket. If White Calf was near, the sound of a snapping twig would pinpoint Raymond's location. Using his flashlight now was out of the question, which meant he had no chance of spotting footprints in the snow. All of it was guesswork. White Calf might not be anywhere in the vicinity. Or he might be following the opposite shore of the river. If the shots Raymond heard turned out to have been fired at White Calf, it meant that he had covered far more ground than Raymond had thought possible. He was sure White Calf knew the rez as well as he did. Just because Raymond and the others assumed he'd try to cross the border near the river didn't make it so. But guesswork was all Raymond had to go on.

He wondered where the others were. Ben, Ryder, and Homer could be anywhere, maybe even at the border by now. Perkins and Jameson, he was sure, were far to the rear. They were so far out of their element that for all Raymond knew they were wandering in circles near where they'd all started. Perkins might be Lakota, Raymond thought, but his Indian blood had been watered down by his years of exposure to white men. Hell, even Perkins' wife was white.

Plunging southwest through the snow, his rifle in one hand, Raymond tried to concentrate on his surroundings, but Perkins continued to intrude on his thoughts. There were times when he admitted to himself that he missed working with the agent, but he couldn't shake the ever-present undercurrent of hostility, hostility that emanated from him, not Perkins. It threatened to bubble to the surface whenever Perkins was around. It puzzled him. What possible reason could there be for his rancor? It made as much sense as the hatred White Calf harbored towards him.

The strange thing was that he found Perkins more troubling in some ways than White Calf. White Calf was simply an Indian gone bad. He had no compunction about killing and he had to be stopped. But one thing was certain—he was Indian through and through. Knowing what he was dealing with made Raymond more comfortable.

Perkins was another matter. It was too simplistic to think that the man's manner of dress offended him. Yeah, he dressed like the average white guy working in an office, right down to the button-down shirt and tie. But so what? Raymond, when in uniform, was dressed no different from any white cop. Did that make him less of an Indian? So what was it that made Perkins the red man's equivalent of the black man's 'Oreo cookie'—red on the outside, white on the inside? Annoyed with himself for dwelling on Perkins when White Calf could be lying in wait for him, Raymond tried to push him from his thoughts. Before he could succeed, the truth bubbled to the surface. It was Perkins' education that aroused his resentment. He made Raymond feel stupid.

You'll get yourself killed, asshole, he told himself, if you don't start thinking about White Calf instead of Perkins. A night hawk startled him, the fluttering of its wings in the silence as dramatic as a helicopter's rotor. Raymond's heart beat rapidly for several moments. From then on he made it a point to pause briefly every five or ten minutes to exercise his senses. He'd listen for the sound of a man's breathing or for footfalls; he would watch for a moving shadow on the snow's surface, and smell the air around him. In a way it was like hunting game, but no animal was as dangerous as White Calf.

Raymond guessed it was taking him at least twenty, maybe twenty-five, minutes to cover a mile of ground in the darkness. He estimated he had moved at least a mile further away from the border, give or take a quarter mile. If he didn't meet up with White Calf within the next half hour, he'd know that his prey had eluded him.

———————

Like Raymond, White Calf grew more alert as he neared the border. It was difficult to be certain in the dark, but the land he traversed and the course of the river was familiar enough for him to believe he was less than two miles from his crossing. He had no idea whether the Mounties had been alerted by the Tribal Police, but even if they had he knew he could elude them. It was a big border and he had the cover of darkness. He worried more about the Tribal Police, Indians who knew the rez as well as he did. If he did meet up with one of them, he'd have to hope the element of surprise would be in his favor. Any adversary would have to be overcome by brute force or dispatched with his knife. Firing his weapon now was not an option, unless he encountered more than one cop. Gunfire this close to the border would not only attract other cops, but also the Mounties, like flies smelling blood. He had no idea what the earlier shots to the east were about, but if luck was with him the police might have been drawn away in that direction.

White Calf hoisted his suitcase onto the top of a small knoll and clambered up after it. He knelt in the snow and listened. Had he heard something or was he imagining it? He peered straight ahead, almost willing his eyes to see in the darkness, then lowered his gaze to the ice-covered boundary of river and rocky shore. Something was moving, following the river's course. He flattened himself on the ground next to his bag and shotgun. Stretching slowly, he withdrew his knife from the sheath on his leg. His eyes grew more accustomed to the dark as he focused his gaze on the spot where he'd heard movement. A shadow emerged from a gap in the cottonwoods. White Calf knew it was a tribal cop even before he saw the man's outline distinctly.

Barely breathing, White Calf waited, hoping the man wouldn't deviate from his course. In less than a minute, he'd be below the knoll where White Calf was hiding. He clutched the hilt of his knife tightly and waited.

———————

Raymond slowed his pace, listening intently. Had he heard something just ahead of him? The skin at the back of his neck prickled and he had a metallic taste in his mouth. He's close, he told himself. He peered into the darkness, frustrated by his inability to give shape to his surroundings. Planting his feet carefully, Raymond moved forward, his rifle held in front of him.

When White Calf leaped, knocking Raymond to the ground, Raymond thought a tree had fallen on him. The impact of his fall took his breath away. What White Calf hadn't foreseen was that Raymond, sensing his adversary's presence, had his index finger curled around the trigger of his weapon. The rifle discharged as Raymond hit the ground. Pain coursed through his fractured ribs. He struggled to roll onto his back and push his assailant off, but White Calf pinned him to the ground with his weight.

Raymond felt a sharp jab of pain at the side of his neck as White Calf, straddling him and pulling his head back by the hair, held his knife to his throat. The point probed Raymond's skin, as if White Calf were seeking the ideal spot to administer a coup de grace. Raymond felt White Calf's harsh, hot breath on the side of his face.

"I was hoping it was you, cop," White Calf hissed in a whisper.

So this is how it will end, Raymond thought.

"There's one thing I hate more than a cop," White Calf said, pushing he point of his blade another excruciating millimeter into Raymond's neck. "An Indian cop. One named Two Teeth."

White Calf's knife jabbed harder and Raymond closed his eyes, submitting to the certainty of his death.

"Get off him!" said a voice behind the two men.

Raymond, rolling onto his side and opening his eyes, was blinded by light. The weight that had been pressing down on him was gone. He sat up in time to see White Calf, caught in a beam of light, vault onto the knoll at the moment Perkins fired his rifle. Before the agent could get off a second round, White Calf had thrown himself prone on the ground and raised his shotgun. Perkins knelt at the base of the embankment, but the blast from White Calf's weapon never came.

"He's running," Raymond croaked, trying to recover his voice.

"Are you okay?" Perkins asked, turning off his flashlight.

Raymond, touching the sore spot on his neck, nodded in the darkness. He felt the stickiness of his blood on his fingertips. "You saved my ass. Thanks."

"That rifle shot was what saved you. I just happened to be close by. I'm not sure if I hit him."

The two men climbed up the embankment and Perkins flashed his light on the ground.

"There's blood," Raymond said. "He's wounded."

"We can't use the light to follow his trail. He'll nail us."

"We don't need the light. He's following the river to the border. If he's wounded it'll slow him down."

"Let's keep some distance between ourselves in case he fires at us. No sense letting him get both of us with the same round."

Perkins drifted off diagonally to the left, leaving about twenty feet between himself and Raymond. They advanced along the river, Raymond backtracking along the route he'd taken earlier, Perkins coming closer only when trying to avoid areas of deadfall. Taking a chance, Perkins hunched over and turned on his flashlight, sweeping the beam along the ground. "There!" he said, his light directed for a moment at blood spatters on the snow.

The two men heard nothing but their own breathing. They'd been on the move for ten minutes when the silence was broken by the barking of a dog, a dog that was not far off.

Raymond again held his rifle in both hands, his index finger within the trigger guard.

A shadow no more than a hundred feet ahead of them darted across the snow toward the river and disappeared into the blackness.

"He's crossing the river," Perkins hissed. "I'll shine my light. Take your shot."

White Calf turned in surprise as the beam illuminated him. Raymond, kneeling, was close enough to see him blinking against the light. Turning his back to them, White Calf, still holding his suitcase and shotgun, stumbled through the shallow waters toward the opposite shore.

Raymond squeezed the trigger when White Calf reached the ice-covered slope. The bag and shotgun fell from his grasp as he crumpled to the ground. Perkins kept his light trained on the body as he and Raymond stepped through the water. Raymond never lowered the muzzle of his weapon. His finger remained curled around the trigger as he moved cautiously forward. The entry point of the round he had fired was clearly visible on White Calf's jacket, a bloody hole between his shoulder blades.

Perkins squatted and placed his fingers on White Calf's neck.

"There's where you got him," Raymond said, pointing to a rent in White Calf's pants along the outer edge of one thigh. The jeans near the wound were soaked in blood.

"He's dead," Perkins said.

"Shine your light a little further ahead," Raymond said.

The beam illuminated the strands of a barbed wire fence.

"Canada?" Perkins asked.

Raymond nodded. "Sonofabitch almost made it."

Perkins had just opened White Calf's suitcase when two flashlight beams appeared in the darkness and a dog, straining at its leash, barked excitedly.

"We're over here," Perkins yelled, shining his light in the direction of the approaching Mounties. "We got him."

Raymond, squatting next to Perkins, withdrew a wad of hundred dollar bills from the open bag.

"When we get back to Browning," he said, "I'll buy you a burger."

irk Aalford was fuming. He had expected White Calf to return on Saturday with the money, but the Indian hadn't made an appearance. By Sunday evening, his growing fear that something had gone wrong gnawed at him. Why hadn't White Calf called? He had to know Aalford would be concerned. Nothing like this had happened in all the years White Calf had been making his deliveries. Had Miguel pulled a double cross and taken the meth from White Calf without paying him? Was White Calf lying dead in a ditch somewhere? Or had the money been a temptation White Calf couldn't resist? One hundred fifty thousand was the most White Calf had ever collected in a transaction. None of it made sense. White Calf and Miguel both knew what would happen if either of them attempted a double cross. Neither Carlos nor the people behind Miguel would have countenanced it. What then had happened?

Aalford sat by himself in his church pondering the situation. He stared abstractedly at the lectern from which he conducted his lessons with the children. Religion was the furthest thing from his mind at the moment. There was one other possibility, one that he often worried about when he first agreed to work for Carlos—apprehension of White Calf by the police. Over the years that concern had slipped away. Until now. The visit of the tribal cop and federal agent made it apparent that they suspected White Calf of his stepdaughter's murder. Aalford had no idea whether or not White Calf knew the authorities were searching for him. If he was aware, and had not been apprehended by them, that might account for his not showing up at the farm. But if that was the case why hadn't he called.

As day followed day with no word, Aalford snapped repeatedly at his three women and at the children. The women trembled whenever he made his appearance in the house and the children hid in their rooms. They all knew what the prophet was capable of when he was angry. Hanging on a hook in his study was a thick leather belt. All of them had experienced its impact against their buttocks or across their back at least once.

Aalford sat by himself in his study every evening. He thought of calling Carlos, but couldn't bring himself to do it. Maybe no news was good news and he was worrying for nothing. Maybe the Indian was simply laying low for the time being, fearful that he'd be spotted if he emerged from wherever he was hiding. Still, White Calf should have made every effort to call him if that were the case. It was not only the missing money that had Aalford sweating. The Indian had too much on him. If he was captured, he could make trouble for Aalford. Big trouble.

By Wednesday the uncertainty was more than he could endure. He glowered at his family, turning every meal into a time of torture for them. Seeing the eight-year-old making a face during dinner, Aalford stood up. He stormed around the table toward the boy, who cowered in his chair. This time the prophet did not resort to his leather strap. He slapped the boy hard across the face, the imprint of his hand clearly visible on the child's cheek. "Get to your room!" he roared. "No food for that child for the next two days," he ordered, glaring at Constance, the oldest of his wives. The silence in the dining room was more profound than usual. Ellen, the youngest wife, trembled as she cleared the table. The dishes rattled in her hands as she carried them to the sink.

"Stop that noise!" Aalford commanded.

Tears rolled down her cheeks as she lowered the soiled dishes into the soapy water. Knowing how much Aalford hated any display of emotion, she brushed her tears away with a dish towel before returning to the table.

On Thursday morning, Aalford made up his mind to drive to White Calf's place. He'd never been there but had a general idea where it was. "Eat without me," he told his wives while they prepared breakfast.

As he headed to the door, the phone rang. Constance answered it. "It's for you," she said. "He wouldn't give his name."

"Have you seen the newspapers today?" a heavily accented voice asked.

Aalford recognized the voice immediately. He and Carlos had never met, but they spoke before every delivery leaving Spokane for Aalford's farm.

"No."

"When was the last time you saw that Indian who works for you?"

"White Calf? It's been over a week, but he knew he had to meet Miguel at Fort Belknap Saturday morning. Why?"

Aalford's heart beat faster at the silence that greeted his question. "What's wrong? What happened?"

"You don't have the money, do you?"

"No. I was just going to drive out to White Calf's house to find out why he hasn't brought it."

"Don't go near his house."

"Tell me what's going on," Aalford said, his irritation mounting.

"You go out and buy yourself a newspaper. I'll call you back in one hour."

Before Aalford could protest, Carlos hung up.

Aalford jumped into his truck and drove to the Prairie Market in Sunburst. He bought copies of three newspapers, the *Shelby Promoter*, the *Great Falls Tribune*, and the *Cutbank Pioneer Press*. The clerk, who knew Aalford by sight, handed him his change.

"Sorry to hear about your trouble," he said.

"What trouble?"

The man looked at him curiously. "The fellow who worked for you. The Indian who was killed?" He gestured toward the newspapers in Aalford's hands. "It's in every paper."

Aalford's eyes darted from the clerk to the papers, then back again.

"You didn't know?"

Aalford turned away and walked quickly to his truck. He held the *Great Falls Tribune* against the steering wheel and looked at the front page. *Manhunt Ends* was the headline. The lead article told of the death of White Calf near the Canadian border in the early hours of Wednesday morning. Aalford read every word and threw the newspaper onto the seat. The fact that White Calf had murdered his stepdaughter, Rebecca, and was also responsible for the deaths of a highway patrolman and an elderly couple did not faze Aalford. Miguel's death was another story. As was the fact that there was no mention of the money or the meth.

The prophet's face was grim as he drove back to the farm. He dreaded the phone call that would be coming from Carlos. With White Calf dead, Aalford was sure he'd be the one held accountable for the missing cash and the meth.

As soon as he returned to the house, Aalford chased the children outside. "Make yourselves useful," he ordered. "There'll be no instruction this morning."

Constance, Jessica, and Ellen stepped aside for him when he entered the kitchen. They watched his every move, anxious not to displease him in any way.

"I'm expecting a phone call and don't want to be disturbed. Go do whatever you have to do."

He sat by the phone trying to anticipate what Carlos would say to him. He didn't have long to find out. The ring shattered the silence of the room. Aalford held his hand over the receiver, took a deep breath, and placed it to his ear.

"You read it?"

"Yes. I'm in shock."

"You said he was reliable, that we could trust him."

"He has been, for years. I don't understand what happened."

Aalford grew uncomfortable with the silence that greeted his remark. "Are you there?" he asked.

"I'm here. Understand this. Thanks to this *loco*, you have caused us some big problems."

"I'm sorry, but—"

"Miguel's people are very unhappy. They were the ones who called me. I'm out the product and they lost their money, but they also lost Miguel. He was family."

Aalford ran his tongue over his lips. His throat was so dry he found it difficult to swallow.

"I'm not to blame," he said weakly.

"They don't see it that way. The Indian was your man."

"What do you want me to do?"

"You saw nothing in the paper about the money or the product, did you?"

"Nothing."

"That's the problem. We don't know how much the police and the feds know. If they suspect you, you'll be receiving a visit from them. They may even tap your telephone."

Aalford's eyes dilated in fear at mention of the phone. He stared at it as if it were a dangerous object.

"As I see it, there are two possibilities—your *loco* hid both the money and the product, or the police are intentionally saying nothing about it."

"Why would they do that?"

"Yes, I ask myself that. It's more likely the Indian hid everything, or gave it to someone to hold for him."

"How can we find out?"

"The article I read mentioned a woman and a tribal cop who were taken hostage. He let the woman go before the cop escaped. You know who this woman is?"

"The paper gave her name. It said she's a nurse at the Blackfeet Hospital."

"We'll have to find out if she knows anything."

"If she was taken hostage, she probably knows nothing."

"But we don't know that for sure, do we? Maybe she and your crazy one knew one another. Maybe they plotted something together."

"That's not likely."

"You have a better idea?"

"I can talk to White Calf's wife. She may know something."

Again, the silence. Aalford began to sweat.

"Which wife?"

Aalford suspected Carlos was mocking him.

"I'm going to send two of my men to you. Do nothing until they get there. And from now on we will no longer use the phone in your house. Get yourself a cell phone. Then call me and give me the number."

There was an abrupt click and the line went dead.

56

The three federal agents relaxed in the small lounge of their Browning office, each man savoring his cup of coffee.

"So Raymond and the Hartmans are all okay?" Briggs said.

Perkins smiled. "All of Raymond's wounds were superficial. The pellets were just below the skin and easy to remove. He did need a couple of stitches for the knife wound. If it had been any deeper we wouldn't be sitting here talking about him. We'd be at his funeral."

"I'm sure he appreciates the fact that you were the one who saved his life," Briggs said, laughing.

"Who told you that?"

Briggs gestured toward Jameson.

"You trying to turn me into some kind of hero?" Perkins said.

"Hey, it's the truth, isn't it? Raymond told me."

"Sounds like you and Raymond are off on a new footing," Briggs said. "So what about the Hartmans? They all recovered from their ordeal?"

"I ran into them while Raymond was in the ER. They were worried about him." He shook his head in wonderment. "It was six-thirty in the morning and even after what they'd been through, there they were in the hospital."

"They are two dedicated people."

"It's a good thing Homer found Mrs. Hartman when he did," Jameson said. "It was pretty damn cold that night and she wasn't dressed for it. The chief told me he could hear her teeth chattering when she was in the back seat of his car."

"You guys had all the fun," Briggs said, grinning. "You could have let me come along."

"Some fun, traipsing around in the woods in the middle of the night, freezing our asses off, and knowing that lunatic, White Calf, was out there."

"Have you gotten any news about the tribal cop who got gored?" Jameson asked. "That was the damndest thing."

"He's still in the hospital in Alberta," Perkins said. "I talked to Homer about him. The horn punctured his lung and tore some vessels in his armpit. He's lucky to be alive."

Geneva Williams, their office receptionist, poked her head into the room. "Phone call for you, Mister Perkins. Chief Whitecloud."

A smile crossed Perkins face as he listened to what Homer had to say. "That's great," he said. "I'll drop by this morning."

"What's up?" Jameson asked.

"Two tribal cops looking around the area where White Calf abandoned the Toyota found two pounds of meth."

"That sounds right," Jameson said. "A hundred fifty thousand for three pounds total."

"How the hell did they find it with all the snow on the ground?" Briggs asked.

"That's the funny part. One of the cops spotted something blue under a pile of branches. There were coyote tracks all around it. It turned out to be an old sweater sticking out of a ground squirrel hole."

"Glad the coyotes are working with us," Briggs laughed. "Well, we have the murderer, the money, and the meth. It's a good case to close."

Perkins slowly shook his head.

"What's the matter?"

"It's funny. Mrs. Hartman said almost the same thing when she learned White Calf was dead. She said she was glad it's over. But it isn't."

"What are you talking about?"

"Don't forget White Calf was working for somebody."

"You mean Aalford?"

"And whoever Aalford's supplier is."

"You don't know for a fact that Aalford was involved," Briggs argued. "Maybe White Calf was running his own operation. And since he's dead, we'll never have the answers."

"We could just push the Toole County sheriff to go after Aalford for polygamy and statutory rape," Jameson said.

"That doesn't help us find out who's supplying him."

"You're convinced he's involved?" Jameson said.

Perkins nodded. "As sure as I'm sitting here."

"Maybe we should bring DEA in on it, see if they can come up with anything on Aalford," Briggs said.

"The 'don't expect anything' people? Aalford's shrewd. DEA will never get anything on him."

"He might be willing to deal on the rape charge."

Perkins shook his head. "Aalford won't talk. He knows what kind of league he's playing in. If word got out that he was the one who led us to his supplier . . . I don't have to draw you pictures."

"We can always offer him witness protection," Briggs said.

Perkins smiled. "With three wives and a dozen kids?"

"So what can we do? If you think it's a waste of time going after him on the sex charges, then we'll have no leverage with him."

Perkins set his coffee cup down. "One way or another, Aalford's going to get the news about White Calf. But he won't hear anything about the money or the meth. We've kept that away from the newspapers."

"So?"

"So the people who supply Aalford are going to want to know what happened to their meth. And Miguel's crowd is out a hundred fifty big ones." Perkins grinned. "Aalford's dealing with a lot of unhappy people, and he's the man caught in the middle. He must be sweating it."

"How's that going to help us?" Briggs asked. "You yourself said he won't talk."

"I might have to pay him another visit and add to his unhappiness. If we light enough of a fire under Aalford, maybe we can get him to make a mistake. As an old Quantico instructor of mine used to say, keep kicking the bush until the shit falls out the other side."

irk Aalford had panicked after the phone call from Carlos. He spent hours pacing up and down the aisle of his church, trying to settle on a course of action. Unbeknownst to his wives, he had squirreled away close to two hundred thousand dollars in five different banks between Shelby and Great Falls. Withdrawing the money and disappearing was one option. Unfortunately, he had enough of a conscience to preclude deserting his family and leaving them with nothing. I can sign the farm over to them, he thought. They can sell it if they're desperate. There was no way he could ever return to Sunburst if Carlos and Miguel's people were after him. The more he thought about it, the more drastic the idea seemed, at least for the time being. Did he really want to spend the rest of his life on the run, unless it was absolutely necessary? There was always the chance that Carlos or Miguel's men might learn where the money was and he'd be off the hook. Better to wait and see how it plays out, he decided.

Nevertheless, Carlos' pledge to send two of his men had him badly rattled. There was no implied threat in that, but better not to take chances. He had to protect himself. The day after his conversation with Carlos, he answered an ad in the local newspaper. Someone was seeking a home for a rottweiler. 'Relocating,' the ad said. 'Good guard dog.' Aalford picked up the dog the same day at a rundown house near Lake Frances. His children stared in disbelief when he walked into the house with the animal. He had never allowed them to have a pet.

"What's his name?" the youngest boy asked.

"Rambo," Aalford said with obvious distaste.

"Can I pet him?"

"Don't spoil him. He's a guard dog."

On the following day the moment Aalford had been dreading arrived as a black Lexus came down his driveway. His dog, tied up in front of the house, barked furiously and tugged at his chain. Aalford, seeing the car's Washington plate, knew immediately who his visitors were. The Lexus parked in front of the house and two Mexicans stepped out. The dog lunged in a frenzy, saliva flying, as the men approached.

"Shut that dog up," the older and taller of the two said.

Aalford kicked at the rottweiler. The dog squealed in pain and cringed away to the extent of his chain. He lay there whimpering softly, his mournful gaze on Aalford.

"Carlos sent us," the tall man said. He had black curly hair receding enough to give him a bullet-shaped expanse of forehead. The shorter man wore a Seattle *Mariners* baseball cap. A prominent scar beginning at his left lower jaw disappeared beneath the top of his tee shirt.

Aalford, wearing his sport jacket, shivered in the late afternoon chill. The cold didn't appear to bother the Mexicans. The older man wore only a light windbreaker. The younger, his cheeks covered in black stubble, wore an unbuttoned denim jacket. His fierce eyes and drooping moustache made him appear a caricature of a Mexican bandit.

Constance stood in the doorway of the kitchen as the men entered the house. "You can eat without me," Aalford told her as he led the two men into his study.

The tall man sat down and stretched his legs out in front of him. The man with the moustache leaned against the wall, his arms folded in front of his chest. Aalford sat down behind his desk.

"That fucking Indian of yours really made a mess of things," the tall man said. "Carlos is very unhappy." His voice had only a trace of an accent.

"But Carlos knows that White Calf was always reliable. He's worked for me for years and there's never been a problem. The newspaper said he killed a girl. That's probably what started all this. How could I know he would do something so stupid?"

"*A girl?*," the tall man sneered. "Carlos told me she was your stepdaughter."

"How did he know that?"

"It's Carlos' business to know everything about the people he deals with. If I had a stepdaughter and some *cabrón* killed her, I'd make sure he died a slow, painful death."

"I had no idea White Calf had done that. He was gone by the time I found out."

"*Sí, con la plata y con las drogas.*"

"What did he say?" Aalford asked.

"Ramon doesn't speak English, but he understands everything. He says the Indian took our money and our meth. So now we have to find out what he did with it."

"How do you know the police don't have it?"

"Because there was nothing about it in the newspaper. Don't you think the police would want everyone to know they were heroes? Not only did they kill the big, bad Indian, but they recovered a lot of money and drugs. No, that fucking Indian hid it."

"How are you going to find out where? White Calf is dead."

"First we go talk to his women. One of them is your other stepdaughter, no?" The man's gold front tooth glinted when he smiled.

Aalford, uncomfortable, squirmed in his chair.

"Manuel, preguntale si él quisiera prestarnos algunas chicas también."

"Ramon wants to know if you'd give us some of your daughters, too."

"Tell your friend I don't find him amusing."

Manuel's smile disappeared. "You don't find *him* amusing? He knows you gave two of your daughters to that fucking Indian. We don't find you very funny either, amigo."

Aalford flushed. Manuel had taken off his windbreaker. He wore a pastel-blue, open-collared shirt with short sleeves. He leaned forward toward Aalford and rested his muscular forearms on the desk. A gold chain around his neck complemented the gold front tooth.

Aalford leaned back in his chair and placed his hands in his lap. He didn't want the Mexican to see them trembling.

"So, now you tell us where that Indian's house is. Ramon and I, we'll go have a talk with the women, the Indian woman and your daughter."

"I'm sure they don't know anything. White Calf wasn't the kind of person to trust anyone, especially a woman."

Manuel regarded him coolly. "We'll find out if that is true or not."

"I can't tell you exactly how to get to his cabin. I've never been there. But he told me it was just south of the Two Medicine River, not far from the road that runs through the southeastern part of the reservation."

"This road, it has a name or a number?"

"358."

"We will find it."

Manuel abruptly stood up. Aalford followed him and Ramon to the front door. The rottweiler issued a low growl as the men came out, abruptly cutting it off when he saw Aalford.

Aalford stood just outside his front door and watched the Lexus' tail lights fade into the distance. The departure of the two Mexicans only increased his anxiety. Thinking about what White Calf's Indian woman and his stepdaughter, Sharon, had in store for them made him shudder. He knew, too, that that Manuel and Ramon weren't finished with him.

58

*I*ra Sands covered the mouthpiece of his phone and called to Raymond. "Hey, Raymond, what was the name of that Blackfeet woman White Calf was married to?"

Raymond, sitting at his desk, looked up in surprise. "You mean Two Bear Woman? Why?"

"Maybe you should take this call. Some guy found two kids walking on the 358 road. They were frozen and half-starved. They told him their mother's name was Two Bear Woman and they couldn't wake her up. The guy offered to take them home but they wouldn't tell him where their house was."

Raymond lurched out of his chair and grabbed the phone. He listened intently. "Thanks," he said. "Stay there with them. I'm on the way."

"What's going on?" Ira asked.

"I'm going to find out. The guy was on his way to Valier, so he took the kids with him. He's buying them lunch at the café in town. I'll pick them up and see what's going on at their house."

Almost a week had passed since White Calf's death. Raymond wondered if Two Bear Woman even knew about it. He had no idea if Homer had sent someone to inform her. He himself had thought of driving out to check on her and the kids, but all the wrapup work involving White Calf had kept him busy. "What the hell could have happened to her?" he mused aloud as he drove.

As soon as he entered the restaurant, Raymond recognized the two boys he'd seen with Two Bear Woman at her cabin. "I'm Officer Two Teeth," he said to the young man with them.

"Dwayne Parker," the man said, shaking hands with Raymond. He nodded at the two boys with his chin. "These kids are hungry. I had to order a second lunch for both of them. Found them walking on the road about five miles south of the river."

"Hi, kids," Raymond said. "Remember me? I was out at your house a few weeks ago."

The boys looked at him but said nothing.

"Where were you going when Mr. Parker picked you up?"

The younger boy shrugged.

"What's wrong with your mother?"

"She's been in bed for two days," the older boy said. "We can't wake her up and we're out of food."

"I'll take you home after you finish eating," Raymond said.

As he drove up to the log cabin, Raymond tensed. He half expected White Calf to step out and confront him with his shotgun. Opening the rear door of the cruiser, he let the two boys out. Raymond knocked on the cabin door, but was greeted with silence.

"Door's open," the older boy said, pushing on it.

Raymond followed the boys in. The cabin was as cold inside as the temperature outside. The boys remained standing outside the bedroom doorway, as if reluctant to go in. Two Bear Woman was lying face down on the bed. Raymond shook her shoulder but received no response. The image of the eyeless girl he'd found in the factory lot flashed through his mind as he rolled Two Bear Woman onto her back. Two Bear Woman still had her eyes, but she'd been beaten badly. Her face was bruised and swollen. The skin of her forehead was covered with black char marks, burns that could only have been made by a cigarette. Raymond felt for a carotid pulse. She was still alive, but barely.

"You boys stay here," Raymond said. "I'm going to my car to call for an ambulance."

The boys were still standing in the doorway, staring in silence at their mother when Raymond returned.

"Ambulance is coming," Raymond said. "Do you know who hurt your mother?"

The boys shook their heads.

"Did anyone come to see her?"

"We heard a car come the other night, but we didn't get out of bed," the ten-year-old replied. "We thought it was our dad."

They still don't know about White Calf, Raymond realized.

"Is she going to die?" the older boy asked, his face impassive.

"When she gets to the hospital, the doctors will help her," Raymond said.

Driving back to town behind the ambulance, the boys once again in his back seat, Raymond put in a call to Homer to tell him what he'd found. "I'll drop the kids off at Social Services on the way to headquarters," he said.

Raymond was not surprised to find Perkins sitting in the chief's office.

"Kids okay?" Homer asked.

"Yeah. I don't know if their mother is going to make it though. According to what the kids told me, she's been in that bed unconscious for two days. The house was freezing. She was barely breathing and her pulse was real slow when I checked it. She was still unconscious when they put her in the ambulance."

"The kids had no idea who might have done it?" Perkins asked.

"They heard a car drive in a couple of nights ago. Thought it was their father."

"It looks like White Calf left a mess of trouble behind him," Homer said.

"Well, we may not know who did this to her," Perkins said, "but I think we know why."

"You think they were trying to find out if she knew anything about the money and the meth?"

"She was tortured. What else can it be?"

"They might go after Sharon next," Raymond said.

"I called Social Services to see if anyone had been nosing around asking about her. All quiet. They've placed her and the kids with a family in Conrad. I think she'll be okay there."

"You suppose Aalford is involved in this?" Raymond said.

"It's not him," Perkins said. "That's not his style. Someone is really pissed off though, and my guess is Aalford isn't sleeping too well either these days. Time for me to have a chat with our Mr. Aalford, let him know he's in our sights, too. Call me if you find out anything from Two Bear Woman when she wakes up."

"If she wakes up, you mean," Raymond said.

59

*T*he ringing of the phone startled Beth Hartman. Putting down her book, she picked up the receiver.

"Hi, it's me," John said. "Sorry I couldn't call earlier."

"I figured you had an emergency." She glanced at her watch. "Wow, nine o'clock. I lost track of time. Shows what happens when you get hooked on a good novel."

"It's been a zoo here. Three admissions since five o'clock. I've got one kid with meningitis, one with pneumonia, and one in diabetic coma. I hope you didn't wait on me for dinner."

Beth laughed. "I forgot all about dinner. I was too engrossed in my book."

"I'll be leaving here in a few minutes."

"Good. I've got plenty of leftovers in the fridge. I'll get the table set while you're driving home. Hold on a minute. There's someone at the door. I wonder who it can be at this hour."

John waited for a full half-minute. "Beth," he called, "are you there? Hello." Puzzled, he looked at the phone in his hand. She couldn't have forgotten about me, he thought. Suddenly, what sounded like a muffled scream came from the receiver. "Beth, are you okay?" he yelled.

John slammed the phone down. "Mary," he called to the ward nurse, "something's wrong at my home. Call the tribal police and tell them to get over there."

He dashed from the hospital in his scrubs and ran to the parking lot. It was only a half mile to his house. John sped through two red lights and was there in less than five minutes. The front door was open. Beth's book and the telephone were on the sofa, the receiver dangling on its cord. An end table had been overturned and the living room carpet was gone. John ran through the house calling for his wife. His heart pounded as he returned to the open front door.

The wail of a siren signaled the arrival of the tribal police. "What's wrong, Doc?" Ben Red Leaf yelled as he stepped out of his cruiser.

"Something's happened to my wife. I was talking to her on the phone from the hospital and she said someone was at the door. Then I heard her scream. I got here minutes later and she was gone. There's a table knocked over and our carpet is missing."

The officer followed him into the house and stared in bemusement at the overturned table and the bare floor. "Was the carpet a valuable one?" Ben asked.

"No. It was a cheap machine-made carpet."

"Have you and your wife been having trouble with anyone?" Ben asked.

"No one. I don't understand this."

"Doc, I'm going to put a call in to the chief."

"The phone's right there." He went to pick it up.

"Don't touch anything in here, Doc. I'll call from my car."

John, hyperventilating and lightheaded, sat on the sofa. The metallic taste of fear was in his mouth. Beth never hurt anyone, he told himself. He had thought that with the death of White Calf their troubles were behind them. How could this be happening? What kind of place is this?

Ten minutes later, Will Perkins' Subaru pulled up at the curb.

John's panic increased when he saw the federal agent. "What's going on here?" he asked, his voice shaking. "Why is the FBI involved? Do you know what happened to my wife?"

Perkins asked John to recount every word of his conversation with Beth.

"You haven't answered my question," John said after he'd finished. "Why is the FBI involved?"

"We'll talk about it when Chief Whitecloud arrives. He should be here soon. It was the chief who told the officer to call me in on this."

"I just checked with the people next door," Ben Red Leaf said, coming back into the house. "They heard a car pull up. Two minutes later it drove away. But they never looked out their window and they didn't hear anything unusual. I'll get more men here to check the entire block." He turned as a car parked in front of the house. "Chief's here," he said.

John sat on the sofa between Perkins and Homer Whitecloud. He fidgeted nervously, close to tears. The look on Homer Whitecloud's face was not reassuring. This is even worse than White's Calf's taking Beth as a hostage, he thought. At least then we knew who we were dealing with. "Why aren't you doing something to get my wife back?" he asked in frustration. "Why are we just sitting here?"

"Here's what we think is happening, Doc," Homer said. "White Calf had a lot of money with him when he was killed. He was trafficking in meth. In fact, the guy he killed at Fort Belknap was the go-between with the dealers. White Calf double-crossed him and took both the meth and the cash. We figure the people behind all this aren't very happy. They want their money and their meth back."

"What the hell has that got to do with Beth?"

"We found White Calf's wife badly beaten the other day. She still hasn't regained consciousness. We figure she had visitors who thought she might know where the money and the drugs were."

"But that was White Calf's wife. Why would they come after Beth? She doesn't know anything about this."

"We know that, but the meth distributors don't. When the newspapers printed the story about White Calf's death, they mentioned his abduction of Raymond and your wife. These people may have gotten the idea that your wife had some knowledge of what White Calf did with the money."

"That makes no sense. My wife was kidnapped by White Calf, for Christ's sake. She didn't go with him willingly."

"I think these people are desperate and trying every angle they can think of."

"So who are they? How are we going to get my wife back before they—" John closed his eyes and shuddered at the thought of what they might do to Beth. If they'd already beaten one woman unconscious . . . "My God, my God," he moaned aloud, covering his face with his hands, "this is a nightmare that won't end." He looked up suddenly, confusion on his face. "Why would they take our carpet?" he blurted out.

"They probably wrapped her in it so no one would see them taking her from the house."

"This is insane. What if we get word out that I have the money, that I'll give it to them for my wife? We could put that in the papers, on the radio—"

"These people aren't stupid," Homer said. "They wouldn't fall for it."

John stared at him intently. "You said White Calf had a lot of money with him when he was killed. I don't remember reading about any money or meth in the newspapers. You have the money and the drugs, don't you? Why didn't the papers print that?"

Perkins and Homer exchanged glances.

"We intentionally didn't tell the reporters," Perkins said softly. "We were hoping we could smoke the distributors out."

John sprang from the sofa and confronted Perkins. His face was flushed and his fists clenched. "You used my wife and that other woman as bait! What the hell is wrong with you?"

"Take it easy," Perkins said. "Obviously, we didn't think they'd go this—"

"You didn't think, that's for damn sure. Well, I'm not going to take it easy. I want my wife back before these people hurt her. How do you plan to go about that? You don't even know who the hell they are."

"We do know a good place to start. I know how difficult this is for you, but give us a chance to do our job."

"Yeah, you do your job. But if anything happens to Beth . . . "

John glared at each of them in turn. He followed them out of the house, standing in the doorway, the door wide open behind him. Still in his scrubs he shivered in the cold. Finally he went back inside and closed the door.

Ben Red Leaf was standing next to his cruiser when Perkins and the chief came out. "A couple of the men checked every house on both sides of the street," he said. "Nobody saw or heard anything."

"That leaves us with nothing to go on," Homer said to Perkins. "If only Two Bear Woman would wake up and give us a description . . . "

"Well, we don't know when or if that will happen and we can't wait around. We still have Aalford. I'll be paying him a visit first thing tomorrow."

"What about Mrs. Hartman in the meantime? The doctor is right to worry. You know what they did to Two Bear Woman."

Perkins opened his mouth to say something, but his words went unspoken. He couldn't argue with what the chief had said.

alford walked slowly along the path leading from the church to his house. The moon was almost full but he paid no attention to it. He had just spent more than an hour alone in the church, ostensibly praying but in reality fretting over his situation. Since learning about White Calf's death and the missing money, he had cancelled his

morning religious instruction sessions with the children and spent more time in the church by himself. Neither his wives nor any of the children dared to ask him the reason for this break in their routine. The women continued to instruct the children in their reading and arithmetic lessons, both they and the children relieved by Aalford's absence. When he was not meditating by himself in the church, Aalford spent most of his time walking the perimeter fence of his property, deep in thought, oblivious to anything occurring on the farm. Hay was now the furthest thing from his mind. If he had received a call requesting a delivery, there would have been no way for him to do it. He'd have to hire a new worker, but that would take time and require more effort than he was capable of at the moment. I hope White Calf rots in hell, he thought.

Although he considered himself deeply religious, and still followed most of the Latter Day Saints tenets except for the one forbidding polygamy, Aalford had had no need of his Redeemer's succor for many years. Dirk Aalford always felt in total control of his life—until now.

It was past ten. All the inhabitants of his household were asleep when Aalford entered the house. Ellen, his youngest wife, opened her eyes, roused out of a restless sleep when the front door closed. All of Aalford's wives knew he'd been troubled ever since he received several mysterious phone calls earlier in the week. That was followed by the appearance of the two strangers, one of whom spoke a language they didn't understand. They knew that somehow their husband's problems involved White Calf, whose name was no longer mentioned and whom they hadn't seen in weeks. Ellen closed her eyes, pretending to be asleep when Aalford entered the bedroom. She was now the wife with whom he usually slept. Mercifully, since his troubles started, he had not inflicted himself on her. Although she accepted Aalford as her master and was obedient to him, Ellen, in her own daily prayers, begged to be freed from his lust.

She remained alert, listening to her husband's every move as he removed his clothes and put on his pajamas. He sat down heavily on his side of the bed. Ellen was aware of his body growing rigid, as if he were listening for something. Ellen heard a car approaching the farm. Moments later its tires crunched on the gravel outside the house. Aalford stood up and pushed the curtains aside. The car he least wanted to see, the black Lexus, was parked in front of his garage.

More than two days had passed since the visit by the Mexicans. Aalford had almost begun to entertain the faint hope that they would not return. He sighed deeply as he took off his pajamas and got dressed. Ellen propped herself on her elbows after he left the room. She listened intently but heard nothing. Tiptoeing from the bed, she lifted the edge of a curtain and peered out the window.

Ramon and Manuel, standing at the rear of the Lexus, looked up as Aalford approached. Manuel walked abruptly toward him, preventing Aalford from getting closer to the car. "Let's talk here," he said.

"Did you find out anything?" Aalford asked.

"The Indian woman knew nothing. Your daughter wasn't there. She and her children left with the police when they first came looking for White Calf. The Indian woman doesn't know where they took her."

"What are you going to do now?"

"Now? Now we need a place for our guest."

"What are you talking about?"

"The nurse who rode in the car with White Calf and the cop."

"What about her?"

Manuel turned and pointed to the rear of the Lexus. "She's in the trunk."

"What? Are you crazy? Why'd you bring her here?"

"Lower your voice. You have a place where we can keep her? Someplace where no one can hear her if she yells?"

A vise of fear closed around Aalford's heart. How could this be happening to him? His involvement with meth dealers was serious enough, but being an accomplice to a kidnapping?

"You've got to get her out of here." His voice trembled.

Manuel fixed him with a cold stare. "Didn't you hear what I said?"

Aalford began to sweat although the nighttime temperature was well below freezing. He shivered more from fear than from the cold. "I'll show you," he said, barely able to get the words out. "We can drive there."

"Get in the back of the car," Manuel said. He motioned to Ramon to get back in.

Ellen, watching the men talk, had been unable to hear anything. She slipped back under the covers. It was all very strange, a real mystery, but she had learned long ago that she had no right to question anything in her husband's life.

The car bounced across the pasture for a few minutes before stopping.

"What is this place?" Manuel asked Aalford.

"It's my church."

Manuel and Ramon followed him from the car. Aalford pushed open the front door and turned on the light. The two Mexicans scanned the interior. Four rows of benches lined each side of the room. Aalford walked toward a lectern at the front of the church. Off to one side was a blackboard and chair.

"You going to preach to us?" Manuel sneered.

Mire! Ramon called to Manuel, pointing to a narrow ascending flight of steps behind the blackboard.

"What's up there?" Manuel asked.

"Nothing," Aalford said. "It goes up to the steeple in case we need to make any repairs. Help me move this," he said, pushing against one side of the lectern.

Manuel pushed with him.

"What is this?" Manuel asked, pointing at the trapdoor that had been covered by the lectern.

"It goes down to another room, a bomb shelter."

"A bomb shelter?" Manuel laughed incredulously.

Ramon, too, laughed, an unpleasant sound that grated on Aalford's ears. *El tiene miedo de un ataque?* Ramon said, moving one hand in a downward arc and mimicking the sound of a falling bomb.

Aalford didn't bother to explain that he had built the shelter years before, at a time when he was convinced Armageddon was upon them. For an entire year he conducted drills, during which he forced his wives and children down into the shelter for an hour or more at a time. Convinced finally that he had been wrong, Aalford ended the drills. The trap door remained closed and covered by the lectern. When he'd led his family up the steps from the shelter for the last time, Aalford had been crushed by disappointment. The apocalypse he had yearned for hadn't come. He disappeared into his study for two entire days, refusing entry to anyone. When he finally came out, Aalford addressed his wives and children. "The Lord spoke to me," he told them. "He reproached me for my laxness." From then on, Aalford became even stricter with his women and children. No child escaped his wrath for the most minor of infractions. The welts inflicted on their buttocks by the leather belt might eventually disappear, but the fear Aalford provoked in all of them remained.

Aalford pulled open the trap door. "You'll need a flashlight," he told Manuel. There's no light down there. I can get one from the garage."

"I have one," Manuel said. He sent Ramon to the car for the light.

Aalford led them down a short flight of steps and pulled back a large sliding bolt. They entered the concrete-walled room. Manuel examined the interior with his flashlight beam and smiled at Ramon. *Perfecto*, he said. "Bring a chair down here," he ordered Aalford. "We'll go get the woman."

Aalford carried a small, straight-backed chair down to the bomb shelter. Ascending the steps again, he met Ramon and Manuel, carrying a rolled-up carpet between them. Ramon had a length of rope wound around his arm. Aalford began to speak but Manuel placed a cautionary finger to his lips.

"I'll wait here," Aalford whispered soundlessly. He removed his handkerchief from his pocket and mopped his face.

Que maricón ese, Ramon grumbled, holding the back end of the carpet as Manuel led the way down the steps.

Manuel paid no attention to his companion's words. He was focused on how to make the woman talk.

61

Beth Hartman was terrified. Trussed up inside her own carpet, a gag in her mouth, she struggled to breathe normally and control her fear. Her nightmare had begun when she answered the knock on the door. A tall Latin-appearing man had held out a piece of paper and asked if she knew where the address written on the paper was. The paper he handed her was blank. Her confusion gave way to alarm when the tall man shoved her back into the hallway. His shorter companion, whom she hadn't noticed before, closed the door behind them.

She dashed for the telephone, its receiver on the end table where she'd left it. The shorter man tackled her, overturning the end table. Beth's scream was cut off by a hand clamped over her mouth. She fought back, kicking and clawing at the man holding her. Her assailant lifted his hand from her mouth. Beth's yell was again aborted as the tall man shoved a wadded up bandanna into her mouth. He followed up with duct tape wound several times around her head to hold the gag in place. The two men shoved her roughly to the floor. She kicked and punched at them as they began rolling the carpet around her. Ramon slapped her hard across the face, bringing tears to Beth's eyes. When she could no longer move, she felt herself being lifted from the floor.

"Let's go," Manuel said.

Beth was aware of being shoved into a small space, the men bending the ends of the carpet so the space could accomodate her. They're putting me into a car trunk, she thought. A sharp thud followed by the sound of an engine confirmed it.

Who are these men? Why are they doing this? Where are they taking me? What are they going to do to me? Question after question tumbled through her mind. Beth was unable to come up with an answer to any of them. Barely able to get enough air in her lungs, she thought of the child she was carrying. She had to keep calm. With so little air in the car trunk, she had to breathe slowly, for her sake and for the baby's.

Taken hostage a week earlier by White Calf and now kidnapped by a pair of strangers, Beth felt she was trapped in a surreal nightmare. When she and John had lived and worked in Gallup, a pneumonic plague epidemic had spread through the Navajo reservation. John had contracted the infection, terrifying Beth, who feared he would die. At the time, she thought those were the most frightening days of her life. They paled when compared to what was happening in Browning. Now she was the one whose death might be imminent.

Beth lost track of time. Eventually, she felt the car slowing and bouncing on a rough road until it came to a complete stop. Two doors slammed, followed by silence. Several minutes later the engine started up and the car moved slowly forward for a short distance. Car doors slammed again and a key was inserted into the trunk lock. The carpet was pulled roughly from the trunk. It was carried by someone on each end. She was tilted head down for a few seconds, the jerky motion telling her they were going down some steps. The carpet was set down and unrolled. She was aware of a cold dampness, but it was too dark to see anything. Rough hands pulled her to her feet and a flashlight beam was directed at her face. As she turned away from the light, a chair was forced against the back of her knees. She fell heavily onto the seat. Seconds later, her arms were pulled behind the chair and her wrists were tightly bound. A second tie was placed around her ankles. Beth, choking on the gag in her mouth, moaned in protest in hopes they would remove it.

She winced as one of her abductors ripped the duct tape away, pulling her hair in the process. The gag was yanked from her mouth. Beth sputtered and coughed.

"Who are you? What do you want from me? Wh—"

"Shut up!" a harsh voice ordered. "I'll ask the questions."

"Can't you take that light out of my eyes?"

The beam was lowered slightly.

"A week ago you were in a car with White Calf and a cop, weren't you?"

The question took Beth by surprise. "Yes. White Calf took us as hostages."

"Did he have something with him?"

"Who, White Calf?"

"Yes, White Calf."

"He had a suitcase."

"Good. And what did he do with it?"

Beth was now totally confused. Was this some kind of joke? "What he did with the suitcase? He threw it onto the back seat of the car."

"After that," the voice said impatiently.

"I don't know," Beth said. "I was sitting up front next to Raymond—Officer Two Teeth. White Calf made me get out of the car and they drove away."

"So you never saw the bag again?"

"Never."

"You're lying. What did you and White Calf do with it?"

"What did—are you crazy? How should I know what White Calf did with it?"

"What about the cop? Did you see him again afterward? What did he say about it?"

"I saw him in the hospital, in the emergency room. He never talked to me about any suitcase."

Ella no sabe nada, Ramon said, disgust in his voice. *Quizás ese pinche policía sabe algo.*

Manuel weighed Ramon's words. The only thing they now knew for sure was that White Calf's Indian wife and this nurse knew nothing. They had no idea where White Calf's other wife, Aalford's daughter, was. The Indian woman had told them the police took her and her children away. Maybe Ramon was right. Maybe the cop did know something, but more likely the Indian had hidden the bag while making his run for the border. If he hadn't, then the cops had it. Either way, they were fucked. They'd never get the bag back.

Tenemos que hablar con ese policía, Ramon said. *Quizás él tiene la maleta. Mucha plata, mucha tentación.*

Although Manuel didn't really believe the cop had the suitcase, they'd never know for sure unless they grabbed him. Carlos would expect that of them. If nothing came out of their efforts, at least they'd have done what Carlos wanted.

Carlos was not a man Manuel wanted to make angry. *Como podemos hablar con el policía?* he said to Ramon. *Será difícil.*

Difícil, sí. Imposible, no. Qué quieres hacer con la mujer?

That was something he had not yet decided. For now the woman could stay where she was. She wouldn't be going anywhere. *No sé todavía. Mientrastanto, ella puede quedarse aquí.*

Estoy pensando, Ramon said. *Como sabemos que ella no habla español? Ella parece más latina que india.*

Ramon was right. The woman did appear more *latina* than Indian. They'd have to find out if she spoke Spanish.

"*Tú,*" Manuel said, moving closer to Beth and raising the flashlight beam so that it shone directly on her face. *Como te llamas?*

"W—what?" Beth stammered. "I don't understand."

Tú entiendes, Manuel said, taking her face in his hand and squeezing it between his thumb and fingers. Beth tried to pull her face away from his grasp but he squeezed harder. *Si no me dices la verdad, yo voy a cortar esa cara bonita con mi cuchillo. Ahora entiendes?*

"Can't you speak English," Beth said. "I don't understand what you're saying."

Basta, Ramon said. *Ella no entiende.*

Manuel removed his hand from Beth's face. He swung the flashlight beam around the room. Its dimensions were twelve by twelve. Walls, ceiling, and floor were all made of concrete. A toilet was placed against one wall and a sink against another.

Corta las ligaduras, Manuel told Ramon.

Ramon removed a switchblade knife from his pocket. Manuel directed the flashlight beam at Beth's bonds while Ramon cut them. Beth rubbed her chafed wrists with her hands.

"You'll stay here," Manuel said. "You know where the toilet and sink are." He directed the flashlight beam at them again.

"How long are you going to keep me here?"

"I'll let you know."

Manuel jerked open the room's heavy door. For a brief instant, Beth caught a glimpse of four dimly lit steps. The door closed and once again she was immersed in darkness. A metallic clang shattered the silence of the room as a bolt slid into place. What is this room? she wondered. Part of a basement? The flashlight's beam had revealed no windows, no skylight. The damp cold penetrated her light sweater. She pushed her chair back until it met the wall behind her. Standing up, she stretched her neck and limbs, trying to relieve the aching of her muscles from her cramped position in the car trunk. With her arms extended, she groped her way to where she remembered the sink was. Following the walls with her palms, she moved slowly around the room, pausing when her leg hit the toilet. She continued moving until her hand let her know she'd reached the wooden door. She pushed against it with all her weight but met solid resistance. Suddenly, she thought of John. How frantic he must be. She remembered their recent conversation about Gallup and Browning. When John had talked about the seemingly insurmountable problems on the Blackfeet reservation, she had tried to convince him that it was no worse than Navajoland, that many good people in Browning did care and wanted to make things better. Was this her comeuppance? At least in Dinetah, no one had ever abducted her.

The only thing that had come out of her interrogation by the two men she assumed were Mexican was that now she knew why she'd been kidnapped. Whatever White Calf's suitcase had contained, it was something they wanted. Now that they seemed convinced she knew nothing, would they let her go? They knew she had no idea where she was, that she could never lead the police here. It would be senseless for them to kill her. She had to believe that eventually they would free her. Otherwise she'd have to surrender to hopelessness, and that was out of character for her. She cut across the room, walking slowly toward where she thought the sink was, her hands held out in front of her. Turning the faucet she was relieved to hear the sound of running water. Beth scooped handfuls of cold water into her mouth. No matter how long she had to remain in this room, she wouldn't die of thirst. She continued groping her way around the room. Once she was comfortable with its dimensions and the placement of the sink and toilet, she counted off steps from the door to the opposite wall. She began to pace back and forth, quickening her steps in an effort to get warm. The one thought she tried to suppress was what would happen to her should the men simply decide to leave. "They won't do that," she said aloud, relieved to hear the sound of her voice in the blackness while trying to overcome her fears.

alford paced back and forth in the church. He stared at the open trap door, trying to envision the woman in the bomb shelter. He had no idea what she looked like, had even forgotten the name given by the newspaper. She must be terrified, he thought. He was afraid to contemplate what Manuel and Ramon intended to do with her. Assuming she was still alive when Carlos' men left, should he rescue her? But how could he do that? If he released her, she'd know his face and she would learn where she was being held. One way or another, it would be the end of him. He'd spend years in jail or eternity underground when Manuel and Ramon caught up to him.

This latest development was more than he had bargained for. Much more. He rued the day he had ever agreed to become a link in Carlos' meth distribution scheme. Aalford couldn't even remember the name of the man who had put him in touch with Carlos. He had a mental image of a smooth-talking service man who had shown up years before to refurbish his baler and do some complicated repairs on his tractor. "It'll hold for a while, but you'll be needing new equipment pretty soon," he told Aalford.

"Too expensive. I have to make everything last."

The man eyed him closely, then scanned Aalford's expanse of farmland.

"You've got a nice place here. Remote, no prying eyes."

"What do you mean?"

"I can put you in touch with someone who can solve your money problems."

"The farm's not for sale."

"I'm not talking about selling your place." He scribbled a phone number on a piece of paper. "Call this number in Spokane and ask for Carlos. Tell whoever answers that Mickey told you to call."

"Is this something illegal?"

Mickey, or Mikey, or whatever his name was, had watched as three different women came out of Aalford's house. One carried a basket of wet wash, which she proceeded to hang on a clothesline; another busied herself cleaning windows. The third, younger than the other two, disappeared back into the house when she saw the stranger watching her.

"No more illegal than some other things," he said, a smile flitting around his lips. "Carlos will explain it all to you. Call him. You won't regret it."

Aalford had not made the call until he received the serviceman's bill. It was higher than he had anticipated. Lately, everything he needed on the farm was expensive, far more than he could afford. His hay prices couldn't keep pace with his rising costs.

Carlos had chatted amiably with him on the phone, not proposing anything until Aalford repeated what the serviceman had said.

"Yes," Carlos said sympathetically, "I know how expensive things are these days. Maybe I can help you." He had outlined a simple plan. Parcels would be delivered at intervals to Aalford. It would be up to Aalford to deliver them to a designated person.

"That's all you have to do. No risk," Carlos had promised him. "You'll be paid very well for every delivery you make."

"What will I be delivering?"

"You don't need to know that. How does ten thousand a delivery sound?"

Aalford was stunned. "And there's no risk?"

"Not if you follow instructions."

It was an offer Aalford found it impossible to refuse. He received his first delivery two weeks after his conversation with Carlos. A young man wearing dark glasses drove onto his property shortly before dusk on a spring afternoon. He remained inside the car, his engine running. "Mr. Aalford?" he called as the hay farmer approached. Aalford looked at him warily. He suspected from the Washington plates that the driver had been sent by Carlos but he had to be sure. Aalford Farm had few visitors and he was immediately suspicious of any stranger.

"Who are you?" Aalford asked.

"Carlos sent me."

"What's your name?" Aalford asked.

"Never mind that. I have something for you."

He picked up a plastic Walmart bag from the floor in front of the passenger seat and handed it to Aalford. "Keep this in a safe place. Carlos will call you about when and where to deliver it." Without another word he drove away. Aalford stepped into his garage with the plastic bag. Inside were two wrapped parcels, each weighing about a pound. Coarse granules and shards, dirty white in color, were visible through the heavy plastic wrap. Aalford had never seen illicit drugs of any kind, but in his imagination he visualized talcum powder when he read anything about heroin or cocaine. He had no idea what the packages contained, but it was obvious to him from the money Carlos had offered that it was an illegal substance.

Aalford had no moral compunction about delivering drugs, not as long there was no risk to him and the drugs found their way to gentiles. His fellow Mormons may have deviated from the precepts of his religion's founder, but at least they were on a road that would someday enable them to see the true path. Gentiles, or non-believers, were another story. They and their institutions were there to be taken advantage of. There was no stigma attached to bleeding the beast.

It was not long afterward that he received his call from Carlos. The dropoff was to take place in Fort Benton. A man named Miguel would be the one to take possession of the packages. In return, Aalford would receive a suitcase with cash. Carlos' man would pick that up at the time of the next delivery to Aalford. Also at that time, Aalford would receive his payment.

Aalford couldn't visualize himself driving all over the state to make deliveries. Besides, should anything go wrong, he did not want to be the one in possession of whatever substance the packages contained. The only solution was to bring his employee in on the scheme. White Calf was the man who made all his hay deliveries. He had proven himself to be dependable during the few years he'd been working for the prophet. Furthermore, the Indian driving Aalford's rig was a familiar sight on the state's roads. He would arouse no suspicion.

"Would you object if the employee who delivers my hay brings the stuff to Miguel?" Aalford asked.

"Who's this employee?"

"His name is White Calf. He's a Blackfeet Indian."

For a moment Carlos said nothing. He seemed amused when he spoke again. "The hay is a good cover," he said. "You can hide the packages inside a bale. You trust this White Calf?"

"Yes."

"Okay then. But you're the one who has to pay him and if anything goes wrong, he's your responsibility."

White Calf listened impassively while Aalford spoke to him about his new duties. He looked at the plastic-wrapped packages and said nothing. Aalford had no idea if the Indian knew what the packages contained. "You'll make five hundred dollars every time you do one of these special deliveries," Aalford told him. "Is that agreeable?"

White Calf took the packages from Aalford. "You know what this is?" he asked, surprising his employer.

"No. What is it?"

"It's meth. Crank. If I'm caught with this I'll go to jail."

Aalford pursed his lips. He couldn't back out now. He was already committed. "You'll receive a thousand dollars for every delivery you make. Is that satisfactory?"

White Calf nodded, his face revealing a hint of a smile.

"Just don't get caught," Aalford cautioned.

"No one will bother me. I'm delivering hay."

After a while, the deliveries became routine, at least two, sometimes three or four, occurring every month. Aalford stashed his money in the banks of nearby towns. He remained circumspect when it came to spending money, but his farm finances were no longer a problem. Everything had gone smoothly until White Calf fouled it up. Now the words spoken to him by Carlos came back to haunt him. White Calf was his responsibility.

His reverie was interrupted by the footsteps of Ramon and Manuel ascending the steps. "Let's push that thing back over the trapdoor," Manuel said.

"Did you find out anything?"

"She knows shit."

"What are you going to do?"

"We have one more person to question. The cop."

"The cop? The one who was in the car with White Calf and the woman? You must be crazy."

"Maybe he took the money."

"You're mad. You think you're going to put him in a rug like you did to her?"

Un cómico, eh? Ramon said to his partner. *Me gustaría cortar su garganta.*

"For your sake," Manuel said to Aalford, "you better hope this cop knows something."

"What do you mean, for my sake?"

"If the cop doesn't know where the money is, you're responsible."

"That's ridiculous. I want to speak to Carlos."

"But Carlos does not want to speak to you." He grinned. "Unless you have his money."

"What about the woman? How long are you going to keep her here?"

"We'll decide that after we talk to the cop."

"I don't want any part of this. I want her off my property."

Manuel glanced at his watch.

"It's very late, *señor*. Tonight, Ramon and I will sleep in the church. We'll leave in the morning."

"What about the woman? She has no food."

"She has water. She has a toilet. All the comforts of home." He smiled mirthlessly. "She'll live. For now."

"I don't like this."

"It's not important to us what you like or don't like. *Buenas noches, señor*."

erkins was on his way to Aalford's by six AM. He had tossed and turned all night, apologizing several times to Liz for keeping her up. "Let's have an early breakfast before the kids wake up," she said finally. Both of them sat at the table drinking their coffee black, trying to clear their fogged brains.

"What's wrong, Will?" she asked.

"I didn't tell you last night," he said. "Beth Hartman, the pediatrician's wife, has been kidnapped."

"What!?"

"This White Calf case won't end. There are people after the money and drugs White Calf had in his possession. They beat White Calf's wife into unconsciousness and now they've grabbed Mrs. Hartman."

"But why Mrs. Hartman?"

"She was in the car with White Calf when he tried to escape to Canada."

"But so was Officer Two Teeth. They were hostages."

Perkins nodded. "When we talked to reporters about White Calf's death, we made sure not to mention the money and drugs he had with him. That money was taken from the drug dealer White Calf killed."

"I'm not sure I understand what you're saying, Will. It still doesn't explain why they'd think Mrs. Hartman would know anything about the money."

"Mrs. Hartman and Raymond were the last ones with White Calf. The people behind this drug operation must think they know something, or were involved with White Calf in some way."

Liz's eyes opened wide as she grasped what he was saying. "Will, why didn't you or the Tribal Police say anything to the reporters about the money? Were you hoping something like this would happen?"

"Don't misunderstand, Liz. We never thought they'd be desperate enough to kidnap Mrs. Hartman. We were hoping to smoke them out, have some strangers show up on the rez asking questions, that sort of thing."

"Oh, Will, this is terrible. After what that poor woman has already gone through. The doctor must be so upset. And angry."

"He is. I can't blame him. Hartman was on the phone with his wife when she screamed. It took him five minutes to reach his house. By then she was gone. I kept thinking about him last night, the agony he's going through. That's what kept me up."

Liz shook her head. "Will—"

"Don't say it. I know I'm partially to blame for this."

"Partially?"

Perkins turned away from his wife's disapproving look.

"Do you think they'll go after Raymond Two Teeth next?"

"I don't know."

"So you have no idea who these men are or where they've taken Mrs. Hartman?"

"We do have one lead," Perkins said, standing up from the table. "I'm on my way now to follow up on it."

His wife looked at him questioningly, but Perkins didn't elaborate. He was already at the door, his jacket on, when she called to him.

"Will. Be careful."

As he headed north on 15 from Shelby, Perkins couldn't get his wife's accusatory look out of his mind. It was hard to make people understand the things he and his fellow agents sometimes had to do. He thought, too, of his wife's question about Raymond. These people had been desperate enough to beat Two Bear Woman into unconsciousness and seize Beth Hartman. It was obvious they'd stop at nothing to get their money and drugs back. But would they go after a tribal cop? He answered his own question. It was a lot of money and to their way of thinking a cop was as corruptible as anyone else.

Raymond hadn't been at the Hartman house last night, but Homer was going to call him. He must know by now what had happened. Raymond was smart enough to realize that the men who abducted the doctor's wife were the same people who had almost killed Two Bear Woman. He'd know that by virtue of his being in the car with White Calf, he, too, was a target. That would put him on his guard. Perkins snorted through his nose. Raymond's idea of being on his guard was the same as that of a pugnacious kid: 'Bring it on.'

In Sunburst, Perkins took the turn that led to Aalford's place. It was early and he hoped to find Aalford still asleep. Always easier to rattle a suspect and trip him up when he was half-asleep.

Fresh topsoil had been graded into place along one lane of the road. It was where federal agents disguised as state road crew had been working during the week-long hunt for White Calf. The FBI didn't truly expect White Calf to appear at Aalford's place, but decided it was best not to take chances. The day after White Calf was killed, Bill Jameson had pulled the road crew off their assignment.

"I'd leave them for a while longer," Perkins had argued. "Maybe we'll learn who supplies Aalford."

"I can't do that, Will. These men have been out there for a week digging their holes and filling them in. They're bored stiff and freezing their asses off. Even the locals are starting to get suspicious."

It would have been reassuring, Perkins thought, to see the men there now and for them to know he was driving in. Not that he expected any trouble from Aalford. It was for that very reason he hadn't bothered to alert Jameson about his intention to visit Aalford this morning. He'd pay his visit, try to put the fear of God into the man, and hope Aalford would lead him to Beth Hartman. Of course, there was always the possibility that Aalford wouldn't cooperate. In that case, the Bureau would have to resort to a full blitz—multiple agents, a search warrant, and a wire tap. The problem was all that took time. And time was what Liz Hartman didn't have.

The sun was just rising, casting a golden glow on the stubbled hay fields.

Although temperatures had risen above the freezing point every day during the past week, mornings were still bitterly cold. Frost glistened on the aspen trees lining Aalford's road. Much of the snow from the previous week's storm had melted, leaving only scattered patches on the hay fields.

Aalford's house and barn looked the same as during Perkins' earlier visit with Raymond. The hay farmer's truck and car were both parked in the garage. Perkins' eye, however, was drawn to the spire in the distance, the building that Aalford referred to as his church. A car was parked directly in front of it. Perkins decided to check it out before stopping in front of Aalford's house. A dog tied up on Aalford's porch barked as Perkins drove past. That's new, Perkins thought. Aalford apparently wanted an alarm system. So much for the element of surprise. He pulled up behind a black Lexus, immediately noticing the Washington plate. Perkins committed the plate number to memory, made a U-turn, and headed back down to Aalford's house. As he parked, he took out his cellphone. If Aalford had visitors it was best to inform Jameson and have him run the plate number through the system. The rottweiler, however, was lunging at his chain and Aalford was standing in the doorway.

Perkins put away his phone and stepped out of the car. Aalford's eyes flitted nervously between Perkins and the church.

"A little early for visiting, isn't it?" Aalford said, his voice unfriendly.

"It looks like you already have visitors," Perkins said. "All the way from Washington."

"What do you want?"

"Do we talk here or go inside?"

"Talk here. I'm busy."

"Found anyone to replace White Calf?"

"What business is that of yours?"

"His death must have posed some problems for you."

Aalford glared at him, but said nothing.

"I'm here to offer you a deal."

"What are you talking about?"

"I'm talking about the nurse who was kidnapped in Browning. Probably by the same men who almost beat White Calf's wife to death. I think you know where that nurse is. Lead me to her and I'll do what I can for you."

"I don't know anything about a nurse or about White Calf's wife." Aalford fidgeted in place, constantly looking toward the church.

"Distributing illegal substances is one thing. Being an accomplice to murder is something else. If anything happens to that woman—"

Perkins was distracted by a movement on either side of him. Using the house as cover, two men had made their way from the church without Perkins noticing.

"Aren't you going to introduce us to your friend?" Manuel said, stepping up to Aalford.

"This man's a federal agent."

Ramon took up a position behind Perkins.

"A federal agent, like in FBI?" Manuel said, his voice flat, evincing no surprise. "Why is the FBI interested in you?"

"He's investigating the kidnapping of a nurse."

"This man is a farmer and we are here to buy hay from him. Why do you bother him about a kidnapping?"

"You're here to buy hay? Long way to come for it. Couldn't find any in Washington?"

Perkins turned to Aalford, his right hand already slipping inside his jacket. "Why don't you introduce your friends?" he said. "I'll give them one of my cards."

Perkins spun around at the sound of a metallic clip. He stared into the muzzle of Ramon's nine millimeter.

"Get your hand out of your jacket," Manuel said, coming up next to him.

He patted down the agent, removing Perkins' revolver from his shoulder holster and the cell phone from his jacket pocket. "Are your keys in the car?" Manuel asked.

"Yes."

"Now, walk in front of us toward that building." He pointed to the church. "And, señor, don't think of running."

"You're aware that you're going to be in a shitload of trouble for messing with a federal agent," Perkins said, addressing his remark to Aalford.

"Walk!" Manuel ordered. "It is you who are in a shitload of trouble."

Aalford trailed behind them in silence.

"You made a big mistake coming here," Manuel said. "But if you're looking for a nurse, maybe we can help you."

They entered the church and Manuel motioned for Aalford to assist him in moving the lectern. Ramon kept his weapon trained on Perkins.

"Now," Manuel said, "go down those steps."

Perkins hesitated, keeping his gaze fixed on Aalford. Manuel spun him around roughly and pushed him toward the steps. "Walk down or go head first."

Perkins stopped in front of the bomb shelter door. Manuel stepped alongside him and slid the bolt back. Ramon pressed the muzzle of his weapon into Perkins' neck as Manuel pulled the door open. Perkins' eyes momentarily met those of a frightened Beth Hartman. Ramon shoved him toward the woman while Manuel slammed the door and slid the bolt into place. The two men ascended the steps to find an ashen Dirk Aalford awaiting them.

"He's a federal agent," Aalford said weakly.

Manuel looked at him menacingly. Aalford knew better than to say anything else.

"A re you all right?" Perkins asked as soon as the door's bolt slammed into place.

"Yes," Beth said. "I can't believe it's you. What are you doing here?"

"I was looking for you. Aalford was the one lead we had so I came here."

"Who's Aalford?"

"The man who owns this farm. White Calf worked for him."

"Who came with you?"

Perkins was glad the room was in blackness. Beth Hartman couldn't see the sheepish look on his face.

"I'm here by myself."

"Does anyone know you're here?"

"Why don't you tell me what happened to you. Start from the beginning."

"Everything happened so fast. I was on the phone with my husband when someone knocked on the door. I opened it and two men grabbed me. They rolled me up in a carpet and threw me into the trunk of their car. The next thing I knew

I was in this dark room."

"Did they talk to you?"

"They kept asking me questions about what White Calf did with the suitcase he had with him. I told them I didn't know, that he still had it when he ordered me out of the car."

"I knew that's what they were after."

"They seemed satisfied with what I told them. I thought they might let me go. But now . . ."

Perkins knew she was right. Beth Hartman had had no idea where the men had taken her. Maybe the Mexicans would have let her go, maybe not. But there was no chance of that happening now, not with him there.

"You didn't tell anyone you were coming here, did you?" Beth said, her voice apprehensive.

"People knew I was planning to come here."

"Planning? When? This week, next month, in a year?" There was no mistaking the anger in her voice.

"You're getting yourself all worked up for nothing. My men and the tribal police know I'm here.".

"If that's the case, how come you're here alone? If this man, Aalford, is a suspect, why would the FBI let you come here by yourself?"

"Why don't you let me worry about our operating procedure?"

"Maybe you can at least explain why they came after me in the first place."

"Because you and Raymond were the last ones to see the suitcase."

"But we were kidnapped. It's not like we were conspiring with White Calf. They must know that."

"There was a lot of money in that suitcase. These men don't have a clue what happened to it. They're grasping at straws. They probably thought there was a possibility you and White Calf were in on it together."

"That's ridiculous."

"Like I said, they're desperate to get their hands on that money. If you convinced them that you know nothing, they'll probably go after Raymond next."

"This is so crazy. Raymond's a policeman."

"These guys are criminals, so they probably think everyone is corruptible. Including policemen."

"What are we going to do? What if help doesn't come as soon as you think? Those men will kill us."

"We're not dead yet. I barely had a chance to look at this room before they shut the door. Why don't you describe it to me."

Beth told him the dimensions of the room. "Give me your hand," she said. "I've paced it enough to know where I am in the dark." She led him around the perimeter several times, stopping by the sink and toilet so Perkins could orient himself. "The door must be six inches thick," she said, as she and Perkins pressed against it. "Even if we pounded on it, no one would hear us."

"Survivalists built these bomb shelters back in the fifties and sixties," Perkins said. "I've seen a couple in the Dakotas."

"They could leave us down here, walk away, and no one would ever find us."

"I don't think that will happen. Aalford is scared of these men. He's a polygamist and sexually abuses children, but he doesn't want to be an accessory to murder."

"It's not only us I'm frightened for. I'm pregnant, Mr. Perkins."

Perkins, moving around the room on his own, stumbled against the chair. "You didn't tell me there was a chair."

"What difference does it make?"

"Now we have a weapon."

"A chair?"

"It's enough to take out one of them."

"Right, then you'd have the other one with his gun pointed at you. You'll have to excuse me for being skeptical

"Did you come in your car?" Beth asked suddenly.

"Yes, why?"

"If anyone comes looking for you, they'll see it and know you're here."

"I wish it was that easy, but these men aren't stupid. The first thing they'll do is dispose of my car. It's probably gone already."

"Then it's hopeless."

"No, it isn't. Get that out of your head."

"Did you see my husband before you came here? He must be frantic with worry."

"I saw him the night you were kidnapped."

"How was he?"

"He was upset, of course, but he's tough. Like you."

"Yes, John is tough. When we were in Gallup, there was an outbreak of pneumonic plague on the reservation. That didn't stop him from visiting people who had come down with the disease. Most of them died. Then John came down with it and I was afraid I was going to lose him."

"But he pulled through."

"Yes."

"And we will, too. You have to believe that."

"We thought we were done with White Calf, that we'd never have to hear his name again."

Perkins nodded in the darkness but remained silent.

"But you knew it wasn't over, didn't you?"

Perkins had picked up on the edge in her voice. "What do you mean?"

"You said there was a lot of money in that suitcase."

"Yes. Aalford and White Calf were distributing meth."

"Who has the money now?"

"We do. And the meth also. But these men don't know that."

"The FBI and the police didn't let anyone know, did they? I certainly heard nothing on the radio and saw nothing about it in the newspaper."

"No, we didn't divulge it. We hoped the missing money would flush out whoever was supplying Aalford."

"And now you're scheme has backfired, hasn't it?" Beth said icily. "Now it might get both of us killed."

"We had no choice. You're a nurse at the hospital. You know how bad the meth problem is on the reservation, in all of Montana, in fact. We have to do what we can to stop it."

"Even if innocent people get killed? People you use as bait?"

Perkins sighed. He'd heard the same accusation from Beth's husband and seen it in his own wife's eyes.

"Why don't you answer me?"

Hearing the anguish in her voice, Perkins wouldn't have been surprised if she were to spring at him in the darkness.

"I don't blame you for being angry, but that's not helping us. Let's do some brainstorming, think of ways we can help ourselves."

Beth's laugh startled him.

"What's so funny?"

"I just remembered a cartoon. Two prisoners in a cell about thirty feet high, their arms and legs manacled to the wall. The only opening into the cell is a barred window in the ceiling above them. One prisoner says to the other, "Now here's my plan.""

"See," Perkins said, forcing a laugh. "Everything is relative. They were in a worse predicament than we are."

"Right, I forgot. We have a chair."

65

"Hello, Ollie," Liz Perkins said when Briggs picked up the phone and identified himself. "Is Will there?"

"We haven't seen him all morning. Do you know where he is?"

"No. He left very early. I just wanted him to know that I'm keeping Lucy home from school today. She's running a fever and has a sore throat."

"Will didn't tell us about any appointments he had this morning. Did he mention anything about where he was going?"

"He told me about the kidnapping of the doctor's wife. He said there was one lead he wanted to follow up on. You mean he never told you what his plans were?"

"Not a word.

"That's not like him. Now you have me worried."

"I'm sure he's fine. I'll talk to Bill and we'll see if we can figure out where he might be. If he comes in, I'll pass on the message about Lucy and have him call you."

"What's that about?" Bill Jameson asked, looking up from his desk.

"Will left his house early this morning, said something to his wife about following up a lead on the Hartman kidnapping, and that's the last she heard from him. One of their kids is sick."

"I wonder why he didn't call to tell us where he was going."

"Maybe because he left so early," Briggs said. "But if he was going up to Aalford's place, which is what I think, he could have called us from up there."

"It's eleven o'clock. We should have heard from him by now no matter where he went. I don't like this."

"What do you want to do?"

"I'm going to call Chief Whitecloud, find out if he knows anything. While I'm doing that, why don't you call the hospital. We need to know if the Indian woman regained consciousness. Without a description from her, we don't even know who we're looking for."

"Still unconscious," Homer Whitecloud said on the phone when Jameson asked if he had heard anything about Two Bear Woman. "The doctor I talked to said she had a severe concussion, maybe some swelling around the brain. If she doesn't come around by later today, they're going to send her to Great Falls to be seen by a neurosurgeon."

"The real reason I'm calling," Jameson said, "is to talk to you about Perkins."

"What about Perkins?"

"When was the last time you saw him?"

"At the doc's house, right after Mrs. Hartman disappeared."

"He left home early this morning without telling anyone where he was going. He told his wife he wanted to follow up on a lead. That's all she knew. Did he mention anything to you?"

"Yeah, he said he was going up to see Aalford."

"Nice of him to inform the Blackfeet Tribal Police but not us," Jameson said, exasperated.

"You haven't heard from him?"

"Not a word."

"You know where Aalford's farm is?" the chief asked.

"Vaguely. Perkins is the only one who's been there before."

"Raymond was with him then. If you're planning to head up there, why don't I send Raymond along. It would simplify things for you."

"I'd appreciate that."

"He's out on patrol, but I'll have him stop by your office within a half-hour."

True to the chief's word, Raymond walked into the FBI office twenty minutes later.

"How are you doing?" Jameson said as they shook hands. Ribs better?"

"The ribs are healing since I stopped jumping out of cars. The chief tells me Perkins went up to Aalford's place this morning."

"That's what we think. He never informed us where he was headed and no one's heard from him. Even his wife doesn't know where he is."

"Not like him to operate like a lone wolf," Raymond said.

"No, it isn't. It has me worried."

"Well, let's go find him," Raymond said.

An hour later, Jameson, directed by Raymond, turned off at the Sunburst exit and headed for Aalford's farm.

"Perkins' car's not here," Raymond said as they drove down the long driveway.

A rottweiler on the house porch began barking and tugging at his chain as the car pulled up.

"A new addition," Raymond said. "I don't remember any dog last time I was here."

Raymond stepped out of the car and scanned the ground. "Lot of tire tracks here," he said. "They look recent. And there are a few drops of oil."

"What does that mean?"

"Maybe nothing. But Perkins told me last time I was with him that he thought his Subaru might have an oil leak. I told him to take the car to my cousin."

"Maybe he was here and drove back to Browning."

"Yeah, but we didn't pass him on the highway. And someone would have called us if he turned up in Browning."

"Easy, boy," Jameson said to the dog as they approached the door. The rottweiler sat on his haunches now that the men were next to him. He sniffed at Jameson's shoes.

"You do the honors," Raymond said. "That dog seems to like you."

Jameson knocked loudly.

The door opened a crack.

"FBI," Jameson said, showing his identification.

"What do you want?"

"We want to talk to you. May we come inside?"

"Just a minute. I'll come out."

Aalford slipped outside, pushing the dog back with his foot. His eyes opened wide when he spotted Raymond standing off to one side. "You," he said, his look revealing a mixture of fear and animosity.

Raymond nodded slowly, studying Aalford. The man's unfriendliness didn't surprise him, but the fear in his eyes did. This was not the same self-assured

Aalford he and Perkins had visited.

"We're looking for agent Perkins," Jameson said. "He came to see you today, didn't he?"

Aalford hesitated, as if weighing which answer was the correct one. Manuel and Ramon had left early that morning, one driving Perkins' car, the other their own. They hadn't bothered to inform Aalford when they would return. Aalford's thoughts tumbled over one another. Perkins and the woman were still in the bomb shelter. If they were found now, he'd be the one to shoulder the blame for their incarceration.

"Well?" Jameson said.

"He was here earlier, but he left."

"Oh?" Jameson said. "And what time was that?"

"I don't know. Ten, ten-thirty maybe."

Jameson caught Raymond's eye. Both knew Aalford was lying.

"You don't mind if we have a look around, do you?"

"Yes, I do mind. You're on private property and I'd like you both to leave."

"I can be back in a few hours with enough agents to make your head spin, and with a search warrant," Jameson said. "In the meantime, Officer Two Teeth will remain here to make sure you don't go anywhere."

Again Aalford's mind raced. If only he had some idea when the Mexicans would return. Ironically, the man they were after, Raymond Two Teeth, was standing no more than ten feet away.

"Go ahead and search," Aalford said. Better now, he thought, while Ramon and Manuel weren't there. He didn't know what would happen if the two Mexicans were to show up. They may have gotten the drop on Perkins, but these two would see the car driving in and be prepared. "Let me call my family outside. I don't want you frightening them."

"I'll take the house and garage," Jameson said to Raymond.

"And I'll do the barn and church," Raymond said.

Aalford stepped in front of Raymond. "Why must you search my church? That's an affront to my faith."

"Better call your family," Jameson said. "We don't have all day."

Raymond headed for the church as soon as Aalford disappeared into the house.

"Watch yourself," Jameson called after him.

66

Y ahora? Ramon said as he and Manuel drove through Shelby. They had just left Perkins' Subaru in a supermarket's parking lot after wiping it down to remove fingerprints.

"Now?" Manuel said, "Now we better take care of business at Aalford's. I want to question that fed."

Y el policía en Browning?"

"I've been thinking," Manuel said. "The woman knows nothing. What if it's the feds and the cops hanging on to the money?"

Que quieres decir?

"Maybe the feds planned it this way from the very beginning. By saying nothing about the money, they made it seem like the money was still out there, hidden by the Indian or given to someone to hold for him. Maybe they were hoping to draw us out into the open."

No lo creo, Ramon said.

"Whether you believe it or not, that's probably what happened. And if that's the case, then we don't need the Indian cop. We have the fed."

Y si el federale no quiere hablar?

"Oh, I think we can get him to talk. Don't forget, we have the woman and you have your knife." He turned to smile at Ramon.

Y después? Ramon asked.

"Afterward? You know the answer to that question. If it was just the woman, I'd consider letting her go. But now?" He shook his head. "We'll finish them off in the bomb shelter and leave the bodies there. They'll become señor Aalford's problem." He laughed.

Carlos no va a estar muy feliz si regresamos sin la plata y sin los paquetes.

"We're not fucking magicians. If the feds have the money, there's nothing we can do about it. Carlos knows that." He tapped his fingers on the steering wheel and said nothing for a few moments. "But then we have to worry about Aalford. One fed came out to see him. What if more of the cabrones show up and put pressure on him? Maybe he'll decide to rat on Carlos to cut a deal."

Tenemos que hablar con Carlos.

Manuel nodded. "Yes, we must talk to Carlos. There's a gas station up ahead. I'll call him while you fill up the tank."

"I told you I had nothing to hide," Aalford said when Jameson came out of the house.

Aalford's three wives and twelve children huddled together behind him. Jameson particularly took note of the youngest woman. She couldn't be more than nineteen or twenty. He wondered how many of the children were hers. With the testimony of Aalford's surviving stepdaughter and this young woman, they'd have enough on Aalford to charge him with statutory rape. But, like Perkins, Jameson had his priorities. Breaking up the meth distribution network and finding out the source of the product took precedence.

Jameson looked toward the church but there was no sign of Raymond. "Open the trunk of the car in the garage," he ordered Aalford.

"That's ridiculous," Aalford said.

"Do it."

Jameson frowned as he looked into the empty trunk. He and Aalford turned simultaneously as the sound of an approaching car reached them. A cloud of dust followed the Lexus down the road into Aalford's farm.

"You have company," Jameson said, observing how pale Aalford had suddenly become.

Manuel and Ramon spotted Jameson's Jeep Grand Cherokee the moment Aalford's house came into view.

"Shit!" Manuel said.

Que quieres hacer? Ramon asked.

"We can't turn around now. They've spotted us. Let's see who it is."

Y si es otro federale?

"If it's one, no problem. More than one we can say we're lost, trying to find our way to the highway. Just be ready for trouble."

No me gusta esto. Mejor si vamos.

"You heard what Carlos said. First we make the fed talk."

Mira! Ramon said. *Todas las mujeres y niños están afuera con Aalford.*

"Friends of yours?" Jameson asked Aalford, noting the Lexus' Washington plate as the car drew up to them.

Manuel parked next to Jameson's car and stepped out. Smiling, he approached Aalford and Jameson with his hands in his jacket pockets. Seconds later, Jameson found himself staring into the muzzle of a Beretta.

"Hands over your head and turn around," Manuel said. "Search him," he ordered Ramon.

Ramon removed Jameson's revolver from its shoulder holster and pocketed it.

"You're making a big mistake," Jameson said. "I'm a federal agent."

"You are the one who made a mistake by coming here."

"There's another one with him," Aalford said. "The tribal cop you're looking for. He's in the church."

"Well, that's convenient. Let's go up there and meet him," Manuel said. "Start walking," he told Jameson. "You can put your hands down. We don't want your friend to think we're unfriendly. Just remember we're right behind you."

67

Raymond scanned the interior of the church as soon as he entered the door. Benches on each side, a lectern, and a blackboard. He walked up and down the rows in front of each bench before stepping up to the lectern. Spotting a narrow staircase behind the blackboard, Raymond trotted up the eight-inch wide steps that brought him to a small platform beneath the steeple. A railing skirted the platform. Raymond peered through a small vertical window facing to the north. A tractor moved slowly across a field. Beyond that was Canada.

Raymond studied the interior of the church from his perch. His bird's eye view added nothing to what he had seen from below. Still, Aalford was nervous when Raymond mentioned searching the church. There had to be something he was missing. He made his way carefully down the steps and walked up to the lectern. A green sliver on the floor behind the lectern caught his eye. Raymond squatted and picked it up. He rolled what appeared to be a piece of plastic between his fingers, studying it carefully. A fleeting smile crossed his lips. Raymond pushed against the heavy oak lectern as if he were back in high school playing tackle. He drew his gun as soon as he saw the trapdoor.

"It's freezing in here," Beth said, alternately walking back and forth in the darkness and jogging in place.

"The dampness makes it feel colder than it is," Perkins said. "Let me give you my jacket."

"No," she said tersely.

It's good that she's angry, Perkins told himself. They were in a serious enough predicament without his having to worry about her panicking.

"Tell me the truth," Beth said. "Does anyone really have any idea that you're out here? Don't feed me a line of bullshit just to make me feel better."

"While I was at your house the night these men took you, I spoke to Homer Whitecloud, the Tribal Police chief, and told him I was coming out here this morning. When my office doesn't hear from me, I'm sure they'll check with Homer."

For the first time since arriving at Aalford's, Perkins thought of his wife and daughters. He had mentioned to Liz that he'd be following up on a lead, but now he wished he'd been more specific. If Jameson had called the house to see if he was there, Liz might be alarmed. He'll figure out where I've gone, Perkins thought, especially after he talks to Homer. For all he knew, Jameson and Briggs were already on their way to Aalford's.

"Even if they come out here," Beth argued, as if reading his mind, "they'll never find us. Who's going to look for a trapdoor under a reading stand?"

"They'll tear this place apart if they have to. But I don't think it will come to that. I still believe that when pressure is put on Aalford, he'll cave."

"Suppose he doesn't."

"Then it'll be up to us."

"Up to us? We're in an empty, dark room below ground. What can we do?"

"Not entirely empty. I told you we have that chair. The next time we hear the bolt being opened, I'll be at the side of the door. I can flatten one of them with the chair and take on the second while you get out of here and try to get help."

"You think I'd run and leave you behind? While you take on the first one, I'll make sure the second one has the worst day of his life."

Perkins had to admire her pluck. "They're armed. If things don't go well, they'll kill you. It's better if you try to get out of here."

"I'll decide that for myself. Maybe we're just deluding ourselves anyway. What if they shoot us as soon as they open the door?"

"Are you always so negative?"

"Okay, what if they just leave us here and do nothing? I mean what if no one ever shows up? How's that for really being negative?"

"I'm impressed. You trumped your previous comment."

"Stop making light of this. It's not funny."

A sharp metallic sound at the door startled them.

"Someone's sliding the bolt," Perkins whispered. He groped his way in the darkness toward the chair. Holding it above his head he stationed himself at the side of the door. "Get on the other side of the door and be ready to run up the steps."

Beth moved quickly so that she'd be behind the door when it opened.

The door swung open and a shaft of dim light from the church entered the room. Perkins' muscles tensed.

"Anybody home?" a familiar voice said.

Perkins, holding the chair above his head, stepped into the doorway and grinned when he saw Raymond. "I never thought I'd be this happy to see *you*," he said.

"Aren't you supposed to sit on those things?" Raymond said, his face deadpan. "I'm glad you're here, too," he said when Beth Hartman stepped out from behind the door. "A lot of people have been worried about you."

"Did you come alone?" Perkins asked.

"No, I'm not as foolish as you. Jameson is with me. He's with Aalford. Let's go join them. I can't wait to see Aalford's face when the three of us show up."

"Aalford didn't tell you where we were?"

"No. You were the one who told me where you were."

"What are you talking about?"

"I found this on the floor." He showed Perkins the green sliver. "It's from your belt."

Perkins looked down and ran his fingers over the quills on his belt.

"Raymond, sometimes you do amaze me. I'll have to thank Mary again for giving me that belt."

"Since it saved your ass, that'd be a good idea.

"Sorry," he apologized to Beth.

"It was you who saved our ass," Beth said. "I'll never forget it. Can we get out of here now. I want to call John."

They filed through the church, Raymond in the lead. Opening the front door, he took one step outside and immediately ducked back in. "Shit!" he said.

"What's wrong?"

"Aalford and two men are headed this way. They've got Jameson walking in front of them. You don't happen to have a weapon, do you?" he asked Perkins.

"They took my gun."

"There's a stairway at the front of the church behind the blackboard. It leads to a platform under the steeple. Get up there and lay flat. Hurry up." Raymond ran with them, shoving the lectern over the trap door before following them up the steps. He reached the platform just as the front door opened. Squeezing in next to Perkins, he lay prone.

Aalford was the first one inside the church. "He's not here," he called to someone outside.

Manuel stepped in and looked around. "I thought you said he was searching the church."

"Maybe he's in the barn."

Aalford and Manuel left, closing the door behind them.

"You two stay here," Raymond whispered.

"There are two of them, Raymond. Let me come with you."

"No. I've got Jameson out there to help me. If anything happens to us and they don't find you in that cellar, they'll think I set you free. It'll be your only chance to escape. Wait here."

68

Shielded by the barn as he raced from the church, Raymond slipped around the building's right front corner. Ramon, his gun pointed at Jameson, stood outside with his back to Raymond.

Manuel followed Aalford out of the barn. "He's not in there," he said to Ramon.

"I don't understand it," Aalford said. "There's no place else he could have gone without us seeing him."

"Is there any other way out of that church?" Manuel asked.

"No, just the one door."

"What about the steps in there? Up in the front."

"Those don't go anywhere. They're only used to do repairs on the steeple."

Que quieres hacer? Ramon asked his companion.

"Let's go back to the church."

Ramon shoved Jameson ahead of them and the four men re-traced their steps toward the church.

"Drop your weapons!" Raymond ordered, coming up behind them.

As Ramon spun around, the 9 millimeter in his hand, Raymond fired. Ramon grunted as the round caught him in the center of his chest. He toppled backward onto the ground. Jameson slammed into Manuel from behind as he raised his Beretta, the weapon discharging harmlessly into the ground as Manuel fell.

"Drop it!" Raymond ordered, kneeling on Manuel's back and pressing the muzzle of his gun against his head.

Jameson picked up the Beretta while Raymond handcuffed Manuel's hands behind him.

"Hey, where do you think you're going?" Jameson yelled to Aalford, who backed away from them.

Raymond headed Aalford off and pushed him back toward Jameson.

"You're in deep shit," Jameson said, patting Aalford down in a search for weapons.

"I didn't do anything. It's those two. They threatened my family and forced me to do what they said."

Jameson looked at Raymond inquisitively as the cop knelt next to Ramon, feeling for a pulse. Raymond shook his head.

"Anything up in the church or barn?" Jameson asked.

"Perkins and the nurse. They're both okay. I left them there."

"Where?"

"Our friend here had them hidden in an underground bomb shelter."

"I never did that," Aalford whined. "It was their idea." He pointed at Manuel, still lying prone on the ground.

"You left them there?" Jameson asked Raymond.

"They're on the platform under the steeple," Raymond said. "I'll go get them while you stay with this one." He indicated Manuel.

Not a bad day's work, Raymond thought as he walked leisurely toward the church.

"You guys planning to spend the rest of the day up there?" Raymond called as he entered the building.

"God, we were so worried when we heard the shots," Beth said, leaning over the railing of the platform.

"Everything's fine. Come on down." Perkins and Beth blinked in the bright light as they left the church, Raymond following behind them.

"You do that yourself?" Perkins asked Raymond as they approached the two Mexicans on the ground.

"I had some help from Jameson."

"You okay?" Perkins asked Jameson.

"I'm supposed to ask you that. Why the hell didn't you tell us you were coming out here? he snapped. "Are you all right, Mrs. Hartman?" he asked Beth.

"I'm fine, thanks to Officer Two Teeth."

"Your husband is going to be mighty happy to hear from you."

"Does Liz know what's going on?" Perkins asked.

"She knows," Jameson said, coming up to him. "How could you do something so stupid, Will?"

"Not very good judgment on my part," Perkins said sheepishly.

"That's one of the men who kidnapped me," Beth interrupted, pointing to Manuel.

"There's the other one," Raymond said, gesturing toward Ramon. A red stain had spread across the front of his jacket.

"Where's my car?" Perkins asked, stepping menacingly toward Aalford.

"I don't know where it is. Ramon drove it away."

"Where'd you leave it?" Perkins asked, kneeling next to Manuel. "And where's my gun?"

Manuel twisted his head around and spit.

"Raymond, give me your weapon."

Perkins rolled Manuel onto his back and shoved the muzzle into his mouth. Raymond winced when he heard the metal hitting Manuel's teeth. "I'm counting to three," Perkins said. "These people may try to stop me but you'll be dead by then."

"Okay, okay." Manuel's words were garbled as he gagged on the barrel of the gun. "The gun's under the seat in the Lexus. Your car is in a supermarket lot in Shelby. We left the key in the ignition."

"Pretty clever," Raymond said. "Guess they were counting on some poor jerk stealing it and getting stopped by the cops. He'd have a tough time explaining his way out of that one."

We can stop there on the way back," Perkins said, handing Raymond his gun. "Maybe we'll get lucky and find it."

"Well, I'd better put in a call for an ambulance," Jameson said.

Raymond took Perkins aside while Jameson made his call. "You surprised me, man. I never saw you so mad. Does the car mean that much to you? Were you really going to shoot him?"

Perkins gave the tribal cop a ferocious glare before grinning. "I'll let you figure that one out. And listen, I really do owe you for saving our lives."

Raymond made a dismissive gesture, his face revealing the closest thing to a smile Perkins had ever seen on the tribal cop. "You federal agents need all the help you can get."

"Thanks a lot."

"Hey, look at it as payback. You saved my ass that time White Calf was ready to cut my throat. Besides, it's nice to see you in trouble for a change. I'm the one who's always getting chewed out by Homer. Now you can take your lumps from Jameson."

"Some pal you are."

"Perkins, in my book you're still a *ee mah tusk kee*."

"I didn't want to know what that was the first time I heard it, and I still don't want to know."

"Now you're being a smart Indian."

"Why, Raymond, that's the nicest thing you ever said to me."

69

Raymond peered out the window of his trailer and yawned. It was Saturday morning and he had a full day ahead of him with no plans. Mary was busy grading papers and preparing lessons and he wasn't meeting her until the evening. She had offered to cook dinner but Raymond had invited her and Delia out.

"My, my, aren't we getting extravagant," Mary said.

"Well, it's a special occasion."

"It is? I know it's not your birthday or mine. What are we celebrating?"

"I'll tell you tonight," Raymond said, smiling to himself as he hung up the phone.

He reached into his pocket and withdrew the small box containing the ring he had bought for her. Raymond had struggled with himself for a long time about asking Mary to marry him. His first marriage had left such a bad taste that each time he considered proposing, it was an ingrained reflex to tell himself not to do it. Gradually, over the past few months, a subtle change had occurred. The few nights a week they spent together were not enough for him. He realized that he was happiest when he was with Mary, not away from her. And he had begun looking upon Delia more as a daughter than simply his girlfriend's kid. Still, what he was about to do required a major effort on his part. He was even more discomfited by not knowing what Mary would say, or how Delia would feel about it. Would Delia accept him as a father? And did Mary feel as strongly about him as he did about her?

A sharp rap on the door interrupted his thoughts.

Standing Bear, his cousin, was outside, hopping from foot to foot and patting himself with gloved hands in an effort to stay warm. The temperature had dropped precipitously since the day before. Standing Bear's breath hovered in a cloud above his face.

"Hey, it's cold out there," Raymond said. "Come on in for some coffee."

"I've had two cups already, but I wanted to drop off these venison steaks. They're as frozen as I am."

"Thanks. Aren't you working today?"

"I'm taking the morning off to go down to Great Falls to see my mother. Why don't you come with me? You're not working today, right? It'll only be for a couple of hours. Crystal Stone says she'd like to see you. It's been a long time."

"Did you ever ask her about that bear claw?"

Standing Bear smacked his forehead. "That's what I forgot. I knew I was supposed to tell her something the last time I was there."

"You getting CRS disease, cousin?"

"What's that?"

"Can't remember shit."

"Very funny. Why don't you come along and ask her yourself?"

Raymond, his curiosity piqued, nodded. "Sure, I'll go with you. But I have to be back by late afternoon."

"No problem. We'll use my truck."

Raymond grabbed a jacket and followed him out.

"Hop in," Standing Bear said. "You'll make my mom's day."

Raymond and Standing Bear stood in front of a small wood-frame house, its peeling paint lying like dandruff on the bare strip of earth adjoining the foundation. The last time Raymond had seen his aunt was when she was a patient in Benefis Hospital, shortly after her stroke. He and Standing Bear hadn't expected her to survive, but she surprised them by walking out of the hospital with the help of a cane after only a month. The old lady had moved in with her daughter, Standing Bear's sister, Lucinda, and her son-in-law, after her discharge from the hospital.

Now, almost two years later, Raymond didn't know what to expect. He shuffled his feet nervously as Standing Bear knocked on the door. Lucinda, a broad-faced woman with a smile for everyone, hadn't changed since Raymond last saw her. She hugged him. "It's been so long we thought you didn't love us anymore," she said. "Charlie had to work this morning, but he'll be home for lunch," she added before Raymond could apologize for not coming more often.

"Mom's in the kitchen," she said in response to her brother's questioning look.

Raymond's aunt, a tiny, wizened woman, sat at the table peeling potatoes. She peered at them through cataract-glazed eyes.

"It's Standing Bear and Raymond come to see you, Momma," Lucinda said.

Each of them bent over and planted a kiss on the old woman's wrinkled cheek.

Oh Kee Nah ah, Raymond said, greeting his aunt in the Blackfeet tongue.

She placed her knife on the table and reached for Raymond's hand.

Mix-ke-mo-te-skin-na, Iron Horn," she said, calling Raymond by his Blackfeet name and clutching his hand tightly.

Raymond smiled. He hadn't heard that name in a long time.

"Sit down, Raymond," Lucinda said, "I'll make coffee."

"How have you been, Auntie?"

"Lucinda takes good care of me."

"And you're a big help to me, Momma."

The old woman mumbled something that Raymond didn't catch. "What did she say?" he asked Lucinda.

"She says 'a big help like a puddle in the path of an ant.' It's her idea of a joke. She knows how much she helps me."

"Not help, just company now that your own children are grown," Crystal Stone said. She went back to peeling potatoes, pausing once to look at Raymond, who sat next to her. "Standing Bear told me you wanted to know about a big bear claw," she said suddenly.

Raymond nodded, surprised at her bringing up the topic. "You didn't forget to ask her," he said to Standing Bear.

"No, but she said she would only tell you."

"I have seen only one person with a claw like that. It's a story I've never told you, but now I think you are ready." She placed the half-peeled potato on the table. "My father, your grandfather, was *Wun-nes-tou,* White Buffalo. He died soon after you were born. He had two daughters, no sons. *In-neo-cose,* The Buffalo's Child, your mother, and *E-eh-ni-skin,* Crystal Stone, me."

Raymond listened respectfully.

"Your mother, who we called Emily, married Little Plume, a Piegan everyone called Oscar. He was a good man with one failing. He was a gambler. Even after you were born, he continued to gamble any money he earned. This led to many arguments with your mother and finally she left him"

Raymond sat back in astonishment. "I don't remember that."

"You were very young, maybe three or four years old. She left you behind because she didn't want to take you away from your cousins, Standing Bear and Lucinda, who were your playmates. She knew I would look after you. She moved to Valier because she had met another man. His name was *Pe-toh-pee-kiss*, The Eagle's Ribs. Everyone knew him as Peter. He was a big man, bigger even than you and my son, Standing Bear, and he wore the grizzly claw you describe around his neck."

Raymond wondered where this conversation was going. The man she described, if still alive, would be very old, certainly not White Calf.

Pe-toh-pee-kiss wore the grizzly's claw because he was a descendant of a Piegan warrior who was a grizzly-bear Brave. In the old days there were two warrior societies, the Braves and the All Brave Dogs. Each society had two men whose duty it was to provide meat at the society dances. These men were very brave and they were feared by all the people. I know this because an old Piegan named *Pi-no-ki-min-uksh*, Tearing Lodge, told it to my grandfather and he told it to me. *Pe-toh-pee-kiss*, like his ancestor, was a good hunter and he was feared by the other Blackfeet. His face was always stern, except when he looked upon your mother. He loved her." She paused and lifted her wrinkled face to Raymond. "She had a son with him, a son they named White Calf."

His aunt's words struck Raymond with the force of a blow. How could all this have been kept hidden from me? he wondered. It was as if she was describing ancient Blackfeet lore, not the life of his parents. Why had they never told him?

"Although your mother loved her new baby, she missed you terribly and asked me to bring you to see her. Your father knew she was living in Valier with *Pe-toh-pee-kiss*. When I told him I was taking you to see her, he asked me to tell her that he no longer gambled and that he still loved her. He wanted her to be with him and with you. I took you and Standing Bear to Valier with me and that was the only time you met *Pe-toh-pee-kiss* and your half-brother, White Calf."

Raymond recalled his dream, the dream of a faceless bare-chested man wearing a grizzly claw suspended like a pendant, and a woman in a blue flowered dress who embraced him.

"I gave your father's message to my sister. She was very upset. She was torn between you and the new baby, between *Pe-toh-pee-kiss* and your father. She loved both children and she loved both men. She shed many tears during the next few days and finally decided to return with me. She knew she couldn't bring White Calf with her. Even if *Pe-toh-pee-kiss* had permitted it, your father knew nothing of the baby and would never have accepted it. *Pe-toh-pee-kiss* was very angry when your mother told him she was returning to Browning. His face was dark, like a black cloud, and his eyes were on fire. I thought he would hurt your mother, but instead, he turned his back to her. His last words were 'I never want to see you again. And you are never to see our son, White Calf.' Your mother wept during the entire trip back to Browning."

Raymond sat in stunned silence. His cousins, Standing Bear and Lucinda, were as shocked as Raymond by their mother's revelations.

"Do you think my mother regretted her decision?" Raymond asked when he regained his voice.

"No. She was happy to be back with you. And your father kept his word. He never gambled again."

"What happened to them?" Raymond asked.

"Your father died before he was fifty and your mother a few years later. You know that."

"I mean to *Pe-toh-pee-kiss* and White Calf."

"People told me that *Pe-toh-pee-kiss* began to drink heavily after your mother left. He lost his life in a car crash. White Calf was about six or seven at the time. I heard he went to live with a relative of *Pe-toh-pee-kiss* near where the Two Medicine and Dupuyer Rivers meet."

"And *Pe-toh-pee-kiss* left White Calf the bear claw?"

"It would have been the custom."

Raymond nodded, his face grim. White Calf must have known Raymond was his half-brother. It was the only explanation for his hatred.

"Now I know why I remembered that claw," Standing Bear said softly. "I was with you that day in Valier."

Raymond looked from him to his aunt. "So you heard no news of White Calf after his father's death?"

Raymond was surprised to see tears coursing down his aunt's wrinkled face. She shook her head slowly. "The last time I saw him was when I took you and Standing Bear to Valier. He was only two years old, but already big. I remember his eyes. They burned like black fire, just like his father's."

Lucinda rested her hand on top of her mother's.

"My daughter reads the newspaper to me," Crystal Stone said. "I know White Calf took an evil path, that he killed people, and that he in turn was killed. I weep for what might have been."

"How?" Raymond asked. "How could it have turned out differently? Your sister, my mother, was the cause of everything that happened."

"Do not make your heart hard against your mother. Everyone bears some of the blame— your father for his gambling, *Pe-toh-pee-kiss* for his drinking that left his son an orphan. My sister tried to make amends by returning to you and to her husband. She thought *Pe-toh-pee-kiss* was strong, that he would be a good father to the child she had with him."

"Auntie, do you know that it was I who—"

Standing Bear raised his hand to cut Raymond off. He gave an almost imperceptible shake of his head. "Nothing can change what is past," he said.

Raymond's coffee had grown cold. He pushed himself back from the table.

"My mother didn't mean to upset you," Lucinda said.

"I'm glad you told me," Raymond said to his aunt, resting his hand lightly on her bony shoulder. Crystal Stone felt no more substantial to him than a wraith. He knew that the shadow of death would soon descend upon her. Standing Bear was right. It made no sense to inflict more pain upon her.

"I should be getting back to Browning," Raymond said, his gaze meeting his cousin's. "If you want to stay, you can drop me at the bus terminal and I'll take a bus back."

"No, we'll go together," Standing Bear said.

"Please stay for lunch," Lucinda said. "Charlie will be home any minute. He'll feel so bad if he doesn't get to see you."

"I'm sorry," Raymond said. "I have to get back. I have something very important to do this evening. Next time I'll stay longer. I promise, Auntie." He wrapped his fingers around her arthritic hand, still resting on the table next to a half-peeled potato.

"Are you okay?" Standing Bear asked as they drove north out of Great Falls.

"I'm okay."

"That was a hell of a story."

"Yeah. A hell of a story."

www.ingramcontent.com/pod-product-compliance
Lightning Source LLC
Chambersburg PA
CBHW011342010726
47493CB00009B/2918